THE SUBLIME SEVEN

By Nicki Huntsman Smith

Copyright © 2019 by Nicki Smith

Acknowledgements

I would like to thank the following:

Lori, my editor, proofreader, and grammar consultant extraordinaire. Her contributions elevated this book to a level I wouldn't have achieved otherwise. She is not allowed to die before me.

My beta readers, Al and Lisa, who provided advice, suggestions, and top-notch cheerleading.

Colby for his help with my Italian words and phrases. Merlin for his invaluable insight into the process of forgiveness.

Lastly and most importantly, my husband Ray, whose encouragement and support makes my books possible. I owe him everything.

Prologue

"Where am I?"

"You're in the In Between. Are you comfortable? Do you need anything? A Coke? Maybe a cigarette?"

"Why would I want a Coke or a cigarette if I'm dead?"

"They can't really harm you at this point. If they offer comfort, you may enjoy them now."

"How? I don't have a mouth anymore."

"Sure you do. You're talking with it."

"It's more the suggestion of a mouth. Or maybe the memory of one. That's what it feels like, at least."

"Well stated. It's true your physical body was left behind in that other place, but taking on its form again here serves a purpose. It will make all this easier to get through. Do you think you can manage that?"

"Let me try."

"Ah, there you are. You were quite handsome in your previous life."

"You're drop-dead gorgeous. Are you an angel?"

"We'll get to all that soon enough. Let's talk about what happened. Before you died."

"I think I got shot in the chest. That Kwik Shop clerk had a sawed-off shotgun behind the cash register."

"He did, but that's not what I'm referring to. Let's talk about your life leading up to its tragic end."

"Where do you want me to start?"

"At your first Pivotal Moment. That's the place in time where, in hindsight, you can see that your life took a Very Good Turn or a Very Bad Turn. Can you identify it?"

"Oh, yeah. That was the summer of '63 when Toby Malone taught me how to shoplift."

"That sounds perfect. Let's begin"

Chapter 1 – Integrity

"What if we get caught?" Johnny said.

"What if we don't?" Toby replied.

Toby was the new kid. Because he had moved from glamorous Hollywood, California, to unglamorous Hutchinson, Kansas, he enjoyed elevated status at Liberty Junior High from the first ear-splitting ring of the 8 o'clock bell. And it didn't hurt that he looked like a younger, blonder version of Ricky Nelson.

Johnny gravitated to him for other reasons, though. The new boy wasn't merely exotic. He was dangerous and therefore worthy of attention. Perhaps even respect. He carried a Swiss Army knife in the front pocket of his Levi's, and smoked Marlboro Reds after school next to the bicycle rack. He frequently snuck out of his bedroom window in the middle of the night while his parents were asleep, and he owned an impressive collection of Superman comic books, which he claimed were mostly stolen.

Among other things, Toby was a thief. A good one, if you believed his stories.

"But what if we do?" Johnny said. "My dad will beat my ass, and I'll be grounded the rest of the summer."

Johnny hated to be the voice of reason, but the other two boys weren't taking on the role. Toby had been accepted into their small group of friends at the end of the school year. Now, summer sprawled before the four boys as languid and enticing as Miss May, 1963, the most recent Playboy edition, and topmost on the hidden stack of Johnny's father's dirty magazine horde. Everyone was excited by the prospect of summer days filled with sleeping late and pickup baseball games at Grover's Field, where they gathered now.

That evening, the four friends had the place to themselves. The drone of the cicadas was dwindling, and they were discussing an adventure. A nefarious, thrilling, vaguely illegal one that would take place that night, if Toby got his way.

"Johnny-boy, you're looking at this all wrong. You're not gonna get caught. This will be a cake walk. Trust me."

"What's a cake walk?" Timmy asked, breaking the tension.

Timmy was the smallest and dumbest member of their group, but he had a big heart. And a big house with a swimming pool. Thus his admittance into the Thunderbirds, named after the coolest automobile ever made and immortalized in the greatest song ever written. Nobody was cooler than The Beach Boys, not even Bobby Darin.

"Man, you're stupid," Toby said.

"Don't call him stupid," Johnny said. "He's just slow."

"So what will it be, gentlemen?" Frank was in his spy phase that summer. When nobody but the Thunderbirds were around, he spoke in a British accent, like Patrick Macnee. He could get away with it because Frank was the smartest kid in school, with a caustic wit that could cut you off at the knees. He had brawn to match his brain, too. You didn't mess with Frank unless you wanted to be embarrassed in front of the other kids, or end up in a choke-hold with your lungs exploding.

"I thought your club was supposed to be cool," Toby said, gazing steadily at Johnny. "Come on, guys. Do something daring for a change."

The word choice sold Frank. "I'm in. Spies need to know how to escape houses without waking dogs or parents. And I'm certain they need to be able to navigate cemeteries in the dead of night as well. This sounds like something a spy would do."

Timmy stared at Johnny, his eyes puppy-like behind the thick-lensed glasses. Timmy would follow Johnny's lead.

"Knocking over tombstones seems wrong, Toby. It feels...disrespectful," Johnny said, hearing the lack of conviction in his own voice. Everyone else heard it, too.

Toby rolled his eyes. "Those people are moldy old bones now. They won't know and wouldn't care if they did. They're dead."

"Fine. I'm in," he said finally, feeling a sense of relief after giving in to the relentless peer pressure.

"I'm in, too." Timmy grinned.

"We'll meet back here at midnight," Toby said. "Wear black clothes and dark sneakers. Don't be late."

***

"Meatloaf again?"

Family dinner was something to get through before Johnny's midnight adventure. Nerves had transformed his stomach into a sloshing goldfish bowl of acid.

His mother narrowed her eyes. "Starving children in Africa would kill for this meatloaf." She placed the casserole dish on the kitchen table, stabbed a steaming wedge of ground beef mixed with god-knew-what, and slapped it down on his plate.

Thank goodness for ketchup.

"Would starving African children have the strength to actually kill someone?" replied Johnny's father with a covert wink in his direction.

"Very funny, Al."

"It's a valid question."

Johnny snickered.

Carol was not amused. "Starving children are off limits from smartass commentary."

"What about starving hyenas, Mother Nature's version of Don Rickles?"

"Hyenas are disgusting, as is Don Rickles. You may disparage them both with impunity," she replied.

"Don Rickles isn't disgusting. I think he's funny," said Johnny, pushing the meatloaf and green beans around on his plate.

"He's rude."

"That's his shtick, Carol."

"I know, but insulting people isn't entertainment to me. I don't understand his appeal."

Al shrugged. Johnny sighed. When his mother got her panties in a wad about something, it was best to change the subject. She could be relentless in her quest to find "teachable moments."

Johnny said, "My stomach hurts a little. I may be coming down with something. I don't think I can clean my plate." It wasn't a total lie. His stomach really did hurt.

"Oh, no," his mother said, placing her hand on his forehead. "You don't have a fever."

"Maybe it's botulism. Or the plague," Al offered. "Don't breathe on me son. I can't miss any more work. Your mother will divorce me and marry someone more worthy of her beauty, brains, and exceptional backside. I must say, those lavender pants look magnificent when you're walking away."

Carol smacked her husband on the head. It was a loving smack.

Beneath the surface of the running divorce joke, Johnny felt his father did worry about it. His parents' combined income placed them at the low end of middle-class. Johnny believed his mother when she said she didn't care about material stuff – she loathed ostentatious displays of wealth, as she put it. But Johnny couldn't help that he was envious of Timmy's pool, Frank's European vacations, and Toby's fancy department store clothes.

And here he was forced to save chore money for a new baseball glove, an item most parents provided without demanding hard labor in return.

Johnny frowned at his meatloaf, thinking about the upcoming adventure later that night. Maybe Toby was right. Maybe those dead people wouldn't really care about toppled gravestones, and if the mission were successful, he'd have bragging rights for months.

He almost smiled when he thought about the respect it would earn him that fall with the other kids at school. Instead, he frowned, acting like his stomach was killing him, and went to bed. He intentionally didn't think about what his father – and especially his mother – would say if he got caught. That only made the goldfish bowl slosh more.

12:37 AM

"You never said anything about this part, Toby," Johnny whispered.

The boys huddled elbow-to-elbow in the oldest section of Fairlawn Cemetery. The graves here weren't maintained like the newer ones near the front gates. No faded silk flowers nor manicured grass in this area, just a smattering of tilted granite slabs positioned at odd intervals. Four of the tombstones now lay supine upon the cracked, bare soil – the sprinklers didn't extend this far in Fairlawn.

"You're getting a bonus," Toby replied. His eyes, night-gray and dilated, glittered in the sparse moonlight.

Johnny shivered, despite having sweated through the armpits of his black t-shirt. "We're not killing a cat," he said, plucking the tabby from Timmy's scrawny arms.

"It's just a stray," Toby replied. "We'll swear a Thunderbird oath with its blood. Brothers forever, right, Frank?"

"Why don't we make a cut in our palms? Isn't that the way they do it in the movies? Why do we need a cat?" Frank no longer bothered with the British accent. They were all alarmed by Toby's sudden divergence from tombstone tipping to animal mutilation. The poor animal with the terrible timing had meandered onto the scene as the fourth slab was toppled.

"Because when you sacrifice a life as part of a blood oath, it becomes stronger. Think about it. It's no worse than dissecting frogs in biology lab. This cat is starving to death anyway. Look how skinny it is."

All eyes turned to the purring bag of bones in Johnny's arms.

"The frogs are already dead," Johnny said, looking down at the scruffy ears and not at Toby's smoldering gaze.

"Fine. I have something better in mind," Toby replied.

At that moment, the sudden squawk of a nearby police car startled everyone, prompting Johnny to drop the cat. With a flash of gray stripes, it vanished into the night gloom, fleeing in the opposite direction of the approaching circles of two high-powered flashlights.

"Run for it," Toby said, knocking Timmy to the ground before taking off.

Frank scrambled after Toby with a backward glance of dismay.

Johnny helped Timmy to his feet, then the two boys followed, barely escaping the snare of those spotlights.

Two days later...

"I still can't believe you did that to me," Timmy said as the boys huddled in an alley off 17th street in downtown Hutchinson. Both hands of the Town Center's giant art deco clock pointed straight up.

The button-down shirts and chinos chaffed in the heat – their Sunday clothes worn on a Thursday, per Toby's order.

Toby shrugged. "I did it because we're not blood brothers. If somebody was going to jail, it would be the slowest one. Not me."

"It's called survival of the fittest, old chap." Frank patted Timmy's narrow back. Two days after the cemetery incident, Frank still wouldn't make eye contact with Johnny.

"It doesn't matter. Nobody got caught. Now let's focus on the task at hand, my friends." Toby's grin was shark-like. Johnny liked it even less than the normal cocky one. "I haven't told you the best part of today's plan. The key to not getting caught is to buy something. It's simple but ingenious. How much money do you have on you?" Toby reached into the pocket that didn't contain the Swiss army knife. "I have thirty-seven cents."

Timmy said, "I have a nickel. I forgot to ask for money this morning."

"Sorry, mates. I seem to have left my wallet at home." Frank pulled empty pocket linings inside out as proof.

Johnny narrowed his eyes at Toby for a full ten seconds, then dug a grudging hand into a front pocket. "A buck fifteen. I was saving up for a new catcher's mitt." It had taken him three weeks to save only one-fifth of the price of the dreamy Ted Williams Pro model.

"Good. We can pool our money, then everyone will get a little. After we stash the candy, we'll find stuff to buy. Bulky stuff that will cover the lumps in our shirts. Maybe those rubber balls in that chicken wire cage in the far corner. You know the ones?"

Timmy's head bobbed.

Frank arched an eyebrow just like Sean Connery in *Dr. No*, then nodded.

Johnny scowled. "If we're pooling our money to buy junk, why don't we just buy the damn candy?"

"Because this is about learning a skill. Get it? The sweets are a bonus. If you get good at this, there's better stuff out there. Like that glove you want. You learn how to do this right, and you won't have to save up for it."

"Stealing is a skill all spies must acquire," Frank said. "They have to be able to slip into fancy dinner parties and purloin documents from the desks of villains. That's why they also know the tango and can drink gallons of champagne without getting drunk. Maybe we can shoplift some champagne tomorrow."

Frank was on board with Toby's plan.

Toby said, "You'll have Lemonheads and Fire Balls to last a month. We're going after the big bags," he added with the rakish grin that made all the seventh-grade girls turn into giggly goofballs.

"No way. Those won't fit in my pockets," Johnny replied. The economy-sized packages were as large as a Pomeranian.

"We don't put them in our pockets. We're going to stuff them inside our shirts. Like this, see? That's why I told you guys what to wear." Toby fiddled with the three lowest buttons of the madras plaid shirt. The gaping hole revealed a tanned belly sprouting five curly hairs. Of course it would be Toby who got the first pubes. Johnny didn't even have armpit hair yet.

"Fine. I'll do this," Johnny said. "But if we get caught, you're out of the Thunderbirds."

The alley extended along one of the many Renaissance-revival buildings of downtown Hutchinson. All the structures were connected and existed in various stages of decay or gentrification. Mel's Grab 'N Go sat in the center of the longest block on 17th Street. That meant that if they had to flee, there would be a half-block of hauling ass before they reached their bicycles, chained like abandoned pets to a Victorian lamppost. From the opposite direction of their targeted destination, the tantalizing aroma of popcorn drifted out of the grandiose Fox Theater. Johnny wished they would scrap the stupid shoplifting idea and take in an afternoon matinee instead.

The temperature had climbed into the low nineties. If it weren't for Toby's stupid plan, they would be sporting cut-offs and white muscle shirts, the standard, comfortable summer uniform for most teenage boys – even those without muscles.

Johnny felt a sudden, unfamiliar surge of hatred for the new kid.

"Mel is half-blind and usually into his second six-pack by now," Toby continued. "Just follow my lead."

Two minutes later, the boys pushed open the glass door of Mel's Grab 'N Go. The cool air washing over them smelled like greasy hot dogs and floor wax. Mixed in was the scent of stale beer wafting from behind the cash register where Mel sat six days a week, from seven in the morning until seven at night. The old man's bristly eyebrows merged at the sight of the boys.

"Just restocked the penny candy." Three empty Blatz bottles stood sentinel behind the cash register. Their contents softened Mel's consonants: *jus resocked the benny canny.*

This might not be so hard after all.

Toby led them to the penny candy aisle.

"Why are we here?" Timmy stage-whispered. "I thought we were going for the big ones?"

Toby elbowed him in the arm, then in a loud voice said, "Look, there's Red Hots this time."

"I'm getting a Jaw Breaker," Frank said loudly with a wink.

"I think I want Pixy Stix," Johnny replied, matching Frank's volume.

"Hey guys, let's check out the ball cage." Toby took off toward the back of the store, detouring down the aisle containing the bulk candy. Johnny saw that the opening in the plaid had appeared again. He fumbled with the buttons of his own shirt. The cold air on his skin felt like a bad omen.

Toby slowed as they walked past the huge bags available in most stores only during Halloween. Johnny watched a lithe hand reach down in passing, grab the mother lode of Fire Balls, then disappear within the madras plaid. Quicker than Johnny would have thought possible, the three lower buttons already secured the lumpish belly. The confident smirk on the tan face was a challenge now.

Johnny grimaced as his own stomach suddenly sprouted a bumper crop of icicles. He ignored the unpleasant sensation, emulating Toby's movements as he walked down the aisle. Seconds later, the bag of Lemonheads nestled securely in his own shirt. He didn't turn to watch the other boys. All his attention was focused on the larceny hidden under the fabric.

He stood next to the ball cage, forcing himself to take deep breaths. The icicles soon vanished, replaced by a mixture of relief and elation. The bulge wasn't that noticeable, and easily hidden behind the bright red ball balancing at the top of the chicken wire.

"They're fifteen cents each," Toby said. "What color does everyone want?"

They spent the next few minutes deciding which boy would buy which ball. Next, they paid for the items, and then escaped into the now-welcome heat. Mel never raised a drunken, wiry eyebrow.

The newly chubby boys ran the half-block back toward their bikes. When they were safely around the corner, they gathered in a tight cluster, comparing the stolen loot.

"So we got the Fire Balls, the Lemonheads, Bazookas...nice, Frank! And for some stupid reason, Charleston Chews. What the hell, Timmy? Nobody likes those."

"They were the closest."

Toby rolled his eyes, then studied Johnny with a smug, appraising expression. "So, how did it feel, Johnny-Boy? Pretty sweet, huh?"

The In Between

"You enjoyed the sensation? The high, so to speak?" said the angel, or whatever she was.

They sat facing each other in cozy chairs, illuminated by a nearby Tiffany floor lamp. No electrical cord was attached to the base, tethering it to some purgatorial outlet located within the impenetrable blackness beyond their circle of light. It was powered by either batteries or magic. Or perhaps God. Johnny noticed that the hues in the lamp's stained-glass shade matched the color of the four rubber balls from Mel's Grab 'N Go. While telling the story of his recent life, he hadn't noticed the chairs appear, nor the lamp, nor the homey braided rug, just like his grandmother's. All these elements came into existence so unobtrusively, that it felt as if they had been there all along.

"I wouldn't say *enjoyed*. More like I had an epiphany. I could have almost anything I wanted without having to work for it. That first time was thrilling, but afterward, I realized I could apply the same concept to bigger and better stuff. I didn't have much growing up, so you can understand the appeal."

"One could say you were rich in love. Your parents adored you."

"That's absolutely right. And I see that now."

"So the stolen candy led to the catcher's mitt, then eventually in your early twenties, to armed robbery. Thus your demise at the hands of an understandably perturbed convenience store clerk."

"That pretty much sums it up. Why am I wearing flannel pajamas?"

"Because the goal is to make you comfortable."

"If I'm comfortable, I'm more willing to talk about how I screwed up my life?"

"Comfort is one of the pleasures of being human. It even beat out sex in one of our surveys."

"Not sure I believe that."

"That's because in this past incarnation you never experienced true discomfort. You slept in a bed every night, had plenty of food to eat, and were rarely too cold or too hot. Not everyone's life is so abundant in comfort."

Johnny nodded. "What's your name? I don't even know how to address you."

"You may call me Sarah."

"That's a pretty name. It suits you."

"Thank you. Let's proceed. You said your Pivotal Moment occurred when Toby taught you how to shoplift. Your life then took a very Bad Turn. Looking back, do you regret it?"

"Oh, yes. If I had stood up to him that day, done the right thing, I never would have learned how to steal. If I hadn't learned to steal, I wouldn't have transitioned to armed robbery. Which means I wouldn't be here now. Shoplifting is a gateway crime, you know."

Sarah's laughter reminded him of his mother's wind chimes – musical, somewhat discordant, soothing.

"I remember just before the guy pulled the shotgun on me, I was thinking, *What the hell am I about to do? This is so wrong. My mother would be so disappointed. I should know better.* It was one of those paradigm shifts. A moment of pure clarity when I saw the situation in a completely different way. From that new perspective, I realized I was a total jerk. Everything my mom and dad had been teaching me finally kicked in. If I hadn't gotten a chest full of lead a half-second later, I would have turned my life around."

"I see. What are your thoughts concerning the act of theft itself, untethered to its potential consequences?"

"You're asking if I think stealing is wrong even if I don't get caught."

"Precisely."

"Of course it's wrong. Looking back on my life now and seeing how messed up it got because of that one day...I think I've seen the light."

"That's not what I'm looking for."

"Give me a minute. These are complex thoughts I'm trying to articulate. Yeah, there's more to it than that. The actual act of taking something from someone, whether by force or through cunning, subtracts from your character. Yes, that 'thing' is in your possession – the bag of candy or the thick wad of cash – but having it diminishes you as a human being. Makes you less of a person. Makes you smaller. Does that make sense? I'm not sure if I'm getting the words right."

"You got them just right." Sarah smiled.

A cup of hot chocolate appeared in his hand. The aroma of Swiss Miss with Mini Marshmallows wafted up from the armrest. He wasn't surprised. That had been his favorite brand growing up.

He took a sip, then said, "Are you going to tell me who you are now? What all this means?"

The beautiful woman tilted her head. Her blond hair cascaded to a shoulder cloaked in lavender polyester-knit. She was wearing a tracksuit. They had been all the rage with his mom's generation back in Hutchinson.

"For now, let's just say I am your Spiritual Guide."

"Like one of those ladies with a crystal ball?"

"No, of course not. You'd be amazed how often I hear that. My job is to mentor you during your development. Advise and instruct you through your evolution."

"Evolution? As in Darwin?"

"Similar, but applied to your soul rather than to a physical incarnation. We want you – your consciousness – that unique spark of the Divine within you, to reach the apex of sublimity. That's always the goal, but we sometimes have a few hiccups along the way."

"You're trying to make me perfect?"

"Perfection is unattainable."

A Marlboro Red had appeared in the hand that wasn't holding the hot chocolate and was already half-smoked by the time he noticed it smoldering between his fingers. In addition to shoplifting, Toby Malone had taught him how to smoke cigarettes. He figured out on his own how to enjoy them.

"Sublime instead of perfect. Got it."

"Did you go to Sunday school in your past life?"

"Until I was fifteen. I have to say, the whole Christian thing, Jesus being the son of God, then coming back from the dead, heaven and hell...all that didn't make much sense to me when I got older."

"That's because those devices were no longer meant for you. They work to a certain point, which varies from person to person. Then they're relinquished, for reasons that will be made clear to you eventually."

"Are you saying Jesus isn't real?"

"Not at all. I'm saying iconic religious figures serve a purpose for a while. Then, when the soul has transcended to a certain level, other methods must be utilized to achieve the ultimate goal of sublimity."

"So this is like a reincarnation thing?"

"That word is frowned upon. It trivializes the process."

"Sorry."

"No problem. It is something like that, however. As I mentioned earlier, you are in the In Between. We are here not only to discuss your most recent life, but also to work out the details of your next one, and the lessons to be learned while living it."

"So I guess in my past life I learned a lesson about not taking what doesn't belong to me?"

"Your lesson was about integrity. You actually lived many lifetimes before you finally, truly, understood that concept during that moment you experienced in the Kwik Shop. The one of *pure clarity*."

"But I don't remember any other life besides the last one."

"That's how this works up to now. From this point on, you will remember your previous lives while you are in the In Between. This is where things get interesting. We'll decide what your next lesson is to be and the optimal conditions under which to learn it. When we meet again, you'll recall your life in Hutchinson, Kansas, in 1963, as well as the new life upon which you're about to embark. And that brings us to my next subject: What would you say are the most crucial human qualities a person should possess to be the best he or she can be? The order doesn't matter. Just say them when you think of them."

"You mean after integrity?"

"Yes. You've done that one."

"I see where you're going with this. Okay, I'll say courage or bravery. Then compassion, which I guess is kind of like empathy, right?"

"This is your list."

"Kindness has to be on there. Also tolerance for others who are different from me, although that could be part of kindness too. Kindness may be a catch-all that many sublime characteristics fall into, like patience and benevolence. Am I right about that?"

Sarah smiled, but didn't respond.

"Okay. I think being responsible is important. Being accountable for my own actions and owning up to mistakes I make, with the ultimate goal of not screwing up to begin with. Maybe that part could come in at the end of one of my lives. What else? Oh, I know. Creativity. I think that's one of the things that sets us apart from the animals."

"You don't think animals can be creative?"

"I wouldn't think so."

"Did you know that dolphins surf the big waves off Western Australia just for the fun of it?"

"I had no idea. That's cool. So I guess the more intelligent ones can be creative."

"Perhaps they weren't always so intelligent."

"You're saying they go through this process too?"

"We'll get to that later."

"Sure. Like whether you're an angel."

"All in good time."

Johnny sighed. "I have the feeling I'll be hearing that a lot in the In Between. All right, back to the list. I think we have to love one another. Unconditional love, like dogs give their owners. Now that I think about it, dogs are probably better at being sublime than us humans."

"Dogs are among the most enlightened of all creatures."

"I believe it. So we'll add unconditional love. What else? Oh, I have one. Leadership. Leadership tied to a solid work ethic. A sublime human wouldn't be lazy, and being an effective, hard-working leader sets the right example for others. So it's kind of a two-fer."

"You're getting the hang of this."

"I think so too. What about moral restraint? Resisting temptation, I mean? Although we could attach that to responsibility-accountability, I suppose. There's humility, curiosity, gratitude, a sense of humor. Oh, and forgiveness. And I mean genuine forgiveness, not just lip service."

"That's a toughie."

"It sure is. We'll put it on the list. I like the notion of combining some of these, if that's okay. Will that make my evolution take less time?"

"Time is meaningless here. It is also non-linear, which you'll soon understand. However, some of these qualities you've chosen could be more effectively accomplished as riders. Two-fers, or even three-fers."

The beauty of Sarah's smile nearly blinded him

"You love your job, don't you, Sarah?"

She nodded. "I do. It's taken me a long time to qualify for it. I worked on my resume for millennia."

"Angels have resumes?"

"Not an angel. Spiritual Guide."

"I know, but I can't stop thinking of crystal balls when you say that."

The tinkling wind chimes again. He could listen to that sound all day.

"Are you finished? Shall we recap now?"

Johnny nodded. "I've done the integrity thing, which I think was important."

"It was. That's why you're here now."

"Cool. Here we go, then, in no particular order. Courage, Bravery, and Leadership with a strong Work Ethic – that's one lifetime. We'll combine Kindness with Compassion and Empathy, and add Patience, Benevolence, and Tolerance too...they all seem to go together. That will take seventy or eighty years, I bet. Responsibility and Accountability with a Moral Restraint rider. Creativity with a bit of Humility thrown in. Unconditional Love. And Forgiveness. What do you think?"

"What matters is what you think. Are you pleased with your list?"

"Yeah, I think so."

"What about curiosity and a sense of humor?"

"Oh, right. Then let's combine Unconditional Love and Forgiveness, and we'll put Curiosity and Sense of Humor together."

"What about gratitude?"

"Dang. How could I have overlooked that? That's a really important one. How about Curiosity and Sense of Humor with a side helping of Gratitude."

"You could do Gratitude by itself. You realize we set no deadline, nor prescribe a specific number of lives in which to complete your journey."

"I've set my own. It just came to me, like the hot chocolate and the cigarette. I want to get this done in seven lifetimes, and I already have one under my belt. Six more to go."

"Why seven? It could be any number."

It was Johnny's turn to smile. "Because I like the sound of The Sublime Seven. It has a nice ring."

"Very well. It's your decision. It's always your decision. You've completed Integrity, so what do you want to tackle next?"

"How about Unconditional Love and Forgiveness?"

"Excellent. Now comes the fun part."

Chapter 2 – Unconditional Love and Forgiveness

Giza, Egypt – 2573 BCE

"Jamila, where is my dinner?" her father said, stooping low to get through the opening of their small mud-brick apartment.

"Sorry, Papa. There was a long line today at the food complex." Jamila scurried to set the bowl containing fish and lentils on a reed mat, freshly shaken and cleaned for the evening meal. With care, she placed two cups of beer next to it, along with a small basin of water.

"Is the water clean?"

"Yes, Papa. I boiled it this morning."

"Very good," he replied, dipping his fingertips into the water, then selecting the choicest fish morsels. "No bread?"

"Right here," she said, removing a scrap of linen and showing him the fine loaf displayed in her basket.

His tired gaze shifted to the basket. A dust-covered eyebrow arched in mild surprise.

"You made this?" he said, between bites.

"I did."

"Well done, child. You'll be an expert baker in no time." He tore off a section of the flat bread and swiped it along the edge of the bowl. "Go ahead, eat. You're working now, so you need to keep your strength up."

"Thank you, Papa." She tore off a piece now, too, dipped it in the broth, and analyzed the texture and flavor. Some said bread was just bread. There's nothing special about it. Its purpose was to fill one's belly. But those people didn't work in the most esteemed bakery of the most esteemed neighborhood within the village of the pyramid builders. This was her first year to become a full-fledged baker in the service of Khafre, Pharaoh of Egypt, whose pyramid would be the second largest in Giza. It was now only half-built, yet its silhouette blotted out the sunrise each morning. It filled Jamila with awe to know her small contribution of feeding the builders would secure her place in the Afterlife.

"The seeds are a nice touch. You're settling in well, then?" Papa said. Exhaustion showed in every line of his dark-skinned face. As a skilled stone mason working in the Friends of Khafre phyle, his services were in high demand. It seemed everyone wanted Akhon to perform the finest, most delicate work. His nickname was 'Iizmil Rayiysiun – Chisel Master – and his talent was the reason he came home every evening almost too tired to eat before falling into the deep sleep of the weary.

"I am," Jamila said, with a satisfied smile. Her labors at the bakery weren't as physically demanding as those of her father, but in their own way, they were as necessary as his. Hungry builders would never be able to erect the pyramids.

"But I like the work very much," she continued. "And this time of year, the heat from the ovens is welcome."

"You won't feel that way come summer."

"True. But for now, I'm enjoying it. Also, there is a boy nearby at the office of the Clerks..." She hadn't decided to enter into this delicate conversation until just that moment. Her father was in a contented mood, and it almost felt as if Hathor, the Cow Goddess of feminine love and fertility, was nudging her in this endeavor.

Her father's eyes had lost their sleepy expression. "What boy?"

"Nephi, the middle son of Makalani, the scribe."

Her father grunted, but didn't reply.

She hurried on. "Nephi is apprenticing with his father. You should see his papyri, Papa. They're almost as elegant as yours."

The moment the words tumbled out of her mouth, she knew they were a mistake.

"It is one thing to scribble ink upon a papyrus and quite another to chisel the glyphs into a block of granite."

His tone did not invite a response, but she persevered. She had gone this far.

"Of course, I know that. I didn't mean to imply that his talent rivals yours. I'm just explaining he may be a good match for me. You're so busy, you might not realize I have become eligible for marriage." She cast her eyes downward in embarrassment. If her mother had survived childbirth, she would be having this conversation with her, not a grumpy father who was at least as embarrassed to think about his daughter becoming a woman as she was in telling him.

"Hmmph. Why didn't you speak of this before?"

"I hadn't yet found an auspicious moment."

He sighed, suddenly looking older than his thirty-seven years. "His father approves?"

She nodded, barely able to suppress a giddy outburst of happy, relieved laughter.

"Very well. I won't forbid it, since his father is respected in Giza. My status is not equal to his, so your beauty must be tipping the scales in your favor."

Akhon's candor was as well-known as his skill. It was one of the characteristics she most loved and despised about him. She had lost track of the times he had noted her clumsiness, usually in the presence of snickering neighbors.

"I'm only average in that area, Papa. You see me as beautiful because you're my father."

He smiled. "Jamila, my dear child, you have no idea how special you are. It is a testament to you that you're not vain, as are most of the females these days."

"But I'm terribly clumsy."

He nodded. "You are that. Nephi must not mind a girl with two left feet. Where are you going? It's getting dark," Akhon watched her clear the remnants of the meal and don her frayed wrap.

"I'm going to tell him the wonderful news," she said, kissing the top of her father's head.

"I'll go with you. I don't want you traveling alone past the beer vendors and cemetery this late."

"Nonsense. You're tired. Go to bed, Papa. I won't be long. I'll be careful of drunkards and demons."

"No drunkard would dare lay a hand on my daughter."

"Exactly. And I can handle myself around the demons."
She grinned. It was a joke between them. Only the truly
superstitious or ignorant believed in them.

"Very well. I'll see you in the morning, my beloved." He
reached for her hand, and pressed his lips against her
fingers. "I'm very proud of the woman you have become.
I'm sorry I don't tell you that more often."

"You have more on your mind than inflating the ego of
your daughter," she said. But she was deeply moved.
Compliments from her father were rare gems. She placed
this one alongside the memories of the others she'd
received over the years.

When she returned home later, her head full of images
of her future husband, Akhon was snoring. She blew out
the oil lamp he had left burning for her, then crawled onto
her pallet. She would be up again before the sunrise, so she
hoped to fall asleep quickly. But she soon realized she was
too excited to sleep. It felt like hours passed by the time she
slipped into the dream realm.

When she awoke, Madjet, the morning boat of the sun
god Ra, was already traveling across the eastern sky.

She had overslept and her father was gone. She
scrambled out of bed, splashed water on her face, and used
the urine jar. She wouldn't have time to take it to the
latrine before work. She would explain everything to her
supervisor and be instantly forgiven for her tardiness.

She hoped.

"Ii-ti!" she called to her neighbor as she scurried out
onto the residential road. It was unusually quiet; everyone

else who had jobs were at them by now. Not Moswen. As
the wife of the Head Clerk, she had only to keep her home
tidy and her husband fed, which gave the older woman
plenty of time to be a nosy nuisance.

"Hello, yourself," Moswen said. "You better have an
adequate excuse for being late. Nedjem is kindhearted, but
only to a point."

"I know, I know. I overslept," she replied, securing the
doorway covering of their apartment.

"And your father allowed it? He spoils you," the stocky
woman said, turning to face Jamila with her hands on hips
in such a way that her copper bracelets would be visible.

Jamila rolled her eyes on the inside. "He is good to me.
I'm a lucky daughter." She tried to walk past the woman,
but it seemed her neighbor was in an especially social
mood. The short legs worked twice as hard to keep up with
Jamila's long, youthful ones as she walked to the bakery.

"So where did you go last night? I saw you leave."

Of course she had. Moswen missed nothing. Every
salacious morsel of gossip within the pyramid builders'
village crossed the woman's path. If you wanted to know
anything about anyone, factual or otherwise, you knocked
on Moswen's door.

"I just went out for an evening stroll," Jamila said.

"Pfft. You went to Makalani's house, didn't you? To
visit his handsome son, Nephi. Your father should have
escorted you. It is unseemly for you to have gone alone."

"He was tired. He needed his sleep."

"If your mother were alive, she would have insisted on it. It's scandalous the way he lets you traipse about the village like a boy or a married woman."

"He trusts me, Moswen. He knows I would never bring shame upon our house."

"That's what all young people say. Then your blood gets hot and your thighs spread of their own volition."

Jamila laughed. She couldn't deny the effect of Nephi's kisses.

"Save your virginity for your wedding bed, young lady. I assume your father didn't instruct you in such matters. What a pity your mother isn't here to do it."

"I'm not ignorant. I know about all that." She felt the heat rising in her cheeks, whether from annoyance or discomfiture, she couldn't tell. Moswen was correct. Her widowed father had never thought to reveal the mysteries of sex to his only daughter. She had learned about all that from friends, whispered revelations told between giggles and graphic pictures rendered in the sand.

"I doubt that. Perhaps you know about the physical aspect – how that part fits into this part – but do you comprehend all the complicated, nuanced, frustrating sides to marriage? You didn't have an example growing up, so how could you?"

"I'll learn as I go. Now, I really must hurry before Nedjem gives me a lashing."

"Nedjem has a soft spot for you. Don't take advantage of that," Moswen added, as Jamila pulled away. The woman had been distracted by a trinket vendor set up near the bakery.

"How much for this hideous piece? It's too garish for anything but costuming."

Jamila smiled. In addition to gossip, Moswen was an expert on haggling. She would negotiate the price down to a quarter of whatever the seller was asking for it. She was happy to be rid of the woman, even if it meant passing the burden onto a hapless street vendor.

"Ii-ti, Nedjem," Jamila said, ducking into the oven room. She hung her wrap on a nearby hook. The roomy, warm space smelled wonderful. Was there anything more delectable than the scent of baking bread? She breathed it in, thinking of the savory herbs she planned to include in one of her batches today.

When she turned to regale her supervisor with a disarming smile, she saw wide-eyed alarm on the kindly face.

"What is it, Nedjem? What is wrong?"

"Oh, Jamila. They came here looking for you." The wrinkled prune of a face had never looked so sad. Jamila felt a stab of terror that threatened to turn her bowels to liquid.

"Who? Who came looking for me?"

"Two of the men from your father's phyle. He's been injured, lamb. Your father is with the physician even now. Go to him. Hurry! There may not be much time."

She darted from the warmth of the room, forgetting her wrap in her blind panic. Which physician? There were several. The most revered physicians served the needs of Egypt's nobility and the pharaoh himself. Her father would not be with them. Her mind scanned a list of names, deciding on one near the middle. She altered her course slightly toward the avenue that would bring her to the apartment building of Kamuzu; it was a respectable address at which to practice the lucrative business of surgery and pharmacopoeia.

It took her ten minutes to run the distance.

She ignored the clerk sitting in the reception hall; she had been to Kamuzu's building before with a badly broken wrist and knew the way to the treatment room. When she rushed through the curtained doorway, the nightmare scenario she'd conjured during her frantic run materialized before her eyes. Her father lay on a raised pallet. Linen gauze encased his torso; bright red spots had soaked through much of it. His left arm – the Master Chisel arm – was also wrapped and dangling from a medical contraption designed to keep limbs elevated.

The worst part was his head.

The bandages there weren't head-shaped. She could see a pronounced crater in the right side of his skull. His eyes were closed, but the torso rose and fell. Barely.

Two men stood next to him; both turned to face the intrusion. Kamuzu himself, not an assistant, was treating her father. For that, she was grateful. The other man's face evoked utterly conflicting emotions within her. She didn't know whether to be happy to see Nephi or terrified that he was here before Akhon's own daughter. What did it mean?

"Jamila, you shouldn't be here," Kamuzu said. "He's unconscious. You won't be able to speak to him. It will only cause you distress to see him in this state."

"He is my father. Of course I should be here," she choked out the words, then walked, dreamlike, to stand beside Nephi. She felt his arm encircle her shoulders, but she didn't look at him. Her gaze rested on her father's bandaged head.

"He is alive, child," Kamuzu said, kindness evident in his voice. "But for how long, I cannot say. And Jamila, you should know it may be better for him if he does not regain consciousness. His brain has suffered severe damage. I have removed some of the bone fragments to allow for swelling, but it won't be enough. The injury should have been fatal."

"But it wasn't," she whispered. "And if the gods saw fit to save his life, I will take care of him."

Kamuzu arched an eyebrow. "A damaged brain can manifest all manner of bizarre, unpleasant behaviors. Nephi, please see Jamila home. I will send word if Akhon's situation changes."

She felt arms guiding her out of the treatment room, past the clerk in the reception hall, and onto the street.

"I don't want to go home, Nephi. I'm going back to work," she said, turning and facing him finally. "Why are you even here? How did you know my father had been injured?"

The luminous dark eyes gazed down at her with something that might have been guilt. Her heart flopped in her chest.

"I had gone to your father at his jobsite. I felt it proper to ask his permission for your hand, despite your nontraditional upbringing."

"You were there when the accident occurred? What happened? Did a stone tumble onto him?"

Nephi's eyes darted everywhere but to her own. The corners of his mouth turned down, and his chin trembled. "It was a fall. He lost his footing on the scaffolding."

"Akhon is the most cautious and sure-footed of all. How could that have happened? Did you see it for yourself?"

"I don't want you to hate me, Jamila."

"Why would I hate you? I love you." It was difficult to force the words past the lump in her throat. She dreaded his reply.

"I distracted him. I should have waited until his shift was over, but I was too excited and filled with my love for you to delay further. And Jamila, this part isn't my fault. A large block had crashed into the scaffolding earlier that morning and weakened the section your father bumped into. Otherwise, it would have held. It was just bad luck. The worst kind of luck."

Her knees buckled and she slumped to the ground. The tears that had been lurking for the past half-hour burst forth from their dam and slid down her cheeks.

"Oh, Nephi. Better I don't say anything than to blurt out words I'll regret later. Please, just go away. I need to be alone for a few minutes before I return to work."

"I knew I shouldn't have told you!"

"You didn't have a choice. I would have heard all the embellished details from Moswen. Just go."

When she looked back up, he had vanished from the street. Passersby glanced at her crouching on the bricks – some with sympathy, and others with disdain. It was not the Egyptian way to display one's emotions so publicly.

She gathered herself, brushing fingertips across a damp face and straightening her shoulders. She pressed her lips together, stared straight ahead, and walked back to the bakery.

Two weeks later...

"Very good, Papa!" Jamila held the door cover open for her father to shuffle through. At least he was able to walk on his own now. She was young and strong, but her father was not a slight man, despite losing weight during his recovery.

"Where am I?" His one viable eye took in the surroundings of their apartment. The impact of his fall had not only shattered his skull, it had also damaged the delicate bones where his eyeball resided. Kamuzu said the misshapen, milky thing it had become should be removed since it was useless, but Jamila had no money to pay for the surgery, and she had already given her a discounted price for treating the worst of her father's injuries. So she had covered the eye with the softest linen she could find, then tied it in place with a gauze strip.

"You're home, Papa." She guided him to his sleep pallet and eased him to its surface.

"Oh, yes. I remember now," he said, though she could tell he didn't. This was a new development, the lying about things he thought he should know. It broke her heart.

"Of course you do. Now why don't you take a nap while I get supper? The line will be short now."

"Jamila, I'm no longer employed. They won't let us get our meals from the food complex if I'm not working on the pyramid."

"Hush. That is not your problem. And did you forget that I am also a worker in the service of Khafre?"

"You're a baker. I remember."

She smiled. It was gratifying when her father got something right. Perhaps with time, the workings of his mind would improve. Kamuzu the physician didn't hold out hope, but she did.

"That's right, Papa. I'm leaving now, but I'll be back soon."

She waited until his good eye closed and his breathing became regular, then she grabbed her market basket and stepped back out onto the street, inhaling air that did not smell like soiled diapers and body odor. She would fetch water from the village cistern after dinner to bathe her father. The notion of washing his naked body was alarming and revolting, but she would do it. She had to.

Her mind wrangled with a hundred problems, so she didn't notice Moswen's pointy nose poking out of the nearby doorway when she walked past.

"Jamila, wait. I'll go with you," the stout woman said, huffing and puffing to catch up to her. Jamila intentionally increased her pace.

"I'm in a hurry, Moswen. I don't have time to chat."

The woman would not be deterred so easily. "Then you'll make time to listen, at least."

She glanced down at the woman who wore an expression that was both unfamiliar and indistinct. She couldn't imagine what useless prattle would spill forth from those thin lips.

"What is it?" she said, distracted by thoughts of the food complex in the distance. She hoped they wouldn't demand to see her credentials; she only had the one chit for herself. Her father no longer qualified for the meal program since he wasn't an active worker on the pyramid, but it depended on the supervisor as to whether she would be given enough for two people or just one. There was leeway in the system, but she knew she couldn't exploit the kindness of others forever.

"I want to help," Moswen replied, breathlessly. "I know you're struggling. I can keep an eye on your father during the day when you're at the bakery. And perhaps I can assist in other ways, too."

"Why would you want to help us? We're neighbors, not family."

Jamila was forced to stop now that she was at the food line. She took a deep breath and turned her attention to the squatty woman gazing up at her with a forlorn expression.

"There's much you don't know, child." Moswen spoke in a whisper, her eyes glancing around, looking for potential eavesdroppers.

"Like what? I have a lot on my mind, Moswen. Please get to the point."

"Your engagement to Nephi...?"

Jamila felt tears well up., and fought them back. She would not cry. She would not weep out here in front of everyone. She wouldn't give them anything else to gossip about.

"What engagement? There is none, and I have no desire to discuss it."

Moswen nodded. "I know. And we won't. He's an entitled dolt," she said, louder now. "You're wise to be rid of him."

Jamila didn't respond. Only two people stood in front of her now, and her anxiety ratcheted up. The supervisor skulking in the background was known for his sharp tongue and sharper oversight. She would get no extra helpings today.

"Anyway, I don't care about him. I want to talk about your father."

"Perhaps later," Jamila mumbled, then stepped up to the counter, withdrawing the household bowl from her basket. She handed it to the attendant behind the food table, who wouldn't meet her gaze, then watched the reduced portion being scooped into it. Just enough for one person's dinner.

"You there," Moswen hissed to the server. "You can do better than that. Akhon's service to Khafre is well-known. Do you want the gods to see your hard heart?"

Jamila noticed the volume was just loud enough for the worker to hear, and no one else. She herself would not have attempted to cajole the hapless man; at least not unless she was much hungrier than she was now.

The man ladled several additional spoonfuls into the bowl, then waved her away. Jamila was happy for the plentiful meal, but embarrassed by his mild disgust.

"Thank you, Moswen. I need to get home, now. May we talk this evening?"

"Yes. I'll be over to help with your father's bath. The stench is wafting into my own apartment," she added in a voice that was not unkind.

***

Among Moswen's dubious talents was her knack for consummate timing. Later that evening, after the meal was gone and Akhon's eyelid was drooping with fatigue and a full belly, Moswen barged through front door. Her chubby arms were filled with towels, brushes, and perfumed soap paste.

Jamila's eyes opened wide in surprise. "We can't afford that. I can barely manage olive oil and ash for bathing."

"It's a gift. Did you get fresh water today?"

"Yes, of course. But it's not boiled. There wasn't time after my shift at the bakery."

"Yes, yes. I know you're working extra hours. Another reason you'll need my help with him," Moswen said, removing her wrap and fixing her gaze upon Akhon. Jamila's heart was moved by the expression she saw on the woman's face; it was mirrored in her own on a daily basis.

Compassion was a side to the pesky woman she had never seen before.

"I'll do his private parts. I'm a married woman. It's not like I don't know my way around down there."

Jamila laughed. She realized it was the first time since her father's accident that she had done so. "That is a kind offer, but I can't ask you to do that. It won't be a pleasant task."

"Clearly," Moswen sniffed.

"Your husband would object to this. I can't allow it." Jamila's tone was unconvincing even to her own ears.

"My husband is attending his whore. He could not care less if I wash the genitals of a camel, let alone a man. Why don't you go fetch some more water? The task will take more than we have. Also, on the way, take this and smash it in the Eastern cemetery."

The pudgy hand reached into a pocket and withdrew a pottery shard. Jamila took the object, reading the amateurish inscription.

"Moswen, we don't believe in demons. The silly practice of smashing shards in the cemetery won't dispel a Sickness

Demon lurking inside my father because it doesn't exist. His condition is due to an accident, not evil spirits."

"Why take a chance? That's the way I see it. Now, just do as I ask, and let me tend to your stinky father. You'll both feel better once he's clean."

Moswen turned her back and went to work on Akhon. When she began pulling off the linen wrap below his waist, Jamila ducked out the front door. Her father's half-hearted protests followed by Moswen's soft scolding made her smile.

The crescent moon floated above the horizon, even though Ra's evening boat, Semektet, had not completed its journey for the day. The air was warmer than it had been, a change she had been dreading. The bakery would be unbearably hot during the warm months, and she would have farther to walk back and forth to her job once she and her father were evicted. The esteemed neighborhood in which they now lived was reserved for the most skilled in Khafre's work force, not lowly bakers nor disabled stone masons. She expected to be moved within the week.

She forced anxiety from her mind and tried to enjoy a moment to herself as she trudged in the direction of the village cistern. She would indulge Moswen on the way and perform the pottery shard ceremony. It was the least she could do in exchange for bathing her father.

What was behind the woman's sudden beneficence? Their nosy neighbor had never struck her as helpful or selfless, yet there she was giving Jamila's father a bath, a task that no one in their right mind would seek out. She remembered the words from earlier: *There's much you don't know, child.* Jamila had been too distracted to ponder their meaning, but she did so now. In her preoccupied state, she didn't see the young man lounging near the beer vendors until a low, familiar whistle caused her to turn.

"What do you want?" she said, watching Nephi detach himself from a group of young men and stumble, drunkenly, toward her.

"I miss you, Jamila. I wish you could find it in your heart to forgive me." There were tears in the brooding eyes, but were they for her or for himself? Nephi's only hardship was not marrying his first choice of female; there were plenty in line to take her place.

"I'm sorry, Nephi, but my mind is made up. There will be another girl for you," she added, feeling a stab of jealousy. She quashed it quickly. There was no longer room in her heart for romantic nonsense.

"I'm not a bad man, Jamila. I just made a mistake."

She noted the chin quiver, and sighed. "Of course, you're not a bad man, but your impulsiveness cost me and my father everything. A happy marriage cannot come from such ominous beginnings. You know this."

He nodded, wearing a comical, lopsided frown. He was too drunk to appear properly miserable.

She hurried on before her conviction wavered. "Go back to your friends, Nephi. Enjoy your evening. I have work to do." She used the coldest tone she could summon.

He stopped on unsteady legs where the road ended and the funerary ground began. She proceeded without looking back.

The moon was higher now and Ra's boat had vanished. Unlike some, Jamila didn't find the builders' cemetery eerie or sinister. Surrounding her were merely the remains of humans who had passed into the glories of the Afterlife. They could do her no harm, and since she didn't believe in demons or evil spirits, she was as safe here as anywhere else. She set her bucket on the sand, located a hefty rock, placed Moswen's shard upon the ground, and smashed it into several pieces.

"There, Sickness Demon. Consider yourself vanquished." She brushed off her hands, gathered her pail, and turned to leave.

Movement in the farthest corner of the grounds caught her eye.

"Who is there?" she called, pivoting and scanning the perimeter. Nephi was gone, and so, it seemed, was everyone else. Even the beer vendors in the distance had packed up for the night.

She refused to allow fear into her heart. Ghosts couldn't hurt her. Demons didn't exist.

She heard a noise now – the scuffling of feet on rocks and sand. She squinted her eyes in the gloom to see what approached. Finally, a form coalesced, still too distant to see clearly.

"What do you want?" she called, keeping her voice steady and clear. It would not do to show unease to whomever – or whatever – was out there. "Reveal yourself."

"Tsk, tsk," came the scratchy reply. The voice made the fine hairs on her neck prickle. "Trust me. You do not want that."

The figure moved slightly closer, then stopped. The ragged linen clothing and bandaged limbs revealed nothing other than a skeletal frame. The head was swathed in gauze strips, mummy-like, except for the glittering eyes visible through a slash within the shredded fibers. The mouth was likewise partially covered, allowing the whispers to escape.

The reflective eyes, the moonlight, and the setting felt suddenly, poignantly familiar, though she had no idea why. "Who are you? What are you doing here?" she said, hoping her voice sounded brave and confident.

"I live nearby. And the same could be asked of you."

"I...I came to dispel a demon," Jamila replied, dismayed as the figure shuffled closer, then relieved when it stopped.

"You believe in demons?" The words slurred, as if the speaker were missing teeth.

"No, of course not. I was doing it as a favor."

"That's kind of you, then. Most young girls aren't brave enough to venture out here after dark." There might be more missing than teeth, so mangled was the creature's speech.

"I am not most girls."

"I can see that. There's nothing wrong with my eyes, at least." The words were punctuated by a dry cough which might have been laughter.

"I must be going. My father is expecting me." She turned to leave. She would not run, but would walk as sedately out of the cemetery as she had when entering it.

"Not yet, please, child. Give me a few moments of your time. It would be a mercy. I don't get to speak to people often."

"Perhaps you shouldn't skulk about in cemeteries, then." Jamila wished she had brought the knife her father had given her on her twelfth birthday. She had forgotten it in her rush to get out of the apartment.

"You are quite lovely. Who are your parents?" The voice seemed wistful now, somewhat diminishing the ghoulish quality.

"What business is that of yours?"

Another dry cough, sounding even more like laughter now.

"None, I suppose. I'm just curious, and as I said, I don't often get the chance to talk to people."

Inexplicably, Jamila felt a flicker of sympathy. "What is wrong with you?" she said in a kind voice. She could afford to be gracious, as long as the figure maintained an acceptable distance. She could outrun the emaciated, shambling creature with ease, especially with a head start.

"You haven't guessed? Are you prettier than you are intelligent?"

With dawning horror, Jamila realized whom – or rather what – she was speaking to.

"You're a leper."

"Of course. Don't worry, though. It isn't as contagious as most believe. You're in no danger at this distance."

Despite the reassuring words, Jamila was filled with fear and revulsion.

"You remind me of someone," the leper continued. "Is your father Akhon, the finest stone mason in Giza? You have his nose and mouth."

"You know him? How can that be?"

Another cough-laugh. "Do you think I was born like this? I knew him many years ago. Is it true about his accident?"

"Yes." Jamila was listening hard to the whispers, not just the words themselves. Was this a man or a woman? It was impossible to tell from the skeletal, shrouded shape.

"Such a pity. May the gods have mercy on him."

"Thank you. How do you know him?"

"It's time you were on your way. The whores and thieves will be out soon. A nice girl like you should be safe in her home."

Abruptly, the leper turned and shuffled away.

"Wait," Jamila called, but the shadowy form was already lost in the gloom.

The creature was right about the late hour. Jamila darted from the cemetery and quickly finished the tasks she had set out to do.

"You took your time," Moswen said, when she returned home.

"I was merely doing your bidding." Jamila placed the water next to her father, who now wore a clean loincloth. His eye stared at her in wordless horror. She stifled a giggle.

"You missed the worst of the bath. Just as I planned." Moswen winked.

"Ah, I see what you did."

"Two birds, one stone."

"Thank you, Moswen. We don't deserve such kindness."

"Of course, you do. All good people deserve kindness. Now, wash his feet. They're disgusting."

Jamila nodded, squatted down, and rubbed soap paste upon her father's feet. Without looking up, she said, "What did you mean earlier? 'There's much I don't know.'"

Moswen combed Akhon's freshly washed hair, taking her time in answering. "Did you know that your mother was not the first woman to whom your father was engaged? There was another, an arranged marriage, not one of love, as was the case with your mother."

"I never knew that. Did he tell you? How do you know?"

The plain face turned melancholy. "Because I was that woman."

"What? What happened?"

"Look at me, child. Do you see a face that might once have been beautiful, even before I got fat? Don't answer that. I was promised to Akhon and thrilled to be so. He was...underwhelmed by the match, but at least pleased to be connected to such a well-respected family as mine. That all changed when he met your mother." Moswen sighed, then continued combing her father's wet hair as gentle snores wafted from his open mouth. Jamila noticed the affection in her movements now. She watched the woman tend to her disabled father – supine, asleep, and drooling – like a devoted spouse.

"You still love him?" It was less a question than a statement.

"Yes. I never stopped."

"But you married someone else. Your husband has provided a comfortable life, much better than Akhon would have given you."

"It's true I have all the material things I want. But I was denied marital love and never produced a child for either my husband or me to cherish. We have an understanding, Jamila. That's why I'm here bathing your father, and my husband is with his mistress."

"I see," she said, looking at the pudgy force-of-nature in a new light.

"And that's why I want to help. Because I'm in a position to do so, and because Akhon will always be the love of my life. Perhaps that sounds pathetic, but I don't care. And I would prefer you not discuss it with anyone. People have forgotten and I'd like to keep it that way." The lips puckered into a tight circle, and Moswen wouldn't meet her eyes. For one so immersed in gossip, the irony of the woman's request was not lost on Jamila. Still, she would respect her wish, for reasons of honor and also because she needed her help. Desperately.

"Of course, Moswen. You have my promise. But once we're forced to move, you won't be close enough to visit often."

"We'll see about that. Perhaps I can put in a good word with the Clerks."

"I would appreciate that very much," she said, then dismissed the idea. Jamila refused to get her hopes up.

"He's all finished, and I must go." Moswen stood, gave Akhon a kiss on his bandaged head, and patted Jamila's shoulder on her way out the door and into the night.

Soon after, Jamila lay on her pallet, pondering the strange events of her evening before her eyes closed in exhaustion.

When she returned home from work late the next afternoon, she decided to talk to Akhon. Her mind had been abuzz all day, and she needed answers. She hoped he would be lucid.

"Papa, I brought you some bread for now. I'll go to the food complex shortly."

Akhon was sitting up, gazing about the apartment as if for the first time. Jamila tore off a piece of the perfectly browned loaf and handed it to her father. He glanced at the object in his fingers as though it were a viper.

"It's bread. Eat it."

"Are you certain it's not poisoned?" His eye was wild now, like a horse about to bolt from its stable.

"Why would it be poisoned?"

He whispered, dismay evident in his voice, "She was here again today."

"Moswen?"

A nod of the head. His jawline had been shaved without even a single nick to the sagging skin. Her father's appearance had aged ten years, but he looked cleaner and healthier at that moment than he had in weeks.

"She did a fine job of shaving you. Nobody wants to poison you, least of all Moswen. She's agreed to help me take care of you. Isn't that wonderful?"

A vigorous shake of the head now.

"Why not?"

"She loathes me," he replied.

"That's not true. She actually loves you. She told me herself last night after you went to sleep. Why did you never tell me you were engaged to her before Mama?"

"I only just remembered it last night, during the...bath." He shuddered. "Perhaps I knew it before the accident. I can't say for sure."

"Oh, Papa. Of course you knew it before. What do you remember?"

"Everything is foggy, Jamila. I recall a beautiful woman who must have been your mother. I see her holding you, bundled in the wrap you wear now when the air is cool."

"My swaddling?"

"I think so. You were a chubby, happy baby with two little teeth that peeked out when you giggled. Your mother loved it when you giggled. It made her giggle too." Akhon's eye closed. The corners of his mouth turned up dreamily.

Jamila frowned. "That can't be right. Mama died giving birth to me."

The eyelid popped open. "No. That's not what happened. But I don't remember what did happen to her, Jamila. I don't remember!" He was getting upset now.

"Sshhh, don't fret. We'll talk about it later. Eat your bread now," she said, taking a portion for herself and chewing it while ruminating on his provocative declaration.

Movement at the doorway interrupted her thoughts.

"Hello, Jamila. I hope you had a good day. I've brought a few pomegranates. Just in case..." Moswen gestured to the solitary chit placed in the market basket next to the bowl.

Jamila studied her neighbor with narrowed eyes, then her gaze traveled to the gifted fruit.

"That's very kind of you, Moswen. Tell me something, please. Why would my father think you might want to poison him?" She saw no need to prevaricate. Best to have everything out in the open with this odd little woman if she were going to accept her help.

"Poison? That's absurd. I told you last night I love your father. I always have."

"Yes, that's what you said. But would a woman scorned still love the man who broke her heart? The man who called off an engagement to her because he was in love with a woman more beautiful than herself?"

The beady eyes narrowed, matching Jamila's expression. "He's out of his mind, Jamila."

"Perhaps not completely out of his mind."

"Perhaps not. But you have it wrong. He wasn't the one to call off the engagement."

Jamila's jaw dropped.

"Close your mouth or flies will get in. I was the one who cancelled it."

"Why would you do that?" she stammered.

"Why wouldn't I? Do you think I wanted to be the heavy, ugly brick Akhon wore about his neck for an entire lifetime?"

Jamila had no answer.

"Even more though," she said, sitting down at the foot of Akhon's pallet and patting his knee. Her father's eye stared at the would-be poisoner on his blanket. "I wanted to release him from an obligation he had no stomach for. Above all else, your father is honorable. Even though I felt the sting of the emotional abandonment, he would never have subjected me to the lurid, painful circumstance of publicly rejecting me. So I let him go instead. I set him free."

"You did that to yourself?"

The close-set eyes peered at her with disdain. "You still don't get it, do you? Of course, you don't. You're too young. You have never experienced all-consuming love for another person. Not the selfish, self-absorbed type most people engage in, but a love that places another person's happiness above her own." Moswen chuckled, a snorting combination of bitterness, amusement, and affection.

"Oh, Moswen. I'm sorry."

"It's long-dead history. Besides, it didn't end well for your father. I doubt he would believe that I felt no vindication when he lost your mother. And I'm here now because I want to be, not because I have any underlying spiteful desire to even the score. That's never how it was."

Akhon's eye watered now, but he didn't speak.

"What about my mother? Akhon said something that makes me question that she died in childbirth. He may be confused, but he seemed quite adamant."

The brown eyes became aloof, suddenly. "I cannot comment on matters that are not my business."

Jamila laughed out loud, then covered her mouth quickly. "You know everyone's business. Why withhold now?"

A reluctant grin tugged at the thin lips. "You have a point. Still, this is not my discussion to have."

"Akhon is not capable of having it."

"Give him time. Maybe he will, or maybe he won't. Either way, what happened in the past is unchangeable. Best to let old bones stay buried."

With that she made her way to the door and out into the late afternoon sunshine. Before she disappeared from view, she said, "There is no stronger force in the world than true love, child. Not that of the Pharaoh, nor his pyramid, nor even the gods themselves."

After Moswen was gone, Jamila studied the door without seeing it, thinking about the words. Then she turned to her father, who was drooling again. She sighed, wiping the moisture from his chin. There would be no further answers that day.

Sleep eluded her for hours. She kept thinking about the kind of love Moswen felt for Akhon and how rare it must be. To sacrifice your own happiness so that your loved one can be happy in your place was almost incomprehensible. When she finally rose with the first blush of pink in the background of Kahfre's pyramid, she saw that her father was up, emptying his bladder in the urine jar by his pallet. She gently cleared her throat so he would know she was there.

"Good morning, Jamila. I'm feeling more clear-headed today."

"Wonderful, Papa. Would you like some beer and bread?"

"Yes, in a minute. I need to talk to you, while I'm thinking straight. Come, sit with me." He patted the place where Moswen had been last night.

She sat down and took his hand, noting how soft the fingers were now that they no longer worked heavy tools and rough stone.

"Do you miss it, Papa? Your job?"

"I do. Perhaps I'll get well enough to do some lowly work on the pyramid. Hauling rubble or delivering water buckets."

"That would be beneath you," she said.

"Nothing is beneath a father who must provide for his family. And that's what I want to talk to you about before I forget again. There are still so many holes in my thoughts...it's nearly impossible to piece everything together. But I do remember that your mother did not die giving birth to you. I don't know why I told you that story for all those years. I have vivid memories similar to the one I told you about, when you were a toddler with your mother. I know she did not perish during childbirth."

"I wish I could remember her," Jamila said. Her mind could summon nothing earlier than images of her father's face.

"She was special, like you. Not just a rare beauty and attentive wife, but an exceptionally devoted mother."

Jamila felt her eyes water.

"Something happened. She was here one day and gone the next. I just can't remember what it was, nor why I didn't tell you the truth."

"I think Moswen knows, but she won't tell me."

"Maybe I can talk to her today, if she comes again."

"That would be wonderful, Papa. You realize now that she doesn't want to poison you?"

The eyebrow arched. "Probably not. Possibly not. Oh, who knows? Everything is so foggy."

Jamila could see his mind clouding up again. Pressing him further would just upset him. Instead, she readied herself for work, then left the apartment with firm directions to Akhon to stay put.

"You may stand outside for fresh air, but don't leave. We don't want you wandering off and getting lost."

"Hmmm." He stood in the doorway with the morning sun shining on his face. She was happy to see his color was a little better every day.

"I mean it, Papa. We wouldn't want people to think you have something they could catch." She was thinking about the leper. Her father's bandaged eye and thin limbs could be mistaken for more than injuries.

She saw that her words had an effect on him, but she couldn't tell what kind. And since she was late for work, she would have to ask him about it later. How strange that their roles had been reversed: she was now the one to give orders, and he must acquiesce. It gave her no sense of satisfaction.

Her day was harder than usual. Even the gentle Nedjem, her supervisor, was cranky and demanding. She was especially relieved to be finished for the day. She placed one of the best loaves in her market basket and ducked out of the bakery. She would go to the street venders on her way home and purchase some fresh beer for Akhon. With a sinking feeling in her belly, she saw Nephi and his friends standing there, already drunk. She pivoted and began walking back the way she had come.

"Jamila, wait," Nephi called, slurring the words.

She sighed. "What do you want? I need to tend to my father. He's been home alone all day."

He caught up to her and tugged on her arm, not ungently.

"I'm miserable, Jamila. I don't know if I can go on."

There was self-pity in the tone, but also genuine heartbreak.

"You can and will," she replied, coldly.

"See? That's what I can't bear. You loved me so and now you can't even look at me without disgust."

"Nephi, if not for your impetuousness, my father would be whole."

"But why can't you see that it was out of love for you that this all happened?"

"Was it? Or was it impatience to get under my dress?" She was shocked by her boldness. Still, it was an opinion she had been harboring, unspoken, since the accident.

Nephi stopped. She begrudgingly did as well, curious to hear his response.

"I love and respect you, Jamila. Of course I felt passion for you. I'm a hot-blooded man. But that's not why I didn't wait for a more suitable time to approach your father. It was because I was eager to begin our lives together. And also, I admit, I was afraid you might get a better offer than me."

This was a new twist. "Jealousy motivated your recklessness?"

Nephi didn't respond, standing in the street and looking miserable.

"You realize this only makes it worse?" she said. "Leave me alone. I want nothing further to do with you." She turned away and began walking.

"I know that, Jamila. And I understand. What I want more than anything else is your forgiveness. Please say that you forgive me. I can't go on if you don't."

"You don't have it. You ruined our lives." She didn't glance back to see the inevitable self-pity on the face of her former suitor. She was in no mood for it.

She meandered through the cobblestone streets of the village, lost in her thoughts and not ready to go home yet. Was she being too hard on him? It was true that if not for Nephi, Akhon would be whole, but Nephi didn't push him off the scaffolding. When the sky turned violet, she headed home.

"Hello, Papa," she said shortly thereafter. She was irritable and exhausted and wanted nothing more than a few moments of relaxation. When she saw distress in her father's face, she knew her desire would be denied.

"She was here again today. That woman who wants to poison me," Akhon whispered, one conspirator to another.

"Moswen does not want to poison you," she said with a sigh. "Here's some bread. I baked it myself. No poison. I suppose this means you weren't able to talk to her about what happened to my mother?"

"What? Your mother died in childbirth," Akhon said. "The poisoner left something for you," he added, pointing to a fragment of pottery on the table next to the doorway. Beside it was a second food chit.

She picked up the shard, glanced at the glyphs, and then set it down again in disgust. "Another demon shard. I won't do it. I'm too tired."

"The poisoner seemed quite insistent. I don't understand what it means, but I know it's very important. You must do it."

She studied her father, noting the anxious look on his face, and forced herself to summon patience from a badly depleted reservoir.

"You don't need to worry about what it means, Papa. I will do it. We can't afford to offend Moswen at this point. She worked some magic and got us an extension on our apartment as well as an extra food chit, it seems."

She placed the second chit in her basket, then trudged back out into the late afternoon sunshine to collect dinner.

By the time her father had eaten, relieved himself, been cleaned up, and settled back into his pallet for the evening, it was dusk. She would have to return from the cemetery after dark. She was so tired she could barely think straight, but she knew she must do this. Moswen's benevolence seemed to depend on it.

She entered through the gates as usual, then found the spot from before. Would the leper show up again? She hoped not. She needed to finish the task and get home before she fell asleep standing up.

She located the same heavy rock, placed the demon shard upon the sand, and smashed it into a miniature rubble pile. She uttered the necessary words, in case Moswen asked if she had, then stood to go.

The shuffling footsteps came from behind, just as they had the last time. The fine hairs on her neck prickled again. When she turned, the leper was close, but not too close.

Moonlight glittered off dark eyes within the linen wrappings. Raspy, labored breathing escaped through a slit in the gauze near the chin. She realized there were no air holes for its nose, and neither was there a lump in the cloth where a nose should be. The image she conjured of the lamentable face beneath the rags filled her with sympathy. As bad as her life had become, it would never be as horrific as this poor creature's existence.

She felt no fear. The shambling bag of skin lesions, lumpy tumors, and bones couldn't hurt her. As long as it didn't approach further.

"I'm happy to see you again." The unearthly voice seemed less frightening this time.

"I was about to leave," Jamila replied.

"Moswen sent you here for a reason. Please sit. I promise I won't come closer."

"I think I'll continue standing."

"You're a sassy one. I like that."

"You know Moswen?"

"Indeed. We were close friends a long time ago."

So the creature was most likely female, which had been impossible to discern from her appearance. The tragedy intensified further. In Egyptian society, it was one thing to be a disfigured, contagious male, but quite another to be a disfigured, contagious female.

"She has been helping my father and me since the accident. I'm in her debt."

"You are that. She's a paradoxical creature, our Moswen. But she does have you and your father's best interest at heart. You can trust her."

"Your endorsement of her might carry some weight if I knew you."

The dry chuckle reminded her of the sound of the laborers' dice games. They used desiccated animal bones for the game pieces.

"I see that you still have no suspicion...no clue as to my identity, despite the recent revelations."

"What revelations?"

"That your mother did not, in fact, die during childbirth."

"Moswen told you that?"

"Jamila, think about it. I know you have your father's quick mind, as well as his good looks."

Suddenly, the world came crashing down upon her. She thought she might faint. She took the leper's advice and sat abruptly on the sand.

"Mama?" she said. Tears streamed down her face.

"Yes, my darling. Oh, Jamila, I've missed you more than words could ever convey. I'm so proud of the young woman you've become."

"H-h-how did it happen?" she said, once she could speak again.

"There was a woman I worked with in the merchants' street. We sold baubles and trinkets from a stand. I carried you to work with me after you were born, but you were a baby and wouldn't remember any of that. I would cover your little face with a cloth so you wouldn't get hot in the sun. I think that may be why you never contracted the disease."

"The woman gave it to you?"

The ragged head nodded. "I noticed a growing white patch on her arm and commented on it. I know now she had suspected she was ill and yet continued to expose me – and you – to it. It took many years to forgive her, but I finally managed. She died recently. I buried her in the colony's plot."

"The leper colony? That's where you live now…" Jamila trailed off, overwhelmed with thoughts of her mother's life all these years. She found it difficult to breathe.

"Yes. It's as bad as you might imagine, but there is life to be had there anyway, and all life is precious."

"Oh, Mama. You left so you wouldn't make me and Papa sick."

"Of course. The two people I loved most in the world could not be exposed to what I had, so I disappeared. Leaving you was the most difficult thing I've ever done. Much worse than living with this disease. Akhon and I decided on the story of my dying in childbirth so you would not be stigmatized or traumatized. Moswen played an important role. Anyone in the village who revealed the truth to you would be subjected to a reputation assassination. She knows everyone's secrets."

Her mother might have been smiling under the bandages.

The raspy voice continued. "We would have carried on with the deception but for the recent damage to your father's brain. Moswen came to me and told me he was no longer able to keep up the pretense, and that you were old enough and strong enough to know the truth. So here we are." The skeletal arms opened wide, gesturing to the gloom of the cemetery. Jamila had the desperate desire to rush into their loving embrace.

"Don't even consider it," her mother said, reading her thoughts. She folded her arms.

"I don't think I can endure it, Mama, thinking of you like this. It's so unfair. How could you ever forgive that woman for making you sick and ruining your life?"

The voice no longer sounded eerie now that she knew it belonged to her mother. With alarm, though, she noticed its strength diminishing. She had to strain to hear the words.

"If I could teach you one thing, it would be forgiveness. Resentment and grudges impact the target only slightly – or perhaps not at all. They cultivate insidious, harmful forces inside the person who harbors them. They are poison and will destroy you. Your young man..."

"Nephi?"

"Yes. You must forgive him. I know it's not easy and it won't happen overnight, but you must work toward that goal. The process of forgiveness – genuine forgiveness – can take a long time. Months, years, even. But the sooner you accomplish it, the sooner you can be happy and whole. Has he asked to be forgiven?"

Jamila nodded.

"Well, then. The process can begin."

There was much truth in the words. Jamila had been nurturing in her belly a tight, angry ball of bitterness, a malignant growth of animosity for her former suiter. It was damaging to them both and served no purpose other than to cause pain for everyone within its influence.

"You're right. I see that now. If you can forgive the woman who made you ill, I can forgive a foolish, impetuous young man."

"Exactly."

"I can come back and visit you tomorrow," she said, excited now at the prospect of gaining a mother after all these years.

Moonlight reflected off moisture in the cloaked, glittering eyes.

"My time draws near, child. I scarcely had stamina enough to walk here tonight. For my sake, because it hurts us both for you to see me like this, I ask that you let me go."

Jamila was weeping again. "But I just found you."

"And that is a blessing in its own way. When Akhon is enjoying a clearheaded moment, he can talk about me. I would much rather *that* woman...that mother...be the one you think of. Not this husk."

"I wish I could hold you," she sobbed.

"That is impossible," her mother replied. "Goodbye, my darling. Be strong, be wise, be gentle, and be kind. Remember that I will always love you more than anything in the world." She turned and shuffled away. Jamila could barely see the shadowy form through her tears.

Three months later...

"Thank you for seeing me, Jamila," Nephi said, sipping his beer instead of guzzling it, as had become his habit.

"I'm happy to see that you're doing better," she said, indicating the nearly full cup.

He chuckled. The handsome face looked older than its years. There were already crinkles next to the eyes.

Have I done that to him?

She reached out to squeeze his shoulder, hoping the gesture felt friendly and nothing more. "I'm sorry to have been so cold to you, Nephi. It hasn't been easy..."

"I know. And I'm so sorry about everything."

She smiled. "I know you are. An enlightened person recently explained to me that forgiveness is a process, and today is the beginning of it. Every day it will get easier for both of us to accept the past and not let it sabotage our future happiness."

"I'm so glad to hear this. Does that mean...?"

She shook her head. "No. But we can be friends. That is my desire."

He sighed, looking down at his cup and then reaching for her hand. "I'll take friendship, Jamila. And be grateful for it. I feel as if I have been dragging a boulder, and you just sliced through its tethering."

"I feel a bit like that, too. Now I have to get home. Papa is waiting for me. You'll be happy to know he's doing better. He'll always need supervision, but his moments of lucidity come more frequently these days. I'm hopeful of further progress."

"Me too," he said, kissing her quickly before she could protest. He was gone the next moment, but not before she saw the glistening on his cheek.

This time on her walk home after talking to Nephi, she smiled.

When she arrived home, Moswen was there, struggling to persuade her father to disrobe so she could wash his clothing.

"Get away from me, poisoner!" he yelled, with a half-hearted swat in Moswen's direction.

"I should poison you and put you out of your misery. Now give me that loincloth. It's disgusting, Akhon. Have some dignity, for goodness sake!"

Akhon's eye widened. He glanced down, then without another word, slipped out of his linen. Jamila was used to seeing his skinny, naked body now, so she merely smiled at the scene.

"I hope you had a nice day," Moswen said. "Your father is being difficult at the moment. Good luck with him this evening. I'll see you tomorrow, dear."

Before the stout little woman left, Jamila stopped her, pulling her into a hug. "Thank you, Moswen. For everything."

"You're welcome, child. Helping with Akhon – even the revolting parts – is my pleasure, as absurd as that may seem."

Jamila smiled, too. "I understand."

The In Between

Jamila suddenly found herself floating in a black void. It took a few moments, or perhaps longer, to remember about the In Between, that period between her corporeal lives. The last time she was here was after her life as Johnny. How different this past life had been from that one. The concept was quite exciting now that she fully understood it: there would be no limit to the choices she had in which to learn her remaining lessons.

She knew she didn't have a physical body, but she remembered Sarah's instructions from before, so she manifested one now – not the aged one from just before she passed, but an earlier version of it. Young and vibrant, as she had been right after Akhon's accident.

With newly fashioned eyes, she glanced down at her white linen shift and the sandals on her feet, dusty from the pervasive chiseling of granite surrounding Khafre's pyramid construction. She imagined the cemetery where she had smashed demon shards and talked to her mother. Tears welled up in her new eyes. She sat down on the sand.

"Hello, Jamila."

It was Sarah's voice coming out of another woman's body. The strange woman sat down in front of her, crossing her shapely brown legs.

"Why do you look like that?" Jamila asked.

"It's helpful for me to appear in the form of someone from your most recent life."

"But I don't recognize you."

The would-be Sarah smiled. "I resemble you, don't you think?"

"I suppose, when I was in my thirties..." She said. Then, "Oh! You're her! That's what my mother looked like?"

The Sarah-Mother nodded.

"How beautiful she was."

"She was even more beautiful on the inside, wasn't she?" Sarah-Mother said.

"Yes. In the short time I had with her, she taught me about forgiveness. Can you imagine forgiving the person who destroyed your life?"

"The more important question is, can you imagine it?"

"Yes. I can and I did. I know what you're doing now. You're quizzing me about the lessons of Unconditional Love and Forgiveness."

"That's correct. Would you elaborate on your experiences in Giza as they apply to your assignment?"

Jamila tilted her head while she pondered her life as a baker in the service of Khafre. She began speaking after a few minutes, or perhaps it was a few days. "I learned Unconditional Love through two examples. The love that my mother showed for me and my father when she went into exile. Leaving her child was the most difficult thing she had ever done. I never had children, but I can understand the pain it must have caused her to do that. The other example, surprisingly, was in Moswen's unconditional, lifelong love for Akhon. She never stopped loving him, even when he married another woman – her best friend – and then later, when he regularly defecated into his underwear. She loved him throughout."

Sarah's appearance was changing before her eyes, back into the one Jamila had first met as Johnny. She still wore the plain attire of a common Egyptian female, and despite the uncharacteristic blond hair, the garb suited her better than the lavender polyester track suit from before.

"And so you believe you've learned the lesson of Unconditional Love?" Sarah said.

Jamila nodded. "I do."

"Let's go back to Forgiveness now."

"My mother forgave, *genuinely* forgave, the person who infected her with a horrific disease and ruined her life. She ended up living with that person in the leper colony and even buried the creature with her own hands as a kindness."

"That's something."

"It certainly is. It almost seems superhuman to forgive such a monumental trespass. So my forgiveness of Nephi pales in comparison."

"His transgression was less severe?"

"Yes. Still, his impulsiveness profoundly altered our lives, and not for the better."

"Who's to say what's better?"

"That's true. Ultimately, it's all about learning the lessons, isn't it?" Jamila smiled.

"That's what all this is about. Do you feel that your forgiveness of him was genuine?"

"I do," Jamila replied, sensing Sarah wanted further elaboration. "But it didn't happen suddenly. Even after I told him I forgave him, I still experienced feelings of resentment and anger, especially when he married someone else and lived a happy life."

"That could have been your life."

"Exactly. Instead, I was stuck for years taking care of my disabled father. At some point though, perhaps because I consciously worked at the process of forgiveness as my mother had, I finally achieved it. The last years of my life, I harbored no trace of animosity toward Nephi."

"Excellent."

Jamila sighed. "Yes."

"Are you ready to move forward?"

She nodded.

"What lessons will you take on this time?"

"I think I'd like to learn about Courage, Bravery, and Leadership with a Strong Work Ethic."

"Perfect. Let's discuss the best framework. This will be fun."

Sarah's smile dazzled Jamila as much now as when she had been Johnny. She hoped the next life didn't have to take place right away. For a while, she was happy to bask in the radiance of her Spiritual Guide.

Chapter 3 – Courage, Bravery, and Leadership with a strong Work Ethic

Pre-history Mesopotamia (Iraq) – 12,000 BCE

Jun-tak walked the hills surrounding the makeshift campsite of the Family. As always, he gathered anything edible as he went. The grass he had come to think of as *barley* was everywhere. He would pluck the grains from the feathery tip and roast them on a concave stone in the fire pit. Something told him, however, that there were other ways to make use of them. He intended to experiment more later.

He had brought with him a satchel to carry all the edibles he gathered on his evening walk. The satchel itself was unusual; everyone made their clothing and accessories from animal skins, and had done so for generations back to the time of the Terrible Ice. But a new plant Jun-tak had discovered on one of his walks provided fiber from which many useful items could be woven. He had wasted no time in utilizing the fine, long strands found within the hard stems. As usual, the Family was skeptical of it. Animals had always yielded what they needed for nearly every aspect of their daily lives.

Why expend so much labor cutting the woody things for just a few threads? Meat fills the belly quicker than those toasted seeds, Jun-tak...so much work for just a mouthful or two. Why must you always do things differently, boy?

That last was from his father, who, like the rest of the Family, did not understand his inquisitive and spirited nature. It wasn't easy being different, but to be any other way felt wrong. Until man-hair had begun sprouting between his legs and under his arms, he had done his best to mimic the behavior of the other children. He played their silly games of Rocks and Sticks or Mammoth Hunter, though he longed to be doing something more interesting. More useful. When he began wondering off on his own every day after chores and before the evening meal, nobody was surprised nor tried to stop him. He believed his father secretly admired this solitary independence of his youngest son, even though it violated one of the Family's basic survival tenets: never go anywhere alone. He almost always came back with something that could be eaten or utilized in their migrant lifestyle, and so far, he had not gotten himself killed.

The beauty of the spectacular orange and purple sunset blossoming above the distant hills was lost on Jun-tak, who was too busy studying grasses. The barley was quite plump this time of year, and he used his flint knife to gather as much as possible before all the light was gone. If he worked late, he need not be too worried, for he knew the direction of the camp by the placement of the stars even now beginning to twinkle to life.

Soon it was too dark to efficiently separate the grain from the stalks. He was just about to head back, when he noticed a rocky outcropping not far ahead. He had been meandering gradually uphill and now stood at the base of a squat mountain. The jutting rock formation looked intriguing, as though it might be the opening to a cave.

A shiver ran up his back, and it had nothing to do with the cool evening air. A cave could be concealing an animal, either predator or prey. A cave could be hiding dangerous people who might look upon his innocent curiosity as a hostile act. A cave, especially one as well-situated as this, could also be the perfect solution to a notion that had been rolling around in his head for a while now.

A permanent home. A home in which the Family could remain during all the seasons. It was an uncommon way of thinking that only made sense if they began doing things in other ways, and Jun-tak had several ideas about that, too. These days, people kept on the move. They were always chasing boar, elk, and aurochs. They stayed in an area long enough to deplete all the edible plants, then they would proceed to the next herd. That was the way it had been for generations, and everyone seemed content to continue.

Everyone except Jun-tak.

Constant migration meant the Family had to carry everything of value, so could never accumulate much. Hauling tools, bedding, and tents, left little space for food. They ate on the go, utilizing whatever was at hand. If the herds weren't where they were expected to be, the Family went hungry. If the season's edibles had already been picked over by other migratory peoples, the Family went hungry. If the fish were sparse at the river, the Family went hungry.

So much is beyond one's control when you are constantly roaming.

Jun-tak eyed the cleft from his lower vantage. He waited, ears straining to hear noises coming from whatever might be dwelling (or hiding) inside. He counted a hundred heartbeats. Then two hundred. He heard the usual dusk sounds of insects and bats, but nothing came from the cave.

Knife in one hand and spear in the other, he scaled the sloping terrain. His leather shoes, stuffed with dried grass, made no sound on the rocky ground. In addition to his intellect, stealth was also one of Jun-tak's talents. If not for his passive, benign personality, he probably would have been the best hunter of all. But much to his father's dismay, Jun-tak had no passion for killing. He would do it to fill his belly, but he had no taste for it.

He reached the cleft just as a fading shaft of sunlight illuminated the opening in the hillside. The angle was perfect, and he could see all the way to the craggy walls at the back. Emboldened now, he stepped inside. Evidence of both humans and animals was everywhere: gnawed bones, a crude rendering of an auroch on one of the walls, and desiccated rat droppings. A shallow section of the floor near the front had once been used as a fire pit. Jun-tak squatted next to it, fingering the lumps of coal and ash. No heat remained.

People had been there, but they were long gone. They would never have allowed their fire to go out if they had planned to return. They would have banked the coals carefully so that a quick stoke would ignite them again. The Family thoroughly extinguished their fire before moving on, but they would bring some of it with them. They had a generations-old pouch used for carrying hot embers. Nobody knew from what animal the skin had come, but it was the only hide that could tolerate the heat. It was much easier to coax a quick campfire from hot embers than to start one from scratch.

He withdrew his fire-making kit from his tool satchel. Even the simple but labor-intensive process of fire-starting could be improved, and Jun-tak had done so. Rather than rubbing the drill stick against the hearth stick with his hands, he had rigged strips of leather which, when pulled in a certain way, increased the speed with less work. It was simple, but ingenious.

Soon he had a fire going. In the enhanced lighting, he conducted a thorough search. It was larger than he had previously thought, and a small secondary chamber lay at the back behind some boulders, invisible from the opening. It could be turned into an effective hiding space for people or their valuables. The cave was also quite dry, not damp like some he had examined in wetter locations. The dryer, the better, when it came to the storing food. He wondered how long grain and other edibles would last there. He pictured rigging an elaborate meat-drying system, more efficient than how they preserved it in their temporary camps. If they stayed in one place, they could build a structure for the sole purpose of hanging meat to smoke and dry.

New concepts and ideas flooded into his mind, and they all depended on that unheard of notion of staying put.

He sighed, then continued exploring as his thoughts pursued their journey down this forbidden path.

Niches in the walls could store tools and utensils; the relatively smooth floor could be made comfortable for sleeping, with the addition of some grass and a few hides; a crevasse in the ceiling served as a natural chimney for the smoky tendrils even now wafting toward it. Jun-tak watched as it drifted up and then out to somewhere else, leaving the air mostly smoke-free. It was a marvel to behold, and it further sparked his imagination.

A rustling sound outside interrupted his musings. His hands flew to his weapons, but before he could get a throwing grip on his spear, he saw a familiar face appear in the opening of the cave.

"Mung, you scared me," he said, his heart racing in his chest. "What are you doing here?"

"Did you think I was a demon?" Mung said, grinning like a fool. The grin coaxed a smile from the normally serious Jun-tak. Mung's grins always did.

"No, I thought you were a giant rat. I found your droppings, see?" he gestured toward the corner.

Mung scrunched his nose in disgust. "That explains the smell," he said.

"Did my father send you?"

"No. I came on my own. I've been tracking you the entire time. You didn't know I was there, did you? My hunting prowess improves every day. I watched you gather the...what do you call those things?"

"Barley."

"They're rather tasty when toasted, but they don't fill you up. Besides, I'd prefer a nice, juicy piece of auroch loin."

"I think those grains have potential. I have some thoughts about how to utilize them in additional ways."

"Of course, you do. That's what the brilliant Jun-tak does. He always comes up with better ways to do everything." Mung's smile was affectionate. He wasn't teasing, merely stating a fact. Most people looked upon Jun-tak's would-be improvements with suspicion; they just wanted to do things the way they always had.

"What do you think?" Jun-tak said to his friend, gesturing to the craggy den and its obvious serviceability.

"I think it's a smelly cave."

"Besides the smell, which a thorough cleaning would improve, what do you think?"

"I still think it's a cave. The nature of caves is to house demons and lepers. Also, they block out the sky."

Jun-tak rolled his eyes. "Don't be superstitious. Think about the possibilities of living in a space like this. Shelter from the weather. A place to stockpile food so you don't go hungry when there's none to be found or hunted. Protection from thieves and raiders."

"Who would choose to sleep in a hole? That's madness, Jun-tak. Humans belong out in the open where we can be seen by the gods. No god would notice you in here."

"Who cares if the gods can see me or not? I'm not sure they exist anyway."

Mung's eyes opened wide in alarm. "Don't say that. You will bring a curse down upon yourself."

Jun-tak smiled. "It's a good thing they can't see me in this hole, then, isn't it?"

"True. So are we ready to go back to camp? I'm sure supper is over by now. I hope they saved us some."

Mung turned to go but stopped again at the cave's entrance when he noticed Jun-tak wasn't following. Mung's handsome face and wavy dark hair was silhouetted against a backdrop of twinkling starlight. Jun-tak looked away after staring a bit too long.

"Yes, I suppose. I'm not finished with this, though. I'm coming back tomorrow for more exploring." He scooped up handfuls of dirt and tossed it onto the flames. "You can come with me if you'd like. You don't have to skulk in my footsteps."

Mung laughed, patting him on the shoulder as they began the descent down the side of the hill. "It's more fun to skulk."

Later that night, Jun-tak lay on his pallet, listening to the soft snores of the Family as they slept. Sleep eluded him. He was gazing at the night sky, but not registering the celestial magnificence above him. His mind whirled and spun as details of this new concept presented themselves. This undertaking would be his most ambitious to date.

His father would not be pleased.

The thought prompted another idea: if he could persuade a few others to go along with his scheme, his father might be less disapproving. As with any adventure, there was safety in numbers, and that wisdom applied to Family disagreements, too.

He would approach some of the other young people, convince them of the cleverness of his bold plan, then he would go to his father. With the backing of some of the up-and-coming members, his father might listen.

He released a long breath into the chilly air, watching it turn to vapor above him. His mind was finally at rest enough to seek slumber.

***

"Have you gone mad?" Mung whispered the words, staring at Jun-tak with mild horror. A young female, Onya, the cleverest of all the newly matured women, also stared. She and Jun-tak had been born on the same day fourteen earth-turns ago.

His prepared speech was not playing well to the hastily gathered audience. All around them, the Family was making preparations for another move. The elk had traveled out of the area, and the people would follow.

"Just listen to me. I've thought it through. Think of the time we spend walking from one place to the next, in addition to the work of setting up a new campsite all the time. That is what's truly mad. It's time that could be used for growing food, drying meat, and making tools."

"What do you mean, *growing food*?" Mung said.

"Have you never noticed that the grasses only come at certain times?"

"Yes, of course. What's your point?"

"Have you also noticed that the grains that fell out of my satchel near the creek last week have begun to sprout? Remember? There was a hole in the bottom when I went to fill up my water-skin. Within a few moon-cycles, barley will be flourishing there."

"How do you know that?" Onya spoke for the first time. Her low voice carried a pleasing quality that was as lovely as her face. Most girls wouldn't have anything to do with an odd fellow like Jun-tak, but Onya wasn't typical. She seemed to see beneath everyone's skin to the true nature that dwelled within. She and Jun-tak were kindred spirits. Not in the same way that he and Mung were, but on a deeper, intellectual level. They were cut from the same hide, but she had been less overt with her own progressive thoughts. Discretion was another of her admirable qualities.

"Because I've seen it happen. Remember that time we stayed for more than a moon-cycle in the valley by the Lesser River? I watched barley grow from mere sprouts. I know what they look like at that stage. Then, when I noticed the dropped seeds sprouting into the very same plant by the creek, I realized what had happened. Do you understand what that means?"

Jun-tak was getting excited now. This was his big play, this notion that grasses – barley and perhaps others –

could be guided by humans. Could be grown in preferred areas, gathered, and then grown again in continuous cycles.

"Think about the possibilities of directing the manner and quantity in which our food is acquired. How many members of the Family did we lose last earth-cycle to starvation? Hmmm?"

Mung's eyes misted suddenly. "Seven, including my youngest sister."

"I'm sorry, Mung, but you see my point even more clearly because of your loss. Her death – due to an empty belly – could have been prevented if we had more control over our food."

"She had always been sickly, though," Onya said, with a quick, sympathetic squeeze of Mung's shoulder. "It wasn't just starvation."

"It was starvation that pushed her over the edge, and we all know it. We were all going hungry and would have died if not for an auroch herd stumbling into our path. We got lucky."

"The gods sent the auroch. It wasn't luck." Mung was getting angry now.

Jun-tak would have to soften his approach. He had no use for the concept of divine beings interfering in his fate, but most did. He was forced to indulge these absurd notions or risk further scorn as a nonbeliever.

He took a deep breath. "Very well, Mung. But what if the gods don't have to interfere to save us? What if we did such a good job of providing for ourselves that all they had to do was smile down upon us with satisfaction?" He exchanged a covert expression of understanding with Onya. She too was skeptical of all things divine.

"Imagine growing so much grain during the warm season that we could save much of it for the winter. For once, we won't go hungry just because there is snow on the ground. I've discovered another way to eat it, too, other than merely toasting it. I grind the raw grains between two rocks until it feels like coarse sand. Then I mix in some water and cook the mixture on a flat stone in the fire pit. It's delicious. I'm calling it *bread*."

"When did you do that?" Mung demanded. Little happened within the Family that Mung didn't know about. Privacy was rare, which is why his friend had become intrigued by Jun-tak's solitary wanderings.

"Soon after I showed you the cave. I thought you might have been skulking in my footsteps again, but I guess you weren't."

"I can't track you all the time. I do have other responsibilities."

"If all this...abundance...truly comes to pass, where would we put it?" Onya said. "How could we carry it on our backs?"

Jun-tak gave her one of his rare smiles. He suspected she already knew the answer. "That's the part I was coming to. The cave I mentioned is perfect for storing everything, including our tools, our food, and ourselves. It's dry and convenient to the grasses and the creek, and I've seen evidence of herds passing nearby."

"Demons live in caves," she said, but it sounded like she was repeating an outdated sentiment that even she didn't believe. "Are you sure it's not damp? Food grows fuzzy in wet places."

"No, it's quite dry." Jun-tak was careful not to seem too excited. "Mung was there a few days ago. It will hold the three of us easily. And the orphan capra you caught by the river last week. We can make a little pen for it, Onya."

Mung laughed out loud. "Now I know you have gone mad. Keeping an animal in a pen inside a cave? What is the point of that? Pens are for herding animals into for easier slaughter. That capra is barely a mouthful, so why even keep it?"

Dismay spread across Onya's face. Jun-tak was probably the only one who had seen her attachment to the creature. When no one was looking, she cared for it as one would care for a human baby, chewing up food and spitting it into the creature's mouth to keep it alive.

He had an answer ready. "Because once it's older, we will find another to breed it with. Then we will have more to keep in the pen. Have you noticed how Onya's orphan follows her around, bleating for her? Have you ever seen an animal do such a thing? I have a theory: I think animals, or at least capras, can be made to not fear people. If you get them as babies, they become used to humans from the very start. It makes sense."

Onya slowly nodded as the brilliance of such a bold endeavor revealed endless possibilities. "I have heard of this before. At the last Great Gathering, I was told of a tribe that collected the milk of the capras. They drank it, and they made it into something else for food. I think they called it curds."

Jun-tak laughed. "See? There you have it. Other people are doing things differently too. We don't want to be left behind, do we? We can continue breeding the capras, using their milk and also their meat when we have a large enough number. We would no longer be at the mercy of the herds. We could simply select one of the penned animals for supper."

Onya winced but didn't respond.

"We won't eat yours. Just the new ones. I promise."

"This is the first time I've heard of influencing and guiding the grasses, though," she continued. "It seems far-fetched. And who knows how long it would take to find a male to breed with my animal? In the meantime, how would we eat by staying in one place? What if no herds came along?"

"We will have plenty of grain to make bread, and the fishing in the Lesser River is excellent. One of us would stay here and work on gathering the grains, while the other two go fishing. We could build a hut to smoke and dry the fish somewhere nearby. Then when cold weather arrives, we will all live in the cave and eat smoked fish and baked bread, comfortable and warm, while the Family continues to wander about, perhaps freezing and starving."

Jun-tak's heart was pounding. He had just revealed the crux of his big plan: the three of them would stay behind when the Family left. The other members of their tribe wouldn't return to this area for many moon-cycles.

Would his friends want to be away so long from their parents and siblings? Jun-tak studied the effect of his words on the faces of the others. The familiar sounds of the Family packing its meager belongings and preparing to move out reached their ears. He saw that Mung and Onya struggled to make such a tremendous decision – not just to live in a completely different manner, but to do so with only friends, not brothers and sisters and mothers and fathers.

"We have everything we need, right here," he pleaded. "I promise we will not be hungry this winter. The Family cannot offer you the same promise. You know this to be true. Not only that, when they return, we will be able to show them our successes. And perhaps...perhaps...we can convince others to join us. With more laborers, we could grow more barley and other grains. We could find more capras or even aurochs for our herd. We will keep improving our methods until no one in the Family will ever die from an empty belly. I give you my word."

At that moment, Jun-tak's least favorite person spoke from behind. He hadn't heard Zorv approach, and neither had the others.

"What is this madness I'm hearing?" Zorv was only one earth-cycle older than Jun-tak but outweighed him by several stones, and his bulging muscles were twice the size of Jun-tak's sinewy ones. Oftentimes, the brains of bulky fellows didn't match their brawn, but Zorv was different. In addition to being the best hunter, he was one of the smartest people in the Family. Still, he and Jun-tak were often on opposing sides of disputed issues. Usually their votes on decisions would cancel out the other's.

"Shouldn't you be packing?" Jun-tak said without turning around.

"I could say the same to you," Zorv replied in a reasonable voice. "But instead, I see you weaving a spell of words over these impressionable young people. Guiding the grasses? Teaching capras to live with humans? Where do you come up with this nonsense?" he said, clapping Jun-tak hard on the back.

Jun-tak sighed. He didn't like Zorv, but he did hold a grudging respect for him. "I wish you had arrived at the beginning to hear the entire speech."

"I didn't need to. I heard the last part about living in a cave while the Family travels south. You remember the south? Where there is no snow and ice? It's irresponsible of you to suggest this, Jun-tak, and even worse to use your cleverness to sway their minds. It's one thing for you to indulge in absurdities, but to recruit others on such a dangerous undertaking is reckless even for you."

The words felt like a physical blow. His enthusiasm, his absolute conviction in his radical but logical ideas, had blinded him to his own behavior. He knew he had a gift for persuasion, and in the end it served others as well as himself when his theories panned out. Despite the disparaging tone, Zorv was right, though. Jun-tak was using coercion to entice his friends into following him on a perilous path, even though he felt with every fiber of his being that it was the best course.

"They have their own minds, Zorv. They're not children." His words sounded petulant even to his own ears. "But, I won't say anything further. I've presented my ideas, and it is now up to them whether they will join me."

"Not yet. Now they shall hear a voice of reason. Onya, do you believe you mother and father will allow you to stay behind and live with two men, neither of whom is your husband? Mung, have you thought about how cold it gets here in the winter? Can you imagine your pretty nose turning black from frostbite and falling off your pretty face? Besides, what will your widowed mother do without her only son?"

Jun-tak's heart fell. He could see the devastating effect of Zorv's words on the others. He would be staying behind alone.

"He's right. I'm sorry I tried to persuade you to stay with me."

"It was rash of you," Zorv said. "You should save your powers of persuasion for more worthy ventures, not this kind of folly." He snorted in disgust. "I thought you were smarter than that."

Jun-tak tilted his head, studying his adversary. Zorv calmly returned his gaze.

"It's not folly, and I will prove it. I'm staying here. When you all return next earth-cycle, you will see I was right."

"I will see your skeleton in that cave."

"You will see food left over in my store room, even after the long winter. I will not starve, as some of the Family inevitably will. I'm not indulging in fanciful notions. I've thought this out, and I have a plan. This is the future for us...for all of us. But I must prove it to everyone, including you. I accept that."

"Exactly. Your promise of full bellies and warm, cozy nights is mere speculation. Show that it can be done first by doing it yourself. Then recruit others for your cause. That should have been your plan all along."

With that, Zorv turned his back and walked away.

The words stung, but their truth was undeniable. He was not surprised by the expressions he now saw on the faces of the other two.

***

Jun-tak stood outside his cave, shielding his eyes from the setting sun as he watched the final straggling Family members vanish over a distant hill.

The silence enveloped him, which was not a bad thing. He wondered how he would feel after a few moon-cycles of being alone. He had never really minded being by himself. He was still grinning when he ducked back inside. His father had not been pleased with his decision to stay, but at fourteen earth-cycles, Jun-tak was considered an adult within the Family and therefore could make his own decisions.

At their time of leaving, his father had presented generous gifts of a hand ax and spear tip. Jun-take had wasted no time in replacing his old, dull tip with the new one. His father was the best at tool-making; no one could flake a sharper edge. Both tools would serve Jun-tak well during the coming earth-cycle. He would utilize the hand ax with its bulbous side and pointed side for chopping, scraping, and cutting. Its design was simple but effective, and the Family had been using versions of them for generations. The exquisitely honed spear tip would pierce even the toughest hides when well-thrown. He was thrilled to have both of these valuable gifts.

His mother, her eyes glistening with unshed tears, had also presented him with a gift, perhaps even more prized than those of his father. Inside the supple pouch was nestled a sizeable quantity of dried moss, the type used to clean wounds so they would not fester. She had included a bit of herb for easing pain, too, utilized by the old people for stiffness and aching in their knees and backs. He imagined with all the hard labor facing him, he would make use of its pain-easing properties, too. He had placed the precious pouch in one of the niches in the rock wall of his new home, then stood back with arms crossed to admire the effect. After a good sweeping, the floor was now clean and covered with fresh grasses that smelled much better than rat droppings. A cheerful fire burned in the pit. His sleep mat lay in a snug corner. From it, he would be able to watch the cave's opening and see the stars beyond, and he would also be in range of the fire's warmth and light.

His heart swelled with pride at what he had accomplished so quickly. After all the work, there was more to be done, and a bit of lingering sunlight accorded an opportunity for it. He reached for his satchel and headed out to the surrounding hillside to gather more of the barley grains before dark. With luck, he might stumble across a hare for his dinner. He studied the new tip and smiled.

He could not remember a time he had felt such a sense of contentment.

***

Later, Jun-tak sat next to his fire, turning three voles on an improvised spit above the flames. Each would provide no more than a mouthful of food, but along with gruel made from the barley, he would have a full belly that night. It was dark now, and despite the firelight, he could see the cold bright stars burning just outside his new home. He hadn't managed to catch a hare, but he knew they were out there in the grasslands. He had seen their scat.

Tomorrow he would build a few snares, which would take time to construct and place, but in the long run would require less effort than hunting. Once they were assembled from rocks, strips of leather, and pliable tree branches, they need only be set at night and checked in the morning. The Family rarely utilized snares because the food they caught was small; their time and energy was better spent pursuing large game or gathering edibles. A few voles or a small hare was enough for one person, so the method would work perfectly for Jun-tak. He would focus on the barley and also wheat; just hours ago he had discovered an enormous swath of it growing to the north of his new home.

The moon had fully risen by the time he finished dinner and banked the fire for the night. He lay on his pallet, not bothering with the blanket. The fire had done a nice job of warming the space. Plus it was late summer, and the weather was mild. He probably wouldn't need to worry about snow and ice for at least several moon-cycles. He really had no idea what to expect since the Family was always long gone by the time winter arrived in the northern grasslands. The thought prompted him to add another item to his mental list: fur and hides. He was not the mighty hunter Zorv was, but he could track game well enough. He had stealth on his side, if not brawn.

As he was beginning to doze off, a noise roused him into full alertness. He held his breath, eyes frozen on the cave's opening. Insects and night birds were all he heard for several heartbeats, then the sound came again: the howling of a wolf – not an unfamiliar sound, and not one to be relished. Wolves provided excellent fur, but their meat was unpalatable except under desperate situations. Even worse, a pack could be dangerous to a solitary human. He reached for his spear, fingering the sturdy length of the shaft and the deadly sharp point at the end.

No wolf would enter his home that night.

Another sound pierced the night. He analyzed it with a sinking heart.

The bleating of a baby capra.

He jumped up, spear in hand, and ran outside. A flat area just beyond the cave's opening was well-positioned for observing the surrounding countryside. The full moon had risen in the starlit sky. The night world appeared almost as bright as its daytime sister. He scanned the hills, the verdant green and splendid gold now awash in shades of gray. His gaze sought movement to the south – a shadow figure ran toward him. He recognized Onya's familiar form even from the lengthy distance. The bleating of the capra confirmed her identity. A second, ominous shape chased her from behind.

This one ran on four legs.

Jun-tak was scrambling down the side of the hill before he even realized he was doing so. His feet flew above the rocky terrain, but would they carry him to Onya in time? Even now he could see the shaggy silhouette advancing on his friend. She was swift, but no human could outrun a wolf. The capra's bleats sounded panicked to his ears; it had caught the scent of the predator. She need only toss the animal down and keep running toward safety. The wolf would choose the smaller, easier meal instead of the larger one that would fight back. But of course she would not sacrifice her beloved pet, which she carried in a sling across her torso.

"Onya!" he yelled as he ran. "Drop it! The capra is not worth your life!"

Did she hear him? He couldn't tell.

He did a quick calculation in his head: his speed; her speed; the distance between them; the dwindling space between her and the wolf; and the range of his spear.

He knew he was about to watch his friend die.

He shouted again, but Onya was either too terrified or too stubborn to abandon the capra.

He increased his speed more than he thought possible; his chest felt as if it might explode. But it would not be enough. The wolf was almost upon her.

Just as it pushed off those powerful hind legs and began arcing toward Onya's exposed back, a shaft came out of the gloom, knocking the predator off its trajectory. It landed on the ground with a single sharp howl of pain.

Onya kept running for a few more paces, then slowed and turned. Jun-tak finally reached her. They both stood gasping for air, watching with disbelief as Zorv appeared from out of nowhere. His grin was not as handsome as Mung's, but it was a welcome sight.

"Is it dead?" Onya asked once she caught her breath.

"Dead, indeed. And Jun-tak will have a fine, new pelt. Good thing I'm here to provide for him," Zorv said with a smirk. "Also a good thing I was here for you, Onya. Running away from the Family at night while carrying a tasty morsel like that capra for the night predators to scent? What were you thinking?"

"I know. It was foolish of me. But they planned to roast Lily! I heard them talking about it." Her eyes glistened with tears.

Jun-tak almost laughed at the dumbfounded expression on Zorv's face.

"You gave it a *name*? You would have gotten yourself killed over an animal? Has everyone in the Family gone mad?" Zorv's exasperation was comical, but Jun-tak was careful not to let his amusement show.

"Not just an animal. She's my pet. I'm keeping her."

Jun-tak recognized the set of Onya's jaw – there would be no denying that jaw. Opposing her wishes once she had set her mind to something was like resisting day turning into night and back again. She was a lovely but determined force of nature.

Zorv saw it as well and sighed. "Jun-tak, it seems you will have some overnight guests tonight, although the notion of sleeping in a hole is quite unpleasant."

"Nobody is forcing you to be here," Onya said. "You followed me. I would never intentionally put any of the Family in danger."

Jun-tak saw the quick frown on the hunter's face, then something unidentifiable, before both were masked in a façade of indifference. "I knew exactly what you were planning. As one of the strongest and most skilled of all the men, it was my duty to protect you. What choice did you leave me?"

Onya snorted in disgust. "Nobody forced you. It was my decision to depart. I didn't want anyone coming with me. If you had been asleep like the rest of the Family, you wouldn't have seen me slip away, and thus, you would not have had to follow."

"I was on watch. You know that."

"Well, it was your job to look for predators from without, not runaways from within."

That evoked a loud guffaw from Zorv. It was the first time Jun-tak had ever heard laughter come from the muscle-bound hunter. It was a surprisingly pleasant sound.

"Very well. You have made your point. What sane person would willingly choose to run away from safety, in the middle of night, carrying a baby capra? Don't answer. Now I have made my point. Jun-tak, lead on," Zorv said, slinging the dead wolf onto his shoulders.

"This way," Jun-tak said with a smile. He wrapped his arm around Onya as they headed back to his new home. "Lily, hmmm? I like the name you selected for your pet. You and she are both welcome to stay as long as you like. And I promise we will not put her in the stew pot."

"Thank you, my friend. And I promise to assist in your undertaking. No matter what that one says," she gestured toward Zorv. "I think you are wise and courageous. And I will help you prove the soundness of this new lifestyle."

When they arrived back at the cave, Jun-tak stoked up the fire. He watched Onya's eyes open wide in surprise at the scene the crackling flames revealed. She performed a slow pivot, taking in all the comforts of his new home, noting Jun-tak's pallet near the opening.

"I'll sleep here," she said, pointing to the farthest back corner. Her meaning was clear.

"Of course. I was thinking that would be the best spot for you. Zorv, you can take the space opposite me. That way we'll both be nearest to anything that might try to enter."

"That would have been my suggestion. But sleep will have to wait. I'll tend to this pelt while it's still warm and pliable." He dropped his bundle on the floor and took the dead wolf outside.

Jun-tak breathed a sigh of relief. Zorv always put him on edge.

"I can't believe you came," he said as Onya squatted next to the fire. "Zorv was right. It was foolish, but brave. I would have done the same thing."

Onya smiled. "I knew you would understand. You have always understood me unlike any other. It wasn't just about the capra. I want to support you because you are smart and creative and also my best friend."

"And you are mine," he said reaching over to squeeze her hand. In the soft firelight, Onya's face looked especially pretty, but Jun-tak's affection for her was platonic. His heart belonged to someone else.

"This is quite an adventure. What will we do tomorrow?" she said

"There is a long list of chores. But the first order of business will be to build a pen for Lily."

Onya's squeal of delight filled him with joy. They discussed plans for their future. Jun-tak felt his eyelids grow heavy now that the excitement waned. He was about to suggest going to sleep when Zorv appeared at the cave's opening, bewilderment evident on the bearded face.

"You people are demented," he said, then pushed a figure in front of him.

Jun-tak's heart leapt with joy at the sight of Mung, grinning like a fool, as usual.

"You thought you could do this without me?" he said.

"You followed me?" Onya jumped to her feet, pulling him into a hug. Jun-tak wrapped his arms around them both. He felt something squirm when he pressed himself against Mung.

"What is that?" he said, drawing away. A whimper came from under Mung's cloak.

"Zorv killed its mother. I figured Onya's capra could use a friend."

Mung opened his cloak, revealing a wolf pup. Jun-tak had never been that close to one. It was the most adorable thing he had ever seen.

He reached out to touch the furry head, scratching the pointed ears. The pup licked his hand. Jun-tak instantly understood Onya's affection for the baby capra. "Perhaps a larger pen is in order?"

Zorv made a disgusted sound and went back outside. The three friends smiled at each other.

***

"What do you call this stuff?" Zorv said the next morning, his mouth full.

Jun-tak had risen early, before the sun, so as to prepare food for everyone. It would be their first meal together in their new home. Also, the sooner Zorv ate, the sooner he would leave.

"Bread. I make it from crushed barley or wheat and a bit of water and salt. I place a flat rock in the fire pit for the purpose of cooking it. It's tasty, don't you think?"

"I would prefer meat."

"If there is not much meat or no meat at all, bread fills the belly nicely."

"I doubt it would keep one from starving."

"I disagree. It could be the very thing that keeps one from starving in the absence of meat."

"When will you be leaving, Zorv?" Mung said. There was no love lost between the two of them.

The brawny hunter chuckled. "Eager to be rid of me? You will have your wish." He crammed the final bits of bread in his mouth, then gathered his things. "Jun-tak, the pelt is drying on the overhang above your cave. It will need to be scraped and stretched often."

"I know how to work animal hides," Onya said, glaring. The chore usually fell to the women in the Family who were taught the process soon after they began walking.

"I know. I have seen your handiwork." Zorv looked at her with that unidentifiable expression Jun-tak had noticed last night. Mung nudged him in the side with an elbow. He didn't need to look at the handsome face to know it was grinning.

Zorv had feelings for Onya. That's what all this was about.

"I didn't know if you had decided to stay," he continued. "I hope you all will be happy here in this hole in the ground come winter. I shall picture you shivering to death while I am in the south, basking in the balmy air and feasting on auroch."

With that, he departed. The remaining three looked at each other, round-eyed and silent. Finally, they burst out laughing. The awkwardness of Zorv's presence was gone. What remained was relief and a giddy sense of freedom.

"Come, friends. Let's build the pen first. I have a small supply of wood outside, but we'll need much more."

They spent the rest of the day enclosing a small area at the back of the cave for the animals, using stones, wood, and leather strips. The result was a sturdy barricade that would keep the wolf pup and the baby capra from escaping while they were still small. What would happen when they grew bigger? Perhaps the animals would be so familiar with the humans they wouldn't want to escape. The concept was fascinating, and the pup added an interesting twist. Two utterly different animals, one prey and one predator. How would they react to each other as they grew? They were playing together now, chasing each other about, but how long would that last?

As the sun descended in the sky, the two newcomers assembled the items they had brought with them. The variety of household goods would be useful additions to what he already had, and Mung's pouch of dried meat was a boon.

"I'm sorry I didn't bring more food," Onya said. "But my mother's old mortar and pestle should prove useful. She has a new one for her herbs and seeds now. I was thinking about it for the barley."

Jun-tak admired the stone implement, imagining the effort it must have taken for Onya to carry it along with everything else. It would do quite well for the task of grinding grains into bread flour – an improvement over his flat-rock system.

"It will be perfect. Perhaps in time, we can devise something even better. Something that will make the work go faster."

"Like your new fire-starter?" Mung said. "Everyone is using those now, you know."

"Yes, exactly like that. Getting more results from one's labor and time – that is always at the back of my mind. Not just to do things differently, but to do them better and quicker."

"You are quite the rebel. It's one of your best qualities." Onya kissed him on the cheek and began making preparations for the evening meal.

"There's still some daylight," Jun-tak said. "You two stay put and rest. Neither of you got much sleep last night. I'm going to gather more grain and check my snares. No, no, Mung. I mean it. Relax now. Tomorrow will be another long day of work."

Mung didn't argue further. Jun-tak was exhausted as well, but he would not let it show. While he was thrilled with how well-stocked their new home was now in terms of utensils and tools, he had done a quick calculation after seeing their combined collection of food. He would need to gather a sizeable quantity of grain to feed everyone for the next few days. He hoped for something bigger than voles in the snares, but he knew he couldn't count on it. The only thing he could control was the procurement of grains. And he knew he must gather as much as possible now, while it was ripe and plentiful, because later, the grasses would be buried under snow and ice.

He stepped up his pace.

***

"Jun-tak, I saved some dinner for you. It's on your bed." Mung's voice, gravelly from sleep, floated up out of the dark.

The fire had been banked, but the coals illuminated enough of the cave that he could find his way to his pallet after dropping the weighty satchel. Every bit of his body ached. He had no idea how long he had been out working by moonlight.

Three sun-cycles had passed since Onya and Mung had joined him. Everyone had full bellies, but only he knew how much work was required to achieve that. If it weren't for the discovery of an enormous field of ripe lentils he had discovered, he might be inclined toward dismay. The pebble-sized seeds would be delicious boiled in water with some salt and perhaps a bit of auroch or boar. The problem was that the field was a half sun-cycle's walk from home.

He was so sleepy that he barely finished the meal Mung had left him before his eyelids shut. That night, while his tired body slept, his mind conjured images of strange structures towering up from a sea of sand. These were not natural mountains produced by nature; their silhouettes were too ordered and symmetrical. In the dream he felt strangely comforted by them, despite their mystifying purpose and origin. By the morning light, the dream had vanished from thought and memory.

***

"Oh my. This is yummy," Mung said with his mouth full of the lentils the two had collected that day.

"Besides the fish, I added some onion tubers and cattails I found by the creek. I'm pleased with the flavor." Onya was not one to brag about her talents. She was an exceptional cook. Jun-tak was fortunate to have both her friendship and her impressive skills in this undertaking. He had a feeling that the two of them could accomplish marvels when they put their heads together. He looked at Mung, eating happily, and smiled. His handsome friend was an average hunter, an average worker, and an average thinker. What he brought to their enterprise was twofold: unwavering loyalty and a relentless sense of humor. If their situation became dire over the winter, both those qualities would be sorely needed.

"The fish were abundant?" Jun-tak asked between bites.

"They were. I hauled as many carp as I could. But I know the fishing won't last once it gets cold. It's time we built a smokehouse next to the river. That way, I can dry them as soon as I pull them out of the water. There's too much time wasted walking back and forth from the river to home. I need to camp there for a while to make the best use of my time. We'll have a nice stockpile of dried fish to add to the bread, lentils, and game."

"It's an excellent plan, but I'm worried about your safety. A lone woman camping alone? Mung should go with you."

"Yes, Onya, I'll protect you." Mung flexed his small bicep muscles.

"No. Mung needs to help with the gathering of grain. I have my knife. I'll be cautious. I just need help building the smokehouse."

Jun-tak knew there would be no deterring her. "Very well. We'll build it first thing tomorrow. Your carp will be a splendid addition to our food hoard. I am also thinking of building a trap for game larger than voles and hares...an improvement to the snares I have in place."

Onya nodded. "A pit trap? I've heard of those."

"Yes. It will take a lot of digging, but a boar would provide much food. We only have to dig it once, but it will continue to produce indefinitely, perhaps even over the winter."

"Boars can't climb out of those," Mung added.

"Right. So we will go to the river to build the smokehouse tomorrow morning. After that, we will dig the pit trap near the southern tree copse. I've seen a boar trail nearby."

"We have a lot to do to get ready, don't we, Jun-tak?" Onya locked eyes with him. She knew better than Mung how much stored food they would need to see them through until spring.

"We do." He flung an empty satchel over his shoulder.

Mung yawned. "You're going back out again? Aren't you exhausted?"

"Not really," he lied. "Rest up, my friend. We'll need those muscles tomorrow."

Mung grinned, exposing teeth more perfect than anyone's in the Family.

***

The moon had risen, providing just enough light for Jun-tak to see where he walked. It was a long distance to the lentil field, and he thought again of how much time he was wasting getting there. If food sources were brought closer to home, they could spend more time doing the work of gathering. He intended to save seeds from all the grasses and edible foliage, including the lentils, and would plant them in a meadow near their home. That was the part of his plan that would be the most difficult. As with many of his ideas, more effort was required in the beginning to make less work later on.

It was a concept the Family disparaged. Except for Onya. Her mind was every bit as quick and forward-thinking as his.

The thought of his two friends sleeping back at the cave warmed his heart. Everything he was doing now...all the sleep he was missing...would benefit them. Eventually, it would benefit the Family, too.

Suddenly, a menacing growl came from somewhere behind him. He stopped, dropping to the ground. He made himself as small a target as possible while analyzing the sound. Was it another wolf? A lion? A jackal? All these were a possibility, and all were night hunters who wouldn't hesitate to attack a lone human. He dropped his satchel and gripped his spear, waiting.

Another growl, closer now. A shiver raced up his back. He identified the vocalization with a wave of terror.

It was a panther, no question. He had heard one on a night hunt with his father several earth-cycles ago. A more lethal predator did not exist.

He estimated how far he had traveled away from the safety of the cave, and his heart fell. No human could outrun a panther anyway, and the worst mistake was to turn one's back. His only option now was to make himself seem as large and fearsome as possible. He stood on tiptoes, waving his arms, and began yelling obscenities into the night.

The big cat screeched a warning in response.

The screech was even closer now than the growling had been before.

He maneuvered his spear into a hunter's grip, the deadly tip pointing toward the beast. The moon chose that moment to disappear behind some night-gray clouds. His vision now was half what it had been. He peered into the gloom, heart pounding, waiting for the inevitable attack.

The man-eater would go for his throat.

He lifted the spear higher. He was happy to see that his hands did not tremble. He had never been more terrified, but he would stand his ground, despite the likelihood of surviving a panther attack.

He continued to shout, his voice hoarse now from screaming. The predator was not deterred. He heard a rustling, scuffling sound in the distance, and more growling. Clouds scuttled across the night sky, obscuring the starlight. He squinted, focusing on the direction from which he expected the inevitable assault.

After what felt like an eternity, he released the breath he had been holding. The scuffling and growling and screeching had stopped. Only silence now. Soon, the chirping of insects resumed, followed by the hoots of an owl. It seemed the other creatures had decided there was no further danger.

"Where are you, vile creature?" he whispered into the blackness. He remained still for some time, unwilling to turn his vulnerable back on such a terrifying beast. Finally, the realization that he wasn't going to die — at least not that night — registered fully. He had no wish to push his luck, and so turned toward home. There had never been a more welcome sight than the opening of his cave framed by glowing firelight.

As he made his way up the side of the hill, he heard the sounds of Onya and Mung talking and laughing. What would have happened to them if the panther had succeeded? The Family was surely too far away by now for them to catch up.

The responsibility for their well-being suddenly weighed on him like a boulder. He must be more careful in the future. Getting himself killed would lead to their more protracted deaths from starvation. He couldn't just work hard into the night, sacrificing sleep, to assure their survival. He must work cautiously too. The Family's lifestyle, unchanged for generations, got one thing right: there was safety in numbers. Without numbers, one had to compensate by doing things differently.

The following night he would bring a torch, an improved version of the type used by the family, which was little more than a lump of charcoal on the end of a stick. He pondered the design of his new torch as well as the items he would need to fashion it. Even as he entered with his empty satchel, his mind worked on this new task.

***

"You can't stay here, Onya. Not after what happened to me last night," Jun-tak said the next afternoon.

The three stood, sweating and panting with exertion, next to the newly built stone structure. Jun-tak's design was ingenious. The little building, filled with racks for hanging fish and game above the small fire pit, would keep the smoke contained but also allow enough ventilation for it not to become too hot inside. The goal was to dry the meat out slowly, not bake it. That was the key to the preservation of food. If any moisture remained, it would soon grow fuzzy and inedible.

"I'm staying. Trudging back and forth every day is not sensible. We've discussed this."

"That was before I almost became dinner for a panther."

"I won't be moving about. I'll be camped right here, and I'll be very quiet." She gestured to a formation of rocks and boulders next to the river. A concaved section at the bottom would provide a place for a small person to lie down. But she would be exposed on all sides except one. "Or maybe I could spend the nights in the smokehouse."

"What, standing up?" Mung laughed. "There's not room for you to even sit down in there, plus it will be smoky. You know, because it's a smokehouse. You'll die from the gray air, if not from discomfort."

Jun-tak wasn't paying attention. He was looking at the recess at the base of the rock pile. The next moment he removed his digging tool and began shoveling out dirt.

"That's it. He finally has gone mad," Mung said, watching Jun-tak at his labor.

Onya watched as well. "No, he hasn't. He's having another one of his ideas. What are you thinking, Jun-tak? You'll make me a nice, safe hole in the ground?"

"Exactly. The soil is not too hard here, so we will shore it up with stones. It won't be pleasant, but it will be secure. We'll make a roof from tethered branches to put on top at an angle, against the boulders. Even if predators can smell you, they won't be able to get to you. I'll devise a way to lock the ceiling from within."

Mung shuddered. "You would sleep in a dark hole, Onya?"

She shrugged her shoulders. "When one's eyes are closed, what difference does it make? It's a brilliant idea, Jun-tak. I don't mind small spaces."

"We can expand it later. When there's time, we can keep excavating farther out, supporting the walls of dirt with more stones. Think about it – a house below ground. It would be safe and cozy. But today, we will only make it deep enough and wide enough for you to lie down comfortably."

"That will require a lot of work," Mung said, reaching for his digging tool. "I guess you're worth it." He grinned at Onya, who already held her root spade.

"I will reward you and that bottomless pit you call a stomach with the biggest, most succulent carp," she said.

***

"I still don't think it is a good idea for you to be out here alone at night," Jun-tak said much later.

Onya's underground space was finished and the sun hung low on the horizon. It was time for him and Mung to head home, but it felt wrong to do so without their third member.

"I'll be fine. Not just safe, but downright comfortable. Look," she said, lifting the roof and sliding down the rock lined wall. She had already placed her pallet on the ground inside the space; the other items she had brought were stacked neatly beside it. "I'm locking it now."

Jun-tak heard her secure the leather roof straps onto the wooden pegs built into the side. Those straps would keep the canopy locked down. No person or animal would be able to lift it easily.

He sighed. "Very well. How long do you think you'll stay?"

"When I have caught and dried all the fish I can carry home," she said, emerging from under the hole. "So perhaps a moon-cycle."

"I will come check on you."

"No. You don't have the time. Jun-tak, listen to me." She took his face between her two hands and gazed into his eyes. "We know what we have to do if we're going to survive the winter. Now leave me to do my part. And please, take good care of Lily for me." She kissed his cheek above the newly sprouting hairs.

"She's quite remarkable," Jun-tak said to Mung later over the flames of their evening fire. "She will make someone a fine wife, someday."

"Umm hmm," Mung replied, his mouth full of food, as usual. "But not me. I see her only as a friend."

"As do I." He was more relieved than he would admit even to himself. Living in close quarters with a pretty female would be quite a temptation for most men.

"What are we doing tomorrow? Tell me it's not more digging."

Jun-tak laughed. "We do need to get that pit trap dug near the boar trail, but if you'd rather gather grain, that can be your job."

"Yes. I'd prefer that, if it's all right with you. I'm exhausted. I don't think I can keep my eyes open any longer. Good night," Mung said with a beautifully tired smile while reaching over and tousling Jun-tak's hair. He was asleep on his pallet within a few moments.

Jun-tak watched the handsome face in the flickering firelight. Then with a deep sigh, he began cleaning up the remains of the meal before heading out into the night to work.

***

The next moon-cycle was filled with long days of hard labor and little rest for Jun-tak. Mung managed to get enough sleep for both of them, though. He wasn't lazy, but he wasn't motivated to the same degree as Jun-tak. More than mere survival was at stake. Thriving in this new lifestyle was necessary to convince the Family it was the way of the future.

The air was beginning to cool and most of the grain within walking distance from home had been gathered. The pit trap had proven successful. Since Onya left, they had added the meat of five boars to their stockpile of lentils, wheat, and barley. There was so much food now that they used a nearby underground cave for storage. The cave remained cool even on warm days. Its mouth, just large enough to wriggle through, was secured by a flat boulder. It took two people to move it, so was inaccessible to animals, and humans wouldn't know it was there. Not that they expected people to be wandering about. The last tribe had passed through recently.

They were all alone now.

Jun-tak woke before dawn. He realized it had been almost a moon-cycle since they had left Onya by the river. He would send Mung to check on her that day. He would prefer to go himself, but the new smokehouse needed to be enlarged, the traps and snares checked and reset, water fetched from the creek, and the animals fed. In addition to the capra and the wolf pup, they now had two piglets – one male and one female – in the pen. Their mother had been butchered and smoked, stored in the food cellar. He hadn't the heart to slaughter her offspring. He knew his kind-hearted friend would be pleased to have more baby animals to raise. Perhaps when they were older, they would breed and make more piglets.

He was finishing up the morning meal when he heard a sound just outside the cave. The wooden door he had constructed to cover the opening stood ajar, and sounds...human sounds...filtered in.

"Mung, wake up," he whispered, grabbing his spear.

"What? What is it?" Mung scrambled up from his pallet.

"I hear someone," Jun-tak began to say when the smiling face of Onya appeared.

"You have a door now? Ingenious!" She bustled through and wrapped him in a ferocious hug. "Come help me get the rest of the bundles down below. I couldn't carry everything up this steep hill."

"I was getting worried about you!" Mung said. "You're skin and bones!"

"I didn't want to eat up all your food, silly boy." She gave Mung's belly a playful jab.

"I want to hear all about your fishing," Jun-tak said. He was filled with joy at the sight of his best friend, safe and sound.

"Oh, there's much to tell. My scariest story is that one night I was working until after dark, when I thought I was about to become a panther's dinner. Just like you, Jun-tak. And then the same thing that happened to you happened to me. At the moment I thought it would attack, the beast went away, never to be heard from again. I did find some blood nearby, but whether it was from the panther or something else, I have no idea. Perhaps another predator got it. But what preys on a panther?"

"Humans." He found the notion troubling. As far as he knew, the three of them were the only remaining people in the area.

"Right. Or maybe a lion. The strange thing is, I heard no sounds of a fight or even a struggle. I'll probably never know why I escaped, but I'm grateful I did. And I have a surprise."

Onya began to unpack all the baskets and satchels they had set on the floor. He was amazed that she was able to carry it all. She had caught and smoked hundreds of carp, had woven baskets from leaves in which to store them, and had devised a clever hauling structure with which to bring it all home. The significance of the woven fronds finally registered.

"You found a date palm tree? Where?"

The Family had encountered only a handful in all their travels. The delectable fruit was prized for its flavor and nutrition, while the bark, roots, and leaves could be used in a variety of medicinal applications. Finding a date palm tree was like stumbling onto a herd of auroch that had already corralled themselves into a canyon.

Onya's smile stretched from ear to ear. "I did. A small cluster of them. Rather a long way from here, but not too far from the river. Look," she said, opening the lid of one of the smaller hampers. Inside were nestled purple thumb-sized fruits that would become more wrinkled and sweeter over time. "There were more. So many more, still yellow in color. Not yet ready for picking. We must go back soon."

"Yes, of course! They may well be our salvation." He was surprised that he let the words slip out. Up until then, he had been doing sums in his head. Even with all the stockpiled food, they simply didn't have enough to get them through the winter. The dates, along with some game, plus the fish, boar, and grain could see them through until spring.

"That's what I thought. We can't travel to the trees, gather the fruit, and make it back here in one sun. We'll have to camp by the river for at least a night. Which also got me thinking about the future. If we expand the sleeping quarters you made there, it could be used as temporary home when we need to venture farther out."

"That is why we are such good friends. We think alike."

"Oh!" she squeaked suddenly when she noticed the animal pen. "Lily has gotten so big! And you have piglets!"

"Yes, for you. And now that the wolf pup is sleeping with Mung – we have been calling him Smokey because of his coloring – there was room in the pen. I don't know what will happen when they outgrow it. And we'll have to feed them all, too."

The burden of feeding animals as well as people weighed on him. Smokey had stolen their hearts. The pup had bonded more closely with Mung, as Lily the capra had bonded with Onya. The concept of animals being affectionate to humans was unheard of, yet it was happening before his eyes. As much as he enjoyed the camaraderie, it made for more mouths to feed.

As usual, Onya sensed his disquiet. "We'll make do. Now, let me see this new food cellar you mentioned."

***

Work continued, and no one labored harder than Jun-tak. The air was turning colder and sunlight lasted for shorter periods now. They had made several trips to the date palm trees and stripped every single piece of fruit – not an easy task. Scaling the trees was a dangerous endeavor, and again he was impressed that Onya had done it by herself. The pit trap had produced three more boars which they butchered and buried, choosing to preserve the meat this time through fermentation rather than smoking and drying.

On one of their missions to the date palms, Mung had speared a beaver by the river before it could slink back under the water to its burrow. Of all the game animals, beavers were the most sought-after. Their flesh was rich and flavorful and their pelts warm and naturally water-resistant. Mung made a hat out of the hide and shyly gave it to Jun-tak one evening over their meal. He treasured the gift even more than those from his parents.

Soon after, the first snow occurred. The three friends stood inside their cozy home and watched the snowflakes dance down from the heavens.

"It's so beautiful," Onya breathed.

"Beautiful, but also a harbinger. You know what this means?" Jun-tak replied.

"Winter is here. We've done everything we can. We're as ready as we can be."

"Thanks to you, Jun-tak," Mung said, draping an arm around his shoulders. "Even though the Family is far to the south by now, they are not as prepared for their mild winter as we are for our harsh one. I wouldn't trade places with any of them."

"Neither would I." Onya squeezed Jun-tak's hand.

He wondered how long they would feel that way.

***

Three moon-cycles later...

"Brrrr. It feels especially cold today," Mung said.

The friends huddled close to the fire, eating their morning ration of bread along with the last of the dates. Nobody had mentioned their dwindling food hoard, but everyone was thinking about it. The grain was more than two thirds gone; enough smoked boar and fish remained to last perhaps one more moon cycle. The fermented meat had been consumed, and the pit traps had produced no additional game since autumn. They were eating the last of the dates as their morning meal.

They could not reasonably expect the ice and snow to melt for at least two moon-cycles. They would soon be forced out into the frigid cold and treacherous weather to hunt for game. It would be an unpleasant, dangerous undertaking.

"Best not to wait until we're completely out of food," Jun-tak said. "We will hunt today. Onya, you should remain with the animals, and it's not just because you're a female. We need someone to take care of them if something happens to the other two."

He could see her wrestling with an internal struggle. At the beginning, they had agreed to distribute the chores equally, not by traditional roles.

"I won't fight you on this," she replied finally. "I'm not as good with my spear as the two of you. The decision makes sense. Just promise me one thing…"

Jun-tak watched her eyes fill up with tears that didn't quite spill over before she blinked them away.

"Anything, my friend."

"Promise that if you don't find game and we run out of food before the winter ends, we won't resort to eating…" A quiet sob escaped her.

Jun-tak didn't respond immediately, taking his time pondering his answer. When he spoke, he knew the words would not be well-received.

"We will do everything we can to make sure that doesn't happen, but I cannot make the promise you desire. If the two people I love most in this world are starving, I will sacrifice these animals, which I have also grown to love. However, I do not love them more than both of you."

Neither of his friends would meet his gaze. His was a difficult and unpopular position. It would have been easier to tell Onya what she wanted to hear and then worry about whether he could keep his promise later. But that would not be the right thing to do.

He sighed, then stood and began preparing for the hunting expedition to come. He and Mung would don every article of clothing they possessed. He hoped it would keep them from freezing. The snow and ice had been relentless. Their world of grassy meadows and gently sloping hills was transformed now into a harsh, glacial landscape. Jun-tak had fashioned footwear from thin branches and strips of leather which, when attached to their fur boots, would keep their feet from sinking into the snow. Even now it was deeper than a grown man's height.

"We should take Smokey," Mung said just as they were about to leave.

"Why would you do that?" Onya replied, alarm in her voice. "He might freeze out there."

Mung laughed. "Can you hear yourself? You're worried about a wolf going outside. A wolf, who would normally live quite comfortably in the cold, without cozy fires and bowls of food given to him by people."

She gave him a grudging smile. "You're right, of course. I'm being foolish."

She rubbed Smokey behind the ears, his favorite place to be scratched. His tongue lolled out the side of his open mouth, exposing white canine fangs that could shred skin and flesh better than that of humans. And his four legs were much faster than two. Jun-tak had a sudden thought.

"Mung, perhaps we could teach him to hunt not just with us, but for us."

"You may be onto something. He could be a tool, like a spear or a fire kit."

"Exactly," Jun-tak said, excited now. "He already does everything you tell him. He takes commands well, and his instinct would be to hunt for himself anyway. The trick will be to get him to bring the prey back to us rather than gobble it all up."

"This could be fun, Jun-tak. If we don't die a horrible death." Mung had lost one of his front teeth during a recent fall, but to Jun-tak, his smile was no less dazzling.

"I hope you're right about the fun part. At the very least, I hope we are successful and don't come back with missing fingers or toes." He gave Mung a playful punch in the arm.

Much later they had travelled far from the warmth and security of home but with nothing to show for all the arduous walking. Evidence of animals lay everywhere – scat and tracks of hares and red deer – but their game satchels were empty. Smokey had startled a flock of geese, but both Jun-tak's and Mung's spears missed their marks. Humans and wolf watched the honking birds fly away, wearing identical expressions of disappointment.

"Roasted goose would have tasted wonderful," Mung said. Then to the half-grown pup, "Some mighty hunter you are."

Smokey sneezed and shook his furry head. Suddenly, the oversized ears perked up. A low growl emanated from deep within the chest. The next moment, he was off at a full run in the direction of a small copse of trees.

By the time Jun-tak and Mung caught up to him, he was gobbling up the steaming intestines of a capra, similar to Lily but larger and with slender horns.

"Smokey, no!" Mung yelled. The wolf lifted his bloody muzzle, regarding Mung thoughtfully. He emitted another growl before returning to his meal. "Smokey, I said no," Mung repeated, using the same stern voice as when he had taught the wolf 'sit' and 'fetch.'

Smokey's growl turned into a whimper. He backed away from the carcass.

"Good boy. You will get the liver and heart. You've earned them," Mung said, squatting down next to the animal. Smokey sat patiently beside his preferred human, as Mung did the work of slicing and gutting.

Jun-tak stood back, watching in amazement, as a man and a wolf shared the job of killing and then butchering their dinner.

"What is this?" Mung muttered.

"What?"

"There's a small gash on the throat. The type made by a knife, not the jagged mark of an animal bite."

Jun-tak hurried over to examine the wound. "Yes, I see. What could it mean?"

"I don't know, but I have a feeling it happened before Smokey got to this capra. Otherwise, I doubt that our little half-grown wolf could have overtaken it."

"Yes, I see your point. So the creature was already weak from the knife wound, making it easier for Smokey to finish the job. But why wouldn't the hunter take the meat for himself?"

"Perhaps he was injured somehow."

"Perhaps."

"It will be enough meat to last a few days. Onya will be so happy!" Mung left the rest of the sentiment unsaid.

"Yes," Jun-tak replied, troubled now. He pondered the enigma during the journey back to the cave and long into the night.

***

Two more moon-cycles passed. Seven more hunting excursions ended in the same baffling manner: the wolf would scent an animal nearby, weakened from a knife wound to its throat, and then take its life. Once it was even an enormous stag – its meat fed them for many days, and its antlers would create neat furrows in the ground for seeds come spring.

He was nearly driven to distraction by the mystery of the wounded prey, but Onya was untroubled. They had made it through the winter with her beloved animals alive and well. Sunlight lasted longer each day now, and the snow and ice soon melted.

At long last, they were able to resume their outdoor chores.

"I want to plant the date seeds over there," Jun-tak said, shielding his eyes from the bright spring sunshine and pointing to the east. "I know it will take many earth-cycles for them to mature, but you have to begin sometime, right?"

Onya and Mung followed the direction of his outstretched hand. At the same moment, they all noticed a dark human-shaped speck moving toward them.

"That can't be the Family this soon. I don't expect them until the grasses are knee-high."

Mung squinted. His was the best vision for distance. "No, not the Family. Well, only part of it. I think that's Zorv."

The three watched in silence as the man approached.

"Yes, definitely Zorv," Onya said.

"You sound excited," Jun-tak smiled.

"What? You're imagining things," she snapped.

Jun-tak and Mung looked at each other in surprise, then burst out laughing.

"Onya likes Zorv!" Mung said. "I bet Zorv likes her too. Remember how he complimented her on her pelt work? That man doesn't compliment anyone. Oh, this is delightful."

"Shut up. What would you know about feelings between a man and a woman? You only have eyes for Jun-tak."

Jun-tak felt a sudden twisting sensation in his belly. Could it be true? He found it impossible to make eye contact with Mung.

"That was mean," Mung said.

"I'm sorry. You just embarrassed me. Now hush. He'll be here soon."

The approaching figure called out, "I guess nobody starved to death, then." When Zorv reached them, they could see how thin he was. His cheekbones jutted out sharply above his dark beard, and pelts hung on a body that seemed to have lost half its mass.

"What happened to you?" Onya said in a horrified voice.

Before Zorv had a chance to answer, Jun-tak exclaimed, "You're wearing panther fur! Now it all makes sense!"

Zorv's reply was only a weak smile within the wiry beard.

"And the knife wounds on the throats of the game animals? That was your work too? In addition to saving me and Onya from the panther?"

"Two panthers," Zorv said, his focus on Onya's pretty face.

"You've been close the entire time?" she whispered.

"Of course. Did you think I was going to let any of you starve? I was intrigued by the notion of training Mung's wolf to participate on a hunt. I thought my...small interventions...would help."

"How did you survive the cold?"

"It wasn't easy. I almost sought the comfort of your gods-forsaken cave on more than one occasion."

"I wish you had," Onya said shyly.

Zorv smiled. "It was important for Jun-tak to do this on his terms, without the interference of someone such as myself. I would have fought him on every decision and probably won. Then we would not know how this great experiment would turn out."

Jun-tak was filled with newfound admiration for his former adversary, and more than a little awe. "It takes a brave, determined man to do what you did."

"And it takes a visionary to undertake what you have, Jun-tak. I did a lot of thinking over the winter. Even though your ideas are radical, I think you are right to pursue them. I'd like to be part of it. But I won't live in that cave. I thought I would build a stone house underground, like you did for Onya by the river. Maybe large enough for two people..." he added with an appraising look at Onya.

The In Between

"Oh," Jun-tak said, slowing becoming aware of his new surroundings. He pictured his face, or at least a reflection of it when occasionally seen in the river, and opened the eyelids of that face.

Memories of his past life flooded into his consciousness...mostly good, a few bad, and one that coaxed tears to flow down the ever solidifying face. He brushed at them with a hand rough from a lifetime of hard labor.

"You're thinking about Mung," a voice said from the void beyond.

"Is that you, Sarah? You sound strange."

Mung appeared in front of him. "That can happen. Especially when my form is aesthetically quite different from the last version."

"You look like him. Oh, Mung. When you died I thought I would die too."

"But you didn't," Mung-Sarah replied with a loving smile. "You lived many additional years and accomplished such remarkable things."

"I did, didn't I?" Jun-tak felt some of his sadness slip away at thought of all that he had done in his recent life.

"You stayed there quite a while, too, yet you had learned your lessons early on."

"I guess I must have been enjoying myself."

"It would seem so. You and a handful of others scattered about in the late Mesolithic period introduced agriculture to humankind. I think there are few better ways to learn about leadership than that." Mung-Sarah squeezed his shoulder.

Jun-take felt a wave of profound bliss when the angel (or whatever he-she was) touched him. He remembered that had happened before in the In Between. He wondered, not for the first time, how such a being had come about.

How long did it seem to you?" he asked. "While I was living my last lifetime? Did it feel like the forty years it took me on Earth? Or was it just a blip to you? I know time isn't linear, but I'm curious about how that part works. Does time in the In Between move at the same pace?"

Mung-Sarah laughed, the familiar tinkling wind-chime sound but deeper now that it came from Mung's mouth.

"Hey, your teeth are perfect again."

"That's because my form is a projection from you and your memories. He was quite handsome, wasn't he?"

Jun-tak nodded. "He was the most beautiful person in the world, even after he lost his front tooth. It wasn't so much his physical body that I loved, but his spirit. He was as kind and as good-natured as he was pleasing to the eye. I miss him so much."

"Perhaps you will see him again."

"Does it work that way?"

"It can."

"Is he here somewhere now? In the In Between?"

"I am not at liberty to say."

"Why? Is that frowned upon, too?"

"Something like that."

Jun-tak sighed. "Fine."

Mung-Sarah smiled. "Do you think you achieved your goal? Did you learn about Courage and Bravery? Leadership? A strong Work Ethic?"

He pondered each part of the question for quite some time before answering. "Yes, I believe so, either through direct experience or observing in another."

"Elaborate, please."

"I learned Leadership through imagining innovative and vastly improved methods for the human lifestyle. I put those methods into effect myself, thus proving they would work and setting the example for others. It took several years for the crops to begin producing enough to feed the entire Family, and then another few years to convince everyone to live in one place year-round."

"Extraordinary."

Jun-tak smiled. "You know, even at the time, I knew I was doing something...revolutionary. Now that I'm back here in the In Between, I realize how profoundly the advent of agriculture and animal domestication impacted the human race. It was a monumental turning point in our evolution. I know I wasn't the only one engaging in it, but I was one of the first. And I worked very hard every day, going without sleep and practically killing myself physically to get it done."

"There's the strong Work Ethic part."

"Exactly."

"What about Courage and Bravery?"

"That was learned through Zorv. That first winter, when the three of us were cozy and warm in the cave, Zorv lived nearby – *outside* – to help feed and protect us. He exposed himself to horrific weather conditions and lethal predators in doing so. I can't think of a better personification of Courage and Bravery than him."

"It seems you have learned what you set out to."

"Yes," Jun-tak said with an energetic nod.

Mung-Sarah was slowly shedding the parts that looked like Mung, while the Sarah elements returned more completely now. He thought he understood what that meant: he was leaving behind his most recent life and the object of his love to embark upon a new journey.

"What's next then?" Sarah asked.

"The one I just got through was a big one. Maybe I'll tackle something more modest."

"But still important, as is everything on your list."

"Of course. How about Creativity with a Bit of Humility Thrown in."

"You think that's a small one? Interesting. Do you have the framework in mind in which to conduct the lesson?"

"I do," Jun-tak's smile widened. "I just need your help on the setting."

Chapter 4 – Creativity with a Bit of Humility Thrown in

Italy - 1465 CE

"Julietta, where have you been? I haven't seen you in days." The boy who spoke was short and skinny – practically malnourished, and not because there wasn't enough food, but because he didn't bother to eat as often as he should. There were always more interesting things to do than to *fill one's belly with substances which will exit via the nether regions smelling much worse than when they went in.*

"I just saw you yesterday, Corto. Did you forget already?" Julietta stepped through the rickety gate and into a well-tended garden.

"Don't call me that," the boy replied, distracted as usual, scribbling on a scrap of paper.

"Why not? You're short. It suits you."

"So does my actual name."

"You haven't grown into that yet. Perhaps in a few years." She smiled with affection at her friend. They had both turned thirteen the past week. Having the same birthday was one of the reasons they had become friends, but it wasn't the main reason. Three years ago, she had taken pity on the oddball local boy and decided to befriend him, even when the other children derided her for it. Much to her surprise, she discovered him to be entertaining, intelligent, and loyal. She preferred his company above that of everyone else.

"Hmmm..." Corto couldn't trouble himself to glance up. He sat cross-legged between the rows of medicinal herbs he had planted earlier in the spring. His father had allowed a small section of the family's garden to be used for his son's experimentation.

"You're making notes? About your plants?"

"Not plants. Medicine."

"Very well. What is this one?" she asked, pointing to some daisy-like greenery.

"You're pathetic, Julietta. Even you should know chamomile when you see it." Indignation finally made him look up. She could almost see the mental tentacles releasing from the paper and onto her. For one so young, his gaze was quite intense.

She grinned. "Got you."

Her friend smiled in return. "I'm sorry. I was concentrating. I still don't know why the oil from the castor bean is beneficial to the digestive organs, but the beans themselves are rather fatal."

"Rather fatal? How do you know? Oh, Corto. You didn't."

"I had no choice."

"Which cat this time? Please don't tell me it was a dog."

"Not a dog. I promised never any dogs, remember? It was the laundress's cat. The thing was on its last life anyway."

"Oh dear."

"Sacrifices must be made in the quest for knowledge."

"I suppose you're right."

"Of course. I always am."

"Usually, not always."

"Hmmm."

His attention had begun to drift back to his work, so she spoke quickly. "I had the dream again."

That did the trick.

"The one about the man with the missing tooth?"

She nodded. Some of her flaxen hair had escaped her caul and framed her face in a way that the older boys would have appreciated.

"That's thrice this week."

"I know. It's difficult to explain how it makes me feel. Sad and happy at the same time, I suppose."

"Nostalgic?"

"How can one be nostalgic for a stranger?"

"True."

"He has the most wonderful eyes...so dark they look like obsidian marbles. And even though one of his front teeth is missing, he is still handsome."

"Dreams are fascinating. I had one this week about a flying contraption that carried people in its belly."

"That's madness. Only birds can fly. People certainly cannot."

"Maybe they can. With the correct vessel."

"How would such a heavy vessel become airborne?"

"There's the rub. The laws of physics must be respected, but I think there may be a workaround."

"I don't believe it. I have some other news, too. About a possible future husband."

"What? You're only thirteen. Your father can't possibly be thinking about marrying you off so young."

"No, of course not, but these things are planned years in advance, you know."

"Only for royalty and the well-heeled."

"Have you been living under a rock? Tradespeople do it as well."

"Is that what we are?"

Julietta blinked, dumbfounded. "Yes, that is what we are. Your father is a notary, and my father is a shopkeeper."

"Whew! I'm relieved to know we're not peasants."

She watched the smirk vanish as quickly as it came. He had been toying with her. For someone as brilliant as Corto, he could be shockingly oblivious to social norms, thus his reputation as an oddball.

"Very funny. Anyway, he's old. Well, not so old, but still old. I think he's twenty-eight."

"Is he handsome?"

"I don't know. I haven't met him."

"Perhaps you should demand to meet him before you agree to marry him."

She sighed. "It doesn't work that way."

"It should," he replied with a thoughtful expression. "I want you to be happy, Julietta. You are my best friend. Actually, you're my only friend."

"I know, amico. And you are mine. We make a strange pair, yes?"

The boy nodded, earnest now. "We have at least two years, though, before we have to worry about this husband?"

"Perhaps. Fifteen is an acceptable age to marry, although sixteen is more common."

"Will you stay here in the village? I couldn't bear it if you moved far away."

She laughed. "You'll be moving before me. Did you forget your father has been discussing apprenticeships for you in Florence?"

He frowned. "I haven't forgotten. I don't want to leave this place. It's the only home I have ever known. Everything I need is here."

"Silly boy. Your talent and intellect should not be limited to this backwater. Florence is the place for you. The pearl of the world," she said wistfully. It was her hope to visit that illustrious city one day.

"I'm not ready for it. Not yet."

"Let's make the most of the time we have now, before we grow up and move on."

"Do you want to play a game? Knucklebones?" he asked.

"You're sweet. I like that game, but I know you don't. It's all luck and no strategy. How about Fox and Geese?"

There was one thing that could tempt her brilliant friend away from his studies and artistic endeavors, and that was any game that involved an intellectual challenge.

She never won at those games. Despite being quite clever, she was no match for Corto and she knew it. She considered it a lesson in humility to submit to his superior intellect. Humility would benefit her after marriage, too, when she would became the possession of a man other than her father.

The thought made her uncomfortable because it went against her independent nature. But there was only so much power a female could wield in this day and age, and it amounted to very little. She knew of a woman – a widow – who had refused to remarry after her husband passed unexpectedly. As no children had been produced during the short marriage, she had inherited a comfortable income from her dead husband's properties. The village elders had been pressuring the woman for years to select a husband – it was unseemly for her to manage money and run businesses. Yet, the woman was doing just that, and from what Julietta could see, flourishing at it.

An idea flashed into her head. "Actually, Corto, I'm not really in the mood for a game. I think I'm going to go have a chat with Signora Moretti."

"Signora Moretti? The property owner?"

She smiled. He hadn't called her the *widow*, a moniker that reduced the woman's importance to only what she was in terms of her late husband. "Yes. I'm curious about how she's doing it."

"Doing what?"

"What only men are allowed to do – owning land and buildings and overseeing them as well."

"Ah, I know where this is going. You're planning a rebellion. I will help you. I don't want to see you wedded to some nitwit who doesn't respect that fine mind of yours. What does a wife do all day? Rearrange the linens? Polish the pewter? Insipid drudgery."

Corto's mother and father had never married, and since he lived with his father, he was ignorant of the variety of services a wife was expected to provide. His father employed two servants: a female to cook and clean, and her husband who tended the garden, chopped the wood, and fixed anything that broke. As a prominent notary, he could afford to pay others to run his household. Corto benefited from his father's success as well. He had no chores to speak of and could use his time and energy on an incredible array of creative and intellectual enterprises. Fortunately for Corto, Ser Piero grasped the genius that was his son.

"Rearranging linens and polishing pewter wouldn't be as bad as working in the fields. Or the tannery," she added. The stench from the leather processing facility pervaded the area when the breeze wafted from the south. Peasants provided the labor for one or both of these industries. The thought made her shudder. Better to be a bored housewife than an impoverished peasant.

Better still, however, to be a self-reliant business woman.

"I'll see you later. Please, no more using the nearby feline population for your test subjects. Someone is bound to find out."

"No dogs, Julietta. That's all I can promise."

His attention had already returned to the scrap of paper.

***

"Buongiorno, Signorina Julietta. What brings you to my home this afternoon?"

The woman standing before her was not beautiful. Most would call the face plain-featured, if not downright homely. Yet the fierce intelligence emanating from the dark brown eyes rendered her captivating.

"Buongiorno, Signora Moretti. Pardon me for coming to your home without invitation, but I wonder if we might talk, solo noi ragazze. *Just us girls.*

"Of course. Caterina, please bring some watered wine." The woman spoke to a pockmarked maid hovering nearby. Julietta had seen the girl on occasion and always felt a stab of sympathy for her. The combination of bad skin and cleft pallet would make finding a husband nearly impossible.

"I know this is forward of me," she said, feeling shy suddenly as the woman led the way to a small but immaculate garden. Two wooden chairs and a table beckoned from beneath the feathery limbs of a towering cypress tree. A light breeze kept the temperature pleasant for June. Did she hear a fountain bubbling somewhere? Utilizing water for something so extravagant bespoke considerable wealth.

"Nonsense. It is my pleasure to converse with anyone for any reason, especially those with so much going on up here." A slender finger tapped at Julietta's caul. Blond ringlets had escaped its confines.

"I apologize for my untidiness." She felt heat rising in her cheeks.

"Again, nonsense. Do I look like someone who worries about such things?" The woman's laughter was low and musical. Her own uncovered hair was a mass of careless, auburn coils.

Julietta smiled. "You don't. I think that's one of the reasons why I wanted to speak with you, Signora Moretti."

"I'm intrigued. And please call me Francesca."

"Francesca," she repeated the name, liking the intimacy of using an adult's Christian name and feeling quite grown up now.

"I'm curious about how you do it. How you own buildings and land in your own name, and how you make a living from them."

"Right to the point. I like that. Saluti," the woman added sipping her wine, and swirling it in its fluted vessel. Venetian glass was another indication of affluence. The cupboards of Julietta's family contained only pewter, plus the prized silver saltcellar included in her mother's dowry.

"Saluti." Julietta took a bird-sip. The vintage was delicious. She must be careful not to drink it all. It wouldn't do to return home tipsy.

"You would like me to tell you my secrets? Of how I elude the village elders who would see me married off to some dull cloth merchant with cold hands and bad breath?"

"Yes! That's it exactly." She felt the intensity of the woman's gaze on her, sizing her up, an event that seemed to be happening more frequently these days. Usually, though, it was done by older boys and men who assessed the length of her eyelashes and the fullness of her lips.

"It is not easy. And, frankly, you may be too pretty for the life I lead." Francesca's hand gesture encompassed the modest but elegant villa and the surrounding garden – symbols of her independence.

Julietta's eyes opened wide. "How so?"

The woman leaned in close now, taking Julietta's hand in her own. "Do you think men would let a beautiful woman, as I can see that you will one day become, slip through their greedy fingers?"

"You're saying I'll be forced to marry because of my beauty?"

Francesca's expression turned thoughtful now. "Perhaps not, if you play the game well. I can see that your intellect rivals your beauty. For us, that combination can be a blessing or a curse."

"I don't understand."

The woman smiled, transforming her unremarkable face into a lovelier version. The change was striking.

"We live in a man's world, mia cara. If we are to get what we want – I assume you desire the same autonomy that I enjoy – we must carefully navigate their egos and their natures. Success requires sacrifices."

"Such as what?"

"Our appearance, for one."

The words compelled Julietta to scrutinize her new friend. Contemporary notions of attractiveness demanded pallor, but Francesca's skin was tan, like that of a peasant. Fashionable women plucked their eyebrows, yet Francesca's were untamed and unshaped. In an age when women of means utilized products to smooth and darken hair, Francesca had allowed gray strands to meander through her coarse, copper tendrils.

"You've intentionally made yourself plain!" Julietta felt her face flush again. She was shocked by her own rude outburst.

"It wasn't that difficult. I'm no natural beauty, like you," Francesca replied, flashing that lovely smile again.

"Look at you. Your teeth are perfect."

"Why do you think I so rarely show them in public, mia cara?"

"If I make myself ugly enough, perhaps the man my father has selected for me will decline my hand."

"It won't be that simple. Some men only want a dowry and children. Who is the man your father has chosen?"

"The middle son of Signor Cavelli. Do you know him?"

She watched the older woman's face with rapt attention, marveling at the trickery that had transformed an attractive woman into a homely one. Was she even now wearing cosmetics to downplay her looks? Facial powder of a drab olive hue? Incredible!

"I do. By all accounts, he is a decent fellow. The family is as well. You could do much worse. Their star is on the rise, and marriage to even the second son would provide a comfortable life with plenty of interesting distractions."

This was the very thrust of Julietta's inner struggle: settle for a life others would be happy to have, or risk everything to gain power over herself and her decisions.

Caterina returned to refill their vessels.

"No thank you, dear," Julietta said kindly. She had taken pity on the poor girl, with her downcast eyes and unfortunate face. "It would be unwise to go home stumbling and smelling of wine."

"And bristling with rebellious notions," Francesca said.

Julietta watched the girl shuffle back into the house. She pondered the life of a lowly servant, but working for Signora Moretti must be a boon. Her reputation was one of flawless morality and a generous nature.

"You must be quite circumspect, I imagine. In your words and behavior."

"Indeed. I see you are grasping the entirety of what it means to be an unmarried woman living as an equal in a man's world."

"Do you miss being with a man? I mean, the physical aspect of it. I've heard some women...find pleasure...in the marriage bed." Again, the heat rose in her cheeks. She was aghast at her own boldness, but her new friend seemed to bring it out in her.

"Yes, I miss him, and I miss that part of it very much. He was a good husband. He treated me well and even indulged my suggestions for improving the businesses. Acting upon my ideas increased our holdings twice over.

He used to call me his piccola genio. His *little genius*." The brown eyes turned wistful.

"That could happen with me, too. Perhaps Lorenzo Cavelli will see me as your husband saw you."

"Perhaps."

"Or he could regard me as a chattel...a plaything to decorate his house and provide him with children."

"That's usually the way it goes."

Julietta sighed. "I'm no closer to knowing what I should do."

"Have you met the prospective groom yet? You might find him comely, and then the decision will make itself. That path is certainly the easiest. I'm only in the position I am now because of my husband and his untimely death. Forgoing matrimony entirely? I'm not even sure how you would go about it. Your father will force you to marry, if that is his wish."

"What if Lorenzo doesn't find me attractive?"

"How could any man not find you attractive?"

"Our family is not wealthy. My dowry is the smallest of all the girls in the village."

"But your beauty compensates for it."

"What if it didn't?" Julietta said, tilting her head to one side and glancing at Caterina, the servant with the unfortunate face.

***

Julietta's thoughts were on everything except the muddy road under her feet and the long shadows stretching out from the surrounding forest. She barely noticed the physical world as she headed home from Signora Moretti's villa a mile from the village proper. It felt wonderful to have a grown-up friend, especially one so wise and worldly. She hadn't intended to stay until evening, but the woman had been positively fascinating. Julietta was no closer to knowing what she should do – or not do – but she had so thoroughly enjoyed herself it didn't matter. Their talk provided plenty of thought-provoking morsels to dissect in the days to come.

"Isn't it late for a young lady to be out walking by herself?" a voice called from the tree line.

Julietta snapped out of her reverie, seeking the source of the voice. She pivoted to face the denser side of the forest in time to see a form detach itself from the shadows. The figure stepped onto the path twenty yards ahead, blocking her route home.

She recognized the man immediately. He was an elder who owned the village's only inn as well as the largest farm in the area. She breathed a sigh of relief. Her first thought had been of the villains who lived deep within the woods and preyed upon travelers.

"And such a comely lass, too," Signor Rizzo said. His voice had taken on an odd, husky tone she had never heard before.

"Buonasera, Signor Rizzo." She gave the man a polite smile. "You startled me. I thought at first you were a blackguard."

The man's sudden laughter was like the braying of a donkey. She frowned, hearing a strange undertone. Nervousness? She dismissed the notion. A man of his stature would never be nervous around a girl like herself.

"Hardly, child." He moved closer, wearing a grin and gawking at her with such intensity that she was compelled to pull her shawl tightly across her bosom.

"I'm just on my way home." She cast her eyes demurely downward as she began to circle around him.

"Not so fast." He grabbed her arm and held it in a painful grip. "There's something I need your help with." His voice was low and raspy. If serpents spoke, they would sound like that.

He yanked her off the road and into a thicket. She started to scream, but his other hand quickly covered her mouth and nose. Within seconds, she felt as if she were suffocating.

"I could snuff the life out of you as easily as the unwanted offspring of the barn cats. Do not make a sound and perhaps I will let you live. If you please me."

Julietta felt a wave of dread wash over her. She was ignorant of the details of carnal acts between humans, but had seen animals fornicate. She had a general understanding of what was about to happen to her.

"Not a sound, remember?" he said, releasing the hand from her mouth and tossing her onto the ground. A sharp stone stabbed her back, making her eyes water from the pain.

Rizzo stood over her, staring at her face, as his hands fumbled with the belt holding his breeches and hose in place.

"You're so very lovely," he muttered, naked below the waist now.

She was shocked by what she saw. She had never seen a man's body without hose. It was horrifying to think that thing could fit inside her. She hadn't bled yet and her hips were narrow even for a thirteen-year-old.

"I am still a maiden, sir. Please..." Her voice sounded like a stranger to her own ears. How could she be so calm under these dire circumstances?

"Precisely the point. Now, lie down. This won't take long."

A glistening trail of saliva slid from the open mouth to the stubbled jaw. He breathed like an ironsmith's bellows. Moans emanated from his throat, while a tongue darted out to capture the escaped drool. A starving man gazing at a forbidden feast would have more dignity than this creature.

The composure she had heard in her own voice seemed to take over her mind. A cool detachedness replaced the panic she had felt moments ago. Rape was imminent unless she acted now.

She locked eyes with the man, willing him to focus on her face, her mouth, her eyes...anywhere but on the hand that searched for a rock of sufficient size and weight.

He grappled with her skirts, thrusting them up above her waist, groaning when he saw her naked, prepubescent body. What kind of depraved fiend desired sexual relations with a child?

He lowered his body, forcing her legs apart.

At that moment, her fingers located salvation, latching upon a rock. Without hesitation, she bashed it against the skull of the man who would defile her. Her next movement was to draw up one knee and jab it into his groin, hard.

He never uttered a sound as he fell to ground, partially trapping her beneath his bulk.

"Despicable monster," she said, rolling him off and standing on shaking legs. She studied the unconscious man with the same cool detachment that had saved her life.

He's breathing. I guess that's a good thing. Now what to do about this?

She walked a few steps away, keeping her eyes on the unmoving body, then sat down on a smooth boulder. The path was just behind her. She could keep her eyes on the would-be rapist as well as the road with just a turn of her head.

What to do?

Finally, a surge of nausea forced her to bend over and empty the contents of her stomach – Francesca's wine and the shared snack of bread and olive oil – onto the ground. She wiped her mouth with the back of her hand, then resumed contemplation of the half-naked man.

He will deny it, of course. And who would believe me over one of the most prominent men in the village?

Her mind raced, not just with a solution to this immediate problem, but with implications of how any action she took now would impact her life. She felt as if the place she now sat was a metaphorical fork in the road. Which way should she go?

***

"It's nothing, Papa," Julietta said to her father, who scrutinized her bruised face with concern and something else. Mild horror?

"I don't understand why you were out so late." Now that he was sure she was essentially unhurt, he became distracted. She knew exactly what preoccupied him.

"I told you. I left Corto's house and decided to go to the woods to gather some herbs." She flashed him a smile meant to be disarming but was rather ghastly now that she was missing a front tooth. "It was growing dark before I noticed how late it was. That's why I stumbled. I didn't see the felled tree branch in the gloom."

"What are we to do?" Her mother injected herself into the conversation, a rare event for the meek woman.

"About what? I'm not seriously injured. Thankfully no fractured bones. Or worse..."

"You know what she means," her father said.

Julietta sighed. "Yes, I know what you both are worried about. Instead of being relieved and happy that a villain didn't rape and kill me, you're afraid my broken tooth will diminish my value."

Neither of her parents bothered to reply. She had anticipated this reaction as she sat on the boulder pondering her future. It was to be expected. A daughter is a burden. The labor she provides rarely offsets the expense of a dowry, which is nothing more than a thinly veiled bribe to another man for taking custodianship of her.

After the near-rape, she thought long and hard about her life. Men already had so much power. Why would she willingly enter into a marriage contract which could strip her of all independence? Signora Moretti – Francesca – had been fortunate. Her husband had respected her intellect, even deferred to it. What were the odds she would also be lucky in her father's choice? Better to remain unmarried and suffer the societal stigma than to relinquish what little self-authority she now had. The devil you know, as they say. Her father was no devil. He had a soft spot for her. She knew how to get her way with him. And although she was no longer comely, he still loved her, of course. An unwed daughter would be an embarrassment to him, but she had a plan to elevate her status within the family and beyond. If she contributed to the family's wealth, surely he would come to see her as an asset rather than a liability.

It was a bold and risky strategy. But when she sat on that boulder, her mouth throbbing from Rizzo's hand and the image of his disgusting genitalia fresh on her mind, she experienced an epiphany. Francesca's servant, Caterina of the unfortunate face, should evoke more respect than a woman who merely married well. The girl worked hard to provide for herself and perhaps a family. There was no shame in that. Shame should be prescribed to the female who abandoned her autonomy to gain a comfortable life. After that revelation, she had picked up a rock – a different one than she had wielded moments earlier – and smacked it against her tooth before she could talk herself out of it.

There was no going back now. She had been tempted to do more damage to her face, but the tooth would surely be sufficient.

She eyed her father appraisingly before casting her eyes down again. She used her most deferential voice. "Papa, I know what you're thinking. You believe Giovanni Cavelli will no longer wish to marry me. I'm sorry."

"It was an accident, bambina. If your dowry were larger, your beauty would not be so important. The fault lies with me, not you." His tone of resignation made her heart soar. "I will go to his father tomorrow, tell him of this development, and release him of any obligation." He sighed.

Julietta fought the urge to smile. She glanced up at her mother who stood to the side, watching her with narrowed eyes. Did she suspect something?

Feeling her mother's gaze still upon her, she fabricated a forlorn demeanor. She thought of the saddest moment of her life – two years ago when her beloved dog Macchiato had been struck by a wine cart – and managed to work up a few tears, which spilled from her eyes and trailed down her cheeks.

"Don't cry, bambina. Everything will be fine." Her father patted the top of her head before lumbering out of the room. Her mother followed silently behind him.

She took a deep breath and released it, careful to contain her jubilation. If she were to succeed, she must learn to govern herself in every way, as Francesca did.

***

"You have a missing tooth. Like your dream man!" Corto said, his mouth agape as he stared at hers. The two friends stood in the boy's kitchen while the female servant hovered nearby, pretending not to hear.

"Let us go outside," she said. "I'll explain everything."

"Signor Rizzo nearly raped you?" he squealed a few minutes later. In the farthest corner of the garden, they were out of earshot of servants and neighbors.

"Yes. At first I thought I might have killed him with that rock, but he was still breathing when I left the forest. This morning I saw the beast strutting about the village, so it seems he suffered no lingering ill effects. I wager he has a pounding headache, though." Julietta grinned, again revealing the gaping hole in her smile. Corto seemed fascinated by it.

"He broke your tooth after you hit him with the rock?"

"No. I did that to myself."

"What? Why would you do such a thing?"

"To make myself unattractive to men."

"I see," he said with obvious admiration. "A drastic move, but probably an effective one. You're still somewhat pretty, though. Your eyes are still blue, and your hair is still flaxen. What will you do if you encounter Rizzo again?"

"Nothing. And neither will he."

"True. Any accusations he makes against you would only implicate himself."

"Exactly. Best just to pretend it never happened. I'll leave him alone, and he'll leave me alone."

Corto frowned. "What if he tries it again with another maiden? Rarely is such a thing a singular event."

"I've considered that. I intend to warn all the girls in the area. I'll be discreet, though. No one will suspect the warning's origin was me. I'll say I'm just passing on a rumor I heard from someone else."

"You're quite clever, you know."

"Yes, I do know. But I need your help for the next part."

"As I said, I'm delighted to facilitate your rebellion. What can I do?"

"Look at these and tell me what you think." She pulled several sheets of vellum from her satchel. She had stolen the blank paper from her father's shop after everyone had gone to sleep. Their living quarters conveniently resided above their business establishment. The thievery had been quick and simple. If everything went as planned, it would ultimately lead to the expansion of the family's fortunes.

"Oh my," he said, examining the sketches.

She laughed at his evident distaste. "I know my artwork is terrible, but try to see past it to the gown designs themselves."

"That won't be easy."

"Please, just look at what I've created."

"Hmmm...yes, yes. Oh, that's quite nice." He pointed to one of the design elements.

"I thought so, too. See how I've raised the waist a bit and also lowered the neckline? And the sleeves are more fitted than what ladies are wearing now. Not so puffy. I think the overall effect is more flattering."

"I suppose you're right," he said, handing them back to her. She could see he was losing interest.

"This is where I need your help. I need you to elevate my renderings. If you make them as lovely as any of your other drawings, I will be successful."

He arched an eyebrow, and gestured for her to return the papers to him. His curiosity piqued, he studied them more intently. "There's no question I can improve upon these. I've never drawn women's clothing before, but it can't be difficult. Shall I add a face? Or just a bizarre oval blob wearing a snood, as you've done."

She took a deep breath. "I would like you to draw the face of Signora Moretti. I will present these to her for my first commission."

"I see your plan. You create these sartorial confections for Signora Moretti, who wears them about town as a form of advertisement. Thus you will gain more work, and so on, and so on."

"Yes. With each client, my business will grow. I will fund future commissions with money from the previous ones. Once I've established myself as the most fashionable seamstress in the village, everyone will want my services, and I can charge more than the going rate. When it comes to ladies of means and their apparel, reputation is everything. If I'm providing something no one else can, I'm justified in charging more."

"I can't deny that. Your designs are remarkable, though the renderings are utterly incompetent. Fortunately, you have me."

"Truly. I couldn't do this without you, Corto."

"Certainly not. I will begin immediately."

Without another word, he walked away. She smiled as she watched him, pondering their friendship. When she had taken pity on the local oddball boy three years ago, she had done it out of kindness, not because she imagined the combination of their creative talents could buy her the independence she craved.

***

"I would like to meet the young man who drew these," Francesca said the following week. Her intelligent eyes were wide in astonishment as she pored over the drawings.

"I'm not sure I can get him here. He's rather averse to socializing. And he's always busy doing something, either of an artistic nature or a scientific one. He's quite brilliant. The only reason I was able to coerce him to help me is because we're friends. I'm his only friend, actually. The other children think he's peculiar."

The two sat under the same cypress tree in Francesca's garden. The weather was cooler, and the sky above the feathery leaves was the color of pewter. Julietta had shared everything that had happened to her since their last meeting, including Rizzo's attack.

"These are exquisite. You have a rare talent for fashion design, but this boy – this artist friend of yours – has a gift from God."

"Yes. Fortunately, his father recognizes that. He intends to send him to Florence when he's fifteen to apprentice with Andrea somebody or other."

Francesca's mouth dropped. "Andrea del Verracchio? The premier artist in all of Italy?"

"Yes, that sounds right. He is important?"

"Santo cielo! Of course, he is important. The father has already secured the apprenticeship?"

"I think so."

"His fortune is thus made. And yours as well when the boy achieves the accolades he deserves and it becomes known he had a hand in your enterprise."

"He's that exceptional?"

Francesca smiled. "Yes, I believe so. I know a little about the arts. I have been to Florence, of course, and Milan, Venice, Genoa. I have met many talented painters and seen their work. Verracchio is the most sought after of all. Everyone wants to commission him. If your friend apprentices with him, his future is bright indeed. And since the boy clearly has talent, there will be no limits. He may even surpass Verracchio himself."

Now it was Julietta's turn to be astonished. "I knew Corto was special, but I didn't realize how special."

"Corto?"

"That's my nickname for him. His real name is Leonardo."

"That's more suitable," Francesca smiled. "You were wise to befriend him and even wiser to entice him to create these for you. Now, back to the more pressing issue: is your dressmaking skill equal to the designs? It is one thing to imagine them and put them on paper, but quite another to bring them to life with the proper fabric and materials, solid construction, and perfect fit."

It wasn't in Julietta's nature to boast. But she knew she had to convince Francesca to give her payment for one of the gowns now so she could purchase the fabrics and launch her business.

"I am the best seamstress in the village, though I'm still just thirteen until next month. Mother says my talent surpasses her own, and my embroidered handkerchiefs sell quite well in my father's shop. I can do this. I know I can." She tapped the top piece of paper. "I'd like to begin with this one, if you agree."

"That is my favorite of the three. Very well. I will fetch the money. I see you have written the amount at the bottom there."

"I know it's high, but I promise you will be more than satisfied."

"Even if I am not, I am happy to assist such an indomitable female in her quest to win autonomy. To say Rizzo is a pig would be an insult to pigs. And his debauchery is not unique in this man's world. We females need to stick together if we are ever to achieve anything near to equality. That you had to disfigure yourself to acquire some control over your own life is a travesty. It makes me sad yet proud."

"Thank you." Julietta felt a heavy weight slip from her shoulders, even though she was shocked by the vehement tone in the woman's voice. It was a side not displayed outside of the villa, she wagered. Francesca navigated this man's world carefully.

"What if your father finds another prospective husband for you? One who doesn't mind the small dowry or the missing tooth?"

"I've thought about that. I may need to take...additional measures."

"You mean further disfigurement?"

Julietta nodded. The notion nauseated her, but she resolved to do whatever was required.

"I hope it doesn't come to that, but I admire your dedication. How does it feel knowing that people no longer see you as a pretty girl?"

She thought a long time before answering. The servant, Caterina, lurked nearby. She thought about the girl's homeliness and her own gap-toothed smile.

"Humbling," she said.

"Yes. And that's not a bad thing. Humility is good for the soul. Now, let me get those coins and you can be on your way before it gets dark."

Later that evening, she gathered her courage to approach her father, who was downstairs, tending to customers. She waited until she heard the jingling of the bell above the door, indicating the last patron of the day had left. She traipsed down the staircase, drawings in hand. When she rounded the corner, taking a deep breath to prepare herself, she stopped in her tracks at the sight before her eyes. The final customer of the day had not left. He was, in fact, chatting with her father, whose countenance exuded pure elation.

"Bambina, I have just received some wonderful news," Father said, clapping Rizzo on the shoulder in a familiar manner. The despicable man turned to face her, regaling her with a venomous smirk. "The Signor has offered you marriage. The nuptials will not take place for two more years," he added hastily. "But I know you will be pleased to be wed to such a prosperous, respected man. And he will be happy to replace his late wife. Youthful laughter will be most welcome in his house, he says."

Julietta feared she might vomit.

Her father saw the expression on her face and stepped in front of the man to block his view of her. "My daughter is overwhelmed by this exciting development. Come, let me walk you out. We shall discuss the details later. I know your word is as sound as any legal document. Nevertheless, I prefer the contract be signed by both parties as soon as possible. I'll have it drawn up tomorrow, if that's agreeable to you."

"Sì, certo," the man replied, allowing himself to be shown to the door. Just as he was stepping out into the evening twilight, he turned in Julietta's direction and gave her a sly wink.

She rushed up the stairs and emptied the contents of her stomach into the water basin next to her bed. Moments later, as she sat on the mattress, tears sliding down her cheeks, she heard her father's footsteps on the other side of her closed door.

His tremulous voice penetrated the cracks. "Bambina, I know he is older than you would like, but in all other ways, he is an excellent choice. You will be well taken care of. He is the most prosperous man in Vinci."

She scrambled off the bed and flung open the bedroom door. "You think it appropriate to marry your daughter off to a man thirty years her elder? He's older than you! How could you do this to me?"

Tears sprang into her father's eyes. She was unmoved by them.

"Be reasonable. You must have a husband, and we can no longer be choosy, thanks to your clumsiness."

The words felt like a slap, which was what she needed at that moment. She knew what must be done, and she would do it before any binding document could be signed.

With narrowed eyes, she gazed at her father. "Very well," she said, shutting the door in his face.

She listened, pressing her ear against the rough wood, then sighed with relief when he shuffled away.

Her gaze took in the details of her tiny space now: grandmother's patchwork quilt tucked neatly around the edges of her bed; a dented brass oil lamp flickering on a hand-me-down table, entirely too cheerful for her mood; a satin box stacked in a corner along with her sewing and embroidery implements. She took three quick steps, then lifted the lid. Golden lamplight reflected off the metal shears.

Their familiar weight took on a new significance.

***

Julietta didn't need to see her reflection in her mother's polished metal vanity to know how frightful she looked. Corto's expression said it all. He was sitting next to a row of medicinal plants. She lowered herself carefully – the wounds on her face would bleed if she moved too vigorously – until she sat cross-legged beside him on the ground.

"Mio dio! What has happened to your beautiful face? What have you done?"

She was afraid he might weep. She couldn't bear it if he did. No tears from him. Not from her Corto.

"I have freed myself," she said. The words gave her courage.

She told him the story of how she had further mutilated herself after Rizzo presented a marriage offer. Told him how furious her father was and how she had covered her grin when he tore up the freshly drafted contract before her eyes. *Signor Rizzo will tolerate a missing tooth, but not the nightmare that is now my daughter's face.* His own had been crimson with anger.

"So it worked," Corto whispered.

"It did."

"Was it worth it? Your freedom? Your independence?"

"I don't think I can answer that. Not yet."

"What will you do now?"

"I'll begin sewing Signora Moretti's gown."

And that is what Julietta did. For the next two years, she labored long days with little sleep. Her back and arms ached constantly, and her fingers grew calloused and rough. But her face healed well, despite the extensive damage she had wrought. Still, the village children and even some of the adults had begun to call her the Dreadful Seamstress of Vinci. It was a moniker she detested, but instead of fighting it, she incorporated it into a professional mystique. She had taken to cloistering herself in her room to avoid being seen. When she ventured out to deliver orders or purchase fabrics, she wore a hood and tied a silken scarf over her face so that only her sapphire eyes showed. Rumors circulated that she dabbled in the black arts, so inexplicably beautiful were her gowns. Thus her success was further propelled.

All the fashionable ladies wanted dresses created by the Dreadful Seamstress.

Her father had stayed angry for months, but as the money trickled in, then flowed like a rain-swollen river, he relented. She thought she now detected traces of admiration when he looked at her.

He could never look at her long, though.

She was sitting in her room, working on a new commission, when she heard the shop bell ring below, then Corto's voice calling up the stairs.

"Julietta! Are you up there?"

He was no longer the short, odd boy she had befriended years ago. He was now a tall, gangly, odd young man with facial hair sprouting in irregular patches punctuated by a smattering of pimples. He would never be handsome, her Corto, but he didn't need to be. He possessed a gift from God. She realized with a sinking feeling why he was here now.

She opened her door and called him in.

"This is where you do it? It seems such a humble setting for such a famous – or is it infamous? – personage," he said, drawing her in for a quick hug.

"Yes, this is my lair where all manner of sorcery conjures the beautiful clothing worn by all the stylish ladies. In addition to a lot of hard work. Look at my fingers!"

"They're appalling. Perhaps they'll distract from your face."

Her scars had become a joke between them. The teasing was a game, but it held therapeutic benefits as well. She no longer cringed when she gazed upon her reflection.

"I know why you're here," she said. "You're leaving for Florence. It's time for your apprenticeship with Andrea del Verracchio, isn't it?"

"Yes. I admit I'm excited. I leave in the morning, and I wanted to tell you goodbye. I will miss you so. You are my best friend."

"And you are mine."

"Will you come visit me? Florence is only fifty kilometers away. You can easily make the trek in two days."

She nodded. "If father will allow it. He's so happy with the windfall my business has brought to our household, I doubt he would deny me anything."

"You have achieved your goal of autonomy."

"As much as is possible for a fifteen-year-old female."

"Be at peace, Julietta. You have gained much these past two years. Your future is under your control."

"I have lost much as well."

"Do you regret it?" he said softly, touching her face affectionately with his long, elegant fingers.

Her smiles were small and tight these days, a result of the painful months of healing as well as knowing how macabre she looked. But when she grinned now at her friend's question, it was broad and sincere.

"No regrets. Not even the smallest one. Farewell, Corto. I shall miss you terribly."

"Farewell, my dear friend, the Dreadful Seamstress of Vinci!"

***

Milan, Italy 1497 – Thirty years later...

"How was your journey, Julietta? Milan is much farther than you're used to traveling for our visits." Corto glanced up at her in the doorway. Typical Corto. She hadn't seen him in five years, and he couldn't be bothered to stop dabbling with his paints and brushes long enough to embrace her.

"It was arduous, to say the least. I have news!"

"Exciting news? Salai, fetch us refreshments," he said to the dark-haired boy who had answered the door and who gave his master a withering glance before scurrying off.

"Salai? Why do you call him that?"

"Because he is a dirty little devil who vexes me on a daily basis."

"Those curls are adorable. Is he a servant or apprentice?"

Corto sighed. "Both, I suppose. The imp has some skill." He set his brush down and walked toward her. His beard was grayer and longer than it had been five years ago.

Finally, she got her hug. Peering over his shoulder, she noticed the painting he was working on and gasped.

"Per l'amor di Dio! Is that a depiction of Jesus and his disciples? It is magnificent!"

Corto released her and nodded. "It's called The Last Supper. I'm rather proud of it. The final rendition will be depicted on a wall in the Santa Maria delle Grazie. It's a commision for Sforza."

"The Duke of Milan?"

"The very one. That version will be much larger, of course."

She nodded. Her childhood friend was now the premier artist in all of Italy and beyond. While apprenticing with Verraccio all those years ago, his talent had quickly been recognized. During Corto's tenure, Verraccio himself had felt so overshadowed by his pupil that it was said he gave up his own career.

"Let us sit outside. It's smells like farts in here. I blame the imp," he said, guiding her out the studio's doorway, through the sprawling tapestry-laden apartments to a small urban garden. Spring had arrived in Milan, but the fragrant flowers and budding trees did little to quell the city's stench. The garden was nothing compared to that of Signora Moretti's country villa, she thought, then felt a wave of sadness. Her friend and mentor had passed several years ago at the impressive age of sixty-seven. Francesca became the largest property owner in Vinci and was still unwed at the time of her death, stubbornly independent to the end.

Julietta almost wished she could make the same claim.

"So what is your exciting news?" Corto asked, sipping at the wine Salai had served before disappearing again. The vintage was excellent, a testament to the lucrative nature of

Corto's brilliance. He cherished his fine wines almost as much as his creations.

She grinned. "I'm married." Even to her own ears she sounded like a silly schoolgirl.

"I don't believe you. After all these years of liberty and all the sacrifices you made to achieve it? Who is he? What is he? *Why*?"

She laughed. "One question at a time, my curious friend. Do you remember the man my father first had selected for me?"

"When we were thirteen? Yes, yes. The middle Cavelli son."

"Lorenzo," she smiled again.

"You are smitten! Not only are you married, a circumstance I never expected to see, you are also in love with your husband."

"I am. Think about the irony. If I hadn't been so determined to win my independence all those years ago, my appearance would be normal now, and I would have likely lived a happy life. Lorenzo is a wonderful man, kind and devoted. He relishes being the husband of the Dreadful Seamstress, and he admires my accomplishments. He says I am the most extraordinary woman he has ever known. Also," she said, feeling the heat rise in her cheeks, "he says he can see past my scars to the beautiful woman within. He loves that I am not vain in my looks, nor boastful of my success. I think that's rather remarkable for a man."

"I love all those things about you, too, Julietta. And I loved you first!" he added, clearly happy for her, but also a little jealous.

"I know. Oh, Corto. I have the best of all worlds. Lorenzo doesn't meddle in my business affairs, nor does he expect me to perform menial domestic tasks."

"No pewter polishing? No rearranging of the linens?"

"None of that. I have been content with my decisions, and I am profoundly so with this one, too."

He stood and kissed her cheek. The scars had faded after all this time, resembling the faint veins of an oak leaf held against the sun – a subtle tribute to her resolve.

"Words ellude me." He was overcome with emotion.

She kissed the cheek above the graying beard. "I know, Corto. I know."

"If you hadn't done those things...to your tooth and to your face...you would never have become the exceptional woman you are today. And you have achieved humility, something I struggle with on a daily basis."

"It's easy to be humble when you're not the most brilliant person in Italy."

"That reminds me, I have something to show you. Salai! Fetch my charcoals. The ones of the flying machine!"

The In Between

Julietta awoke in a black void. She constructed a mouth, then whispered, "I'm back in the In Between."

The memories of her most recent life flood into her consciousness. She remembered how this part worked and created a comfortable setting for the inevitable discussion with Sarah.

She closed her eyes and imagined the enchanting garden of Signora Moretti's villa – the feathery leaves of the cypress trees; the nearby bubbling fountain; the fragrant, warm air on her skin. When she opened her eyes again, the void had been delegated to the perimeter, and she sat in a chair beneath those soft branches. She glanced down where her lap should be and saw only the wooden slats of the seat. She concentrated, remembering her recent appearance, then watched her legs emerge, covered in her favorite azure brocade. When sewing only for herself the last few years, she had created one of her most stunning gowns from the expensive fabric. Self-indulgent, yes, but after a lifetime of making others feel beautiful, it had been her turn at the end.

The empty space in the chair next to her gradually became denser. She knew what was happening and closed her eyes again, anticipating the form Sarah would choose.

When she opened them, her beloved childhood friend sat beside her.

"Hello, Corto-Sarah." Julietta felt the tug of her scars when she smiled at her Spiritual Guide. Or angel. Or whatever she was.

"Hello, Julietta. It's lovely seeing you again. How did it go? Did you learn about Creativity and Humility?" It was Sarah's voice coming from Corto's mouth. Under different circumstances, the effect might have been unsettling. Here, it felt normal.

"I believe I did."

"Tell me all about it."

"I learned about Creativity through my dressmaking and also through Corto's example. I think the juxtaposition of our two talents – mine small, his enormous – was particularly effective. One doesn't have to be Leonardo da Vinci to be creative. There are many smaller ways to express it as well."

"What else?"

Julietta thought for several moments. "I learned about Humility when I transitioned from pretty to ugly. Being an unattractive female wasn't easy in a time when women were prized for their beauty and little else. I would see the expressions on the faces of the villagers when I ventured out, before I began covering my scars."

"What did those expressions reveal?"

"Disgust. Revulsion. Hatred, even. Before my disfigurement, everyone was pleased to see the pretty little Julietta scamper by. After, my ugliness almost seemed like an affront to them...as if my very existence offended them."

"Sadly, that reaction is not rare, especially within the less enlightened segment of humankind."

"I think I got a bonus on this one, too." The notion had occurred to her just before her spiritual guide had fully materialized.

"How interesting. Please explain."

"In my quest to learn Humility, I also learned about Independence and Personal Liberty. Living during the Renaissance, I was exposed to a wealth of creative genius. Many of the world's greatest painters and sculptors were producing masterpieces practically every week, and there was an explosion of scientific advancement as well, which is another form of Creativity, yes? You were wise to propose this time period. Despite all that imagination and ingenuity, it was a horribly oppressive time during which to be a female. Male privilege existed at every level of society, from peasants to kings. It was the female's burden to acquiesce to her husband, her father, her brother or uncle, merely because she wasn't born with a penis. How clever to suggest incarnating as a woman this time. I would never have experienced all that I did if I had been a man."

Corto-Sarah smiled as she transitioned back into the original Sarah. But now, instead of the lavender track suit, she wore one of Julietta's most spectacular gowns, the very one which had sheathed Francesca Moretti during that dear lady's burial.

"I love it when a bonus lesson happens. In my line of work, that's one of the most thrilling perks," Sarah said.

"Do you think I can go forward, then? Did I get everything right?"

"Do you think you got everything right?"

Julietta leaned back in the chair. She brushed her fingertips against the soft cypress leaves; took in a deep lungful of air that smelled of rich soil, herbs, and wildflowers; gazed at the wispy clouds scuttling in the blue sky between the tree limbs; thought about the seventy-one years she had recently spent on Earth.

"Yes. I think I got everything right."

"Very well. What will you tackle next?"

"Let's do Responsibility and Accountability with a Moral Restraint Rider."

"Excellent. I have some ideas on that one," Sarah added.

"Whatever they are, I want my next life to take place in a time when humanity has evolved a bit further in terms of gender equality. I've done four of my Sublime Seven so far, and looking back on them, I recognize a pervasive disparity in that regard."

"As with all areas of enlightenment, these things take time," Sarah replied.

"I understand. I have some ideas of my own, too.

"Chapter 5 – Responsibility and Accountability with a Moral Restraint Rider

Mars Southern Pole Colony (United Nations jurisdiction) – 2157 CE

Jaeda sipped the last dregs of her coffee. It had been cold an hour ago, and now it was practically java slush. Even with the base's advanced climate control system, nothing stayed warm for long here, including human bodies. She shivered as she sat in the small combination work office and sleeping quarters, peering at the IT screen on her desk. It was archaic, one of the reasons she loved it. Everyone else had long ago switched to AVR implants, or at least headsets, which connected them effortlessly to the HIVE and to each other. The problem with the AVRs, however, was twofold: first, the privacy setting was easily hacked, and second, there was too damn much thought-noise. All those colonists, both enlisted and civilian, and all their brain activity while on the HIVE created a kind of ambient background hum that was annoying as hell.

They said she was imagining that hum, but she knew better.

Mars should be quiet, but it wasn't. Jaeda knew exactly how loud an overpopulated planet could be. She had been born on Earth with its eleven billion souls, all of whom lived on the thirteen percent of the planet's remaining habitable land surface. From a young age, she knew what her future would look like. She had been genetically engineered for it. Jaeda could tolerate increased radiation and low gravity better than the Norms on Earth. She had spent much of her childhood in a pressurized dome in Colorado to prepare for an off-world career – and also because of the frequent air-quality alerts.

Before arriving at the MSPC, she expected to be more at ease in its artificial atmosphere than she had ever felt in any forest or on any mountain or seashore. Some might consider that a sad thing, but not Jaeda. What was disappointing was the noise. Through all the years of training, she had looked forward to the peacefulness of Mars. But after landing on the red planet, she realized she would have to venture outside the biosphere without a suit to find the anticipated silence.

But if she did that, she would be dead within three minutes.

Her fingers tapped mid-air at the v-board, which was connected to the IT screen, which was connected to the HIVE, otherwise known as the High-Functioning Integrated Virtual Ethernet. Besides her, the only people who used the virtual keyboards were the old guys in Command. And the Colonel, of course. It didn't get more old-school than him.

The thought made her smile. Then she turned her attention back to the newest requisition order from the colonists in Omega pod. Those Meggies were a tush-twinge.

A sharp rapping at her office door made the v-board disappear under her fingertips. That happened when her concentration wavered.

"JD, the big guy wants you. In his quarters, not COM," a young male voice said through the speaker.

"What? Why?" she said, pressing a fingerprint against a button on the side of her desk. Her office door slid open with a whoosh. Bonzo stood in the opening, looking annoyed and exasperated as only the young and deeply impatient could. At forty-three, Jaeda was old-school herself.

"I didn't ask him. I like my head attached to the rest of my body."

If she hadn't been anxious about the summons, she would have laughed. Bonzo was a favorite among the grunts. He was one of the CRISPR-4 kids who had arrived two years ago. The latest batch was impressive, too. They could endure more than three Sieverts of radiation without batting an eyelash...or losing any eyelashes sixty days later.

"Damn," she mumbled, rolling her chair back. She took a quick pee in the tiny attached latrine, checked her reflection in the mirror above the sink – tired, but her dark curls were still neatly tucked under her cap – and stepped into the corridor.

"S'up, JD," said another of the CRISPR-4 kids, brushing past her in the busy hallway. The short, stocky young woman had won first place in the base's annual weight-lifting competition, ousting the previous three-time champion and propelling her to instant celebrity. Jaeda liked her. Her arrogance rivaled her intellect, plus she was a muscled-up bad-ass. It was always good to possess the second and the third qualities – if you also possessed the first.

"Hey, Shroom. You hear anything come down the PVC?"

The woman stopped and turned, tilting her head. "Why would I hear anything that you hadn't?"

"Because you're plugged in. You know what I mean."

An impish grin appeared on the young face. "Girl, you gotta get an upgrade. You're in dinosaur territory."

"Tell me about it."

"But to answer your question, I haven't heard a whisper. The usual shite from the Meggies, but nothing to be worried about."

"What shite?" Jaeda asked, concerned now.

"That you're a vindictive bitch who denies some of their requisitions based on their pod address."

Jaeda nodded, somewhat relieved. This was data-mold.

"Thanks, Shroom."

"Catch you later, Dark Lady," said the young woman with another grin before disappearing around the corner. Jaeda had a second nickname other than JD. She had never been able to determine who coined Dark Lady, but assumed it had something to do with her skin color. What else could it be?

The notion made her smile. If anyone thought they could get a rise with a stupid nickname, they had another think coming.

When she arrived at the Colonel's door, she took a deep breath, rapped twice, then stepped through the opening after it swished aside. She hadn't even identified herself through the speaker – a bad sign. Curious and alarming that he had sent the summons via human messenger, too.

"You wanted to see me, sir?"

"Yes, Captain. Come in, sit down." If rocks crashing down a cliff could talk, they would sound like Colonel Khandar, known to the young enlisted as 'the Kraken.' When she heard the term three years ago, a HIVE search had revealed its meaning and origins. She'd laughed her ass off for the next hour. A menacing, multi-limbed monster summoned for the purpose of teaching painful lessons about respect to unsuspecting victims was just about perfect for the Colonel.

He swatted away the HIVE's v-screen and pivoted in his chair to face her. Her heart sank. She had seen him wear that expression only one other time in her life: when he had received the Deep Space Network transmission about her parents' accident. Despite having just emptied her bladder, she felt the need to urinate again.

"Go on. Sit down," he said again, gesturing toward the only empty chair in the small room, then pressing his fingertip against a hidden panel. The door closed.

She sat on the metal chair, ramrod straight, resisting the urge to cross her legs.

A restless hand raked through hair that was more salt than pepper these days. Golden eyes bored into her, seemingly taking her measure before the brain that controlled them decided what to say. Or what not to say.

Something in those eyes shifted, telling her he had made up his mind. With another tap on the panel, the room began to buzz. If she had still been on Earth, she might have expected a swarm of honeybees to emerge through the vents – not that she had ever seen an actual honeybee swarm, just the old vids.

Shite. He turned on the hack block.

Nobody anywhere outside that room, whether through the HIVE, augmented ears, or any kind of remote listening device, would be able to hear whatever terrible thing he was about to tell her. The hack block was completely impenetrable.

"We got a message through the DSN yesterday," he said. Instead of continuing, he closed his eyes.

It was a relief to no longer be the focus of that intense gaze. She waited, stomach churning. The announcement would be world-altering. She sensed it just as she sensed the thought-noise on the HIVE, the noise people said she imagined.

"We made contact," he said.

"Contact?"

"Yes."

"Oh, you mean...*contact*?"

He frowned, gave her a scathing look, and then said, "Yes, Captain. Alien contact."

"Feck," she whispered, then, "Sorry, sir."

He waved a dismissive hand in her direction.

"There's more, though. Right?" she said.

"Oh, yeah. A lot more and all bad. They exploited the DSN. Hijacked our own damn interplanetary communication network to tell us they're coming."

The two words sent a frisson of dread throughout her body.

They're coming.

She swallowed. "I'm guessing the tone wasn't friendly?"

"You could say that. They used mathematics to communicate. We always knew math was our best chance for inter-species dialogue. The brains at NASA decoded it pretty quickly." He rubbed at the ashen crescent-moon patches under his eyes. "I'll paraphrase for your benefit. They intend to take over our home planet, but before doing so, they're making a stop here."

"What do they want from us?" Her mouth was so dry she could barely get the words out.

"That part isn't completely clear. The thrust of their communique implied displeasure at how humans have been running things in our miniscule corner of the universe for the last millennia. The astrobiologists at NASA are divided in their interpretation of the alien intent. The optimists believe they're coming to teach us how to be better planetary caretakers. The pessimists think they're disgusted with our 'raping of the cosmos.' That one came from Dr. Muehler, not surprisingly. And that they plan to eliminate the humans, thereby allowing the two planets and one moon which we currently occupy to eventually return to their natural, human-free state."

"If they meant us harm, why would they notify us ahead of time? Wouldn't they just show up and kill us?"

"That was Dr. Nguyen's argument. Muehler shot it down fast. She said the aliens probably don't need the element of surprise to overpower us. The fact that they have the ability to travel to our solar system from a world possibly light years away indicates a level of technology we couldn't begin to withstand. In other words, they don't need to use stealth because they're not afraid of us."

"But why bother telling us at all?"

"Dr. Muehler had an answer for that as well. She believes these aliens possess some kind of ethical directive which dictates they give us advance warning. A handful of scientists interpreted an ambiguous fragment of the communication that way."

"They're giving us time to prepare for our demise?"

"That's become the popular consensus on Earth."

She nodded, finally crossing her legs, hoping her bladder would hold out for a few more minutes. "What's the timeframe?"

Khandar arched a shaggy eyebrow, leaned back against his chair, and said, "Two months."

"What's our plan?"

"That's where you come in, Captain."

***

The plan involved fast-tracking the Subterranean Biosphere that had been under construction for the past decade. The facility was largely ready for habitation but not yet outfitted, nor would it ever be adequate to house, feed, hydrate, and oxygenate a thousand colonists and military personnel.

In other words, not everyone would get to hide in the bunker when the aliens arrived.

A week of sixteen-hour work days had passed since Jaeda's conversation with Khandar. Not only was she charged with managing the logistics of servicing the three hundred souls who would fit into the SB, she had to do it all covertly.

The Colonel had sworn her to secrecy, of course. The last thing anyone wanted was panic, or worse, anarchy. Life in a hermetically sealed habitat on a planet hostile to human life was fragile at best, and deadly at worst.

Much of the complicated business of keeping everyone safe – from radiation, structural breaches, starvation, and dehydration – fell to her as quartermaster, an archaic title still in use in the modern military of the twenty-second century. Provisioning an army in the wilderness of the Louisiana swamps or the Siberian tundra would have been demanding. Provisioning an army plus civilians on a planet with a gravitational field strength less than half that of Earth's, with a median temperature of −55°C, and a thin, unbreathable atmosphere inadequate to protect against a constant barrage of cosmic radiation and solar wind, was a colossal task.

But she did it, and she did it well. It satisfied her deep-seated need to minister. As a child, she had fussed over a multitude of dolls, moving on to animals during her teen years. When she had taken the aptitude test to determine her future career, nobody was surprised by the result, including herself. Despite the physical, emotional, and intellectual challenges of living on Mars – and the noise – she loved every minute of the life she spent taking care of the needs of others.

Until now.

Entwined with the extra work was the burden to her conscience. She wasn't told whose names were on The List other than her own. She assumed the officers had made the cut, as well as the medical and science people, both military and civilian. Khandar would have selected those with the most experience, knowledge, and skill sets. During the past week, she had exchanged more than a few speculative looks with people: *Are you one of the lucky ones, too?*

When she thought about the hundreds who would be staying topside, it made breathing difficult. The evacuation plan for those on the list was diabolical in its simplicity. There would be a non-emergency drill to analyze the orderly process of getting from the base to the SB. Not everyone would participate, and since people hated drills of any kind, they would feel relieved when the alert went out and they hadn't been chosen. They would eat their dinners, play ping-pong or poker, read or nap, delighted to be exempt from another tedious drill.

When the aliens showed up, the blissfully unaware folks would be easy targets, while the lucky ones hunkered below, watching annihilation on the monitors.

Every time she imagined the scenario, her stomach hurt.

"JD, got a sec?" Shroom stood in the doorway of her quarters.

Jaeda had been leaving it open as a way of appearing more approachable and less sneaky. Her guilt felt palpable to her; she imagined the word *betrayer* tattooed on her forehead. The open door and the excessive smiling was overcompensation, but she didn't know how else to behave. She had never intentionally deceived anyone in her life until now.

"Sure. What's on your mind?" she said, rearranging her face to appear friendly and candid.

"See? That right there. That's what's on my mind," the short woman replied with a frown. "Permission to speak frankly, ma'am?"

"Permission granted, Corporal Eckland," she said, crossing her arms against her chest.

"You are acting like a crazy person, and you're creeping me out."

"Perhaps that's a bit too frank."

"Sorry, but I had to tell you. I don't think everyone has noticed, but I have. I'm a CRISPR-4, as you know, but I'm also a Psi. I assume you're aware of us?"

"I've heard about the program, but my security clearance doesn't give me access to certain sections of personnel files. I wouldn't know who was and who wasn't."

"Honestly, this may have nothing to do with my Psi, since I'm also really good at reading body language."

Jaeda didn't respond. There hadn't been a question yet. She hoped her expression now was one of mild interest and nothing more.

"For the two years I've been here, you have been up-front and open, tough but fair – never mind what the Meggies say – and tuned in to not only what people need but what they want. And what will make them happy. Not all QMs are like that, you know. It's what makes you exceptional."

"Thank you, Corporal. I try."

"That's just it. You're no longer trying. It's like you've cut yourself off from everyone."

"Cut myself off? I'm sitting right here with my door open."

"Right. Why did you start doing that? We know you hate the clamor. By the way, since we're being frank, I hear the thought-noise on the HIVE too. The implant was mandatory for my generation, so sometimes I just pop out the Li-air battery so I don't have to hear it, and pretend I'm still connected."

"I'm pretty sure that's against protocol."

"It is. I don't care. It's more important to keep my sanity."

"That I understand. Not sure about the rest, though." She was finding it increasingly difficult to return the young woman's steady gaze.

"You know why people call you Dark Lady?"

Jaeda snorted. "I figured it had something to do with my pigmentation. Racism is mostly dead in the twenty-second century, but not entirely."

"Please. You older peeps are the only ones who carry that stigma."

"Gee, thanks."

"They call you Dark Lady because even though you're too old to have the Psi upgrade, people think you're telepathic or empathic. Maybe both. Remember the gypsies? The wandering Romani tribes of Eastern Europe? There was some lame song a million years ago about one of them who could read minds, or tell fortunes, or some such crap."

Jaeda's mouth fell open. "You've got to be kidding me. There's not a psychic bone in my body."

"Then why do you hear the thought-noise?"

She had no answer. She had always figured it was some kind of side effect of the system, despite the techies' denials.

"You hear it on a psychic level, just like I do."

"But I'm not a Psi."

"I know, trust me. You're much too old."

"You mentioned that already."

"The thought-noise doesn't matter anyway. What matters is that you possess some kind of innate telepathic ability, and because I do as well, even though mine was genetically engineered, I pick up on your vibes."

"Vibes? Seriously?" Jaeda said, injecting a mocking tone.

The blue eyes narrowed. A hint of distaste flashed across the youthful face.

Jaeda not only liked this strong-willed young woman, she respected her. And she desired nothing more at the moment than to have that respect returned. She bit her lip and waited.

"Yes, vibes," Shroom continued. "And they're telling me some wicked shite is about to go down. But it's not just the vibes and the weird body language. You've been putting in long hours even though there are no special projects under way."

"The SB drill is coming up," she said, breaking eye contact and studying the antiquated solar system pictures on the walls.

"Right. I think that's part of it."

Jaeda's gaze shifted away from the pictures and back to the young woman, taking the smooth, strong hand in her own. "Even if something terrible were about to go down, you know I couldn't talk about it."

"So that's an affirmative on the wicked shite? One blink for no, two for yes."

A small, hysterical chuckle worked its way up from her diaphragm. She blinked twice in rapid succession.

"Feck," the young woman said, wide-eyed now. The expression made her look like a twelve-year-old.

Jaeda's stomach roiled and knotted.

"You're not going to say anything else?"

"I can't," she mouthed.

"On the wicked-shite scale of one to ten, how does it rate?"

Jaeda held up all eight fingers and both thumbs.

***

Sleep eluded her that night. Her brain struggled with the logistics of servicing the three hundred people in the Subterranean Biosphere, but her thoughts strayed to the more than seven hundred souls who would remain topside. There had to be a way to ensure their safety, too, when the aliens arrived. She had toyed with several ideas but dismissed them all for their impracticality.

This wasn't Earth. To say their options were limited would be an understatement. Mars provided plenty of hidey-holes, none of which were habitable. To live or travel anywhere required a bio-pod, a bio-ATV, a bio-suit, or a combination thereof. Without one or more of these, humans could handle the low gravity, but they couldn't tolerate the cold, nor breathing ninety-six percent carbon dioxide.

The location for the Subterranean Biosphere had been well thought-out. The engineers selected a natural cavern two clicks from home base, inflated the specialized pod built on Earth specifically for the space, then outfitted it with ductwork connected to a smaller version of the MOXI unit used at home base. The large MOXI unit – Mars OXygen In situ, a machine which converted carbon dioxide into heated oxygen – generated breathable, warm air for a thousand people within the topside bio-sphere. The smaller unit in the SB would barely be adequate for the three hundred people housed there when the aliens arrived. Even if the additional seven hundred people could fit into the small space below ground, there wouldn't be enough air.

Everyone would suffocate in half an hour.

Of course it made sense to save as many people as possible. Jaeda didn't resent anyone for making that call. But it wasn't in her nature to let people go without basic necessities, let alone die a horrible death, if there was any chance she could do something about it.

She tossed and turned on the narrow cot, her mind scanning on-hand inventory lists as well as the manifest of a supply rocket due to arrive in three days. It would be the last one before ET's ETA. She had almost committed everything to memory at this point, having dissected it dozens of times since her meeting with Khandar. Its cargo was fairly standard – food, medicine, etc. – as well as a few unusual items Omega pod had requested, which she had grumbled about but allowed.

It was those items her subconscious invoked while she tried to focus on other issues. As she lay awake in bed, the Meggie requisition list appeared again on the back of her eyelids.

- *Carrot seeds (at least a gross for hydroponics facility)*
- *Expanding foam (insulation for rec center...it's COLD in there!)*
- *10 meters synthetic silk (children's craft projects)*

Finally, after days of scrutinizing but not really seeing the line item on both the HIVE database as well as in her thoughts, its significance bobbed up to the surface. The expanding foam. It offered a solution, or at least part of one. The rest would be up to the engineers and the officers.

She leaped out of bed, fumbled with her headset, and sent an urgent missive to the Colonel. Seconds ticked by. Was he asleep? Was he ignoring her? Either option was profoundly aggravating. How could anyone sleep at a time like this? How could he ignore her when she had been the loyal soldier for the past week, doing his bidding despite the heavy cost to her conscience?

"What the hell is it, Johnson? Do you know what time it is?" The face that appeared ghost-like on the monitor befitted the Kraken nickname; she could imagine those blazing eyes unleashing a firestorm.

"I've thought of a solution. For the others."

"We've been over this, Captain. You are dangerously close to a write-up."

A write-up? Really? Who the feck cared at a time like this?

"Please, just hear me out," she managed, swallowing the expletives that formed on her lips.

"Not on the HIVE, JD. You know better than that."

The Colonel's quarters were suddenly illuminated in the background behind the pillow-spiked hair. "Get your ass over here fast."

The screen went black.

It didn't get more by-the-books than Khandar. He had staked his entire military career on wise but safe choices and proper chain-of-command. His orders as to how they would address the alien contact came from his superiors on Earth, just as Jaeda's orders came from him. Getting the man to go off-script would be the most monumental challenge she had ever faced.

She needed more than just a persuasive argument.

She conjured the v-board, typed some code and text into the HIVE's message center, and threw on some clothes before heading to see the Colonel.

"Sit," Khandar said a few minutes later, then, "Here," thrusting a cup of black coffee at her. He wore pajama pants and a thermal shirt, donned for her benefit, thankfully – she had noticed his bare chest on the HIVE screen earlier. She didn't think she could have this, nor any, conversation if he was half-naked.

"Now, what is this all about?" He took a sip from his cup. A stranger might assume the Colonel liked his coffee strong and black, but he preferred it spiked with milk and sugar and a sprinkling of cinnamon on top. Nobody had the balls to tell him it was a sissy way to drink coffee.

The cinnamon smelled wonderful. She took a deep breath and dove into the fight of her life.

"Do you remember Oxblood Cavern a half-click to the south?" It had been so named for the interior color of its rock formations.

"Yes, of course. It was unsuitable for the SB location, so it was abandoned ten years ago."

"Right. Too small for a bulky biosphere habitat and all the outlying support systems. But there's enough room for the seven hundred people that the SB can't accommodate. It would be tight, but they would fit...for a little while."

He sighed. The burden of suffering Jaeda's idiocy seemed too much for him to bear. "Yes, we could wedge them all in there, and they would be dead in four hours when their suits ran out of air."

"What if they only needed to wear their suits to get there?"

"You're making no sense, JD. Are you sleep deprived?"

"Yes, but I'm thinking clearly. Hear me out."

He waved a tired hand in a circular motion, then took another sip of coffee.

"What if we sealed up the cave? We have fifty liters of expanding foam coming on the next supply ship and a surplus of beryllium panels from that requisition...uh...misunderstanding three years ago." The misunderstanding had been a screw-up on the part of a superior officer who had inserted an extra zero in front of a decimal. She had caught it, questioned it, then been accused of insubordination. She had never gone to the Colonel about it, but nothing escaped his notice. Along with the foam, those panels, sitting unused in a remote supply pod close to Oxblood, might well be their salvation.

"And then what, JD? Sealing it off might save people from the worst of the cold, but they're still going to run out of air."

"Not if we rig up some ductwork and reroute home base's MOXI unit to the cavern."

A salt-and-pepper eyebrow arched. She could see he was intrigued by her unorthodox plan. But just as she was beginning to get her hopes up, the eyebrow's mood changed, falling back to its normal position, then meeting with the second eyebrow in a skeptical frown.

"That's a ridiculous idea. It will never work for three reasons."

"What reasons?"

"First, we don't have enough poly-tubing to run ductwork from the home base MOXI unit to the cavern. Second, even if we did, the aliens would see it, identify its purpose, and follow it from the suspiciously people-free base to the cavern, probably stepping on it with their giant alien feet in the process and cutting off the oxygen. And third, even if we had enough tubing and were able to hide it somehow, everyone would know what we were doing. Everyone – the three hundred people we can protect and the seven hundred people we can't – would know what was going on. If that sensitive information got out there, it would spark mass chaos and a breakdown in the polite society we've taken such pains to achieve here."

The Colonel's expression softened. He squeezed her shoulder with a rare display of affection. "JD, it was a good try. I'm proud of you for thinking of it."

Her stomach constricted in the now-familiar knots of anxiety. She had anticipated his reaction and was ready for it.

She shrugged his hand from her shoulder, took a deep breath, and said, "There's poly-tubing in the supply pods – I've checked. If we scavenged a bit more from around here, we could just get it done. Some areas of home base would have to be sealed off and those residents moved to other pods temporarily. It would be cramped for a few weeks while the project was underway, but we could do it. Second, we use the ATV excavator to dig a trench, lay the tubing, cover it up, and scatter the excess soil somewhere inconspicuous."

Khandar snickered, started to respond, but she cut him off.

"Third, everyone will already know what's going on because I plan on telling them."

The eyebrows shifted from skeptical to thunderous.

"What did you just say, Captain? I think I must have misheard you, because it sounded like you said you intend to disobey a direct order. You have exactly five seconds to rephrase that final statement or be thrown in the brig."

"You can do that, but it won't keep me quiet. I programmed a communique to be sent to all one thousand and seventeen colonists and military personnel, timed to be delivered..." she glanced down at her antique watch,

"Now." She lifted her gaze back up to the Colonel's face as his HIVE unit blared with incoming alerts.

"What does the message say?" Khandar said through clenched teeth.

Jaeda gave his shoulder an ironic version of the squeeze he had given hers moments earlier. "I kept it short. I instructed people to stand by for an announcement from Colonel Khandar regarding imminent alien contact. I said that he will provide instructions for how we're going to get everyone safely through it. I also programmed a future communique to be sent in the event I had been...detained...and wasn't able to delete its directive."

"And what does that one say, Captain?" He leaned back in his chair, wearing a carefully neutral expression now.

Jaeda wanted to think she saw a hint of grudging respect in those fierce eyes, but she might have been mistaken. It might have been hatred.

She gave him a shaky smile. "It explains that the officers intend to turn their backs on seven hundred people while they and their handpicked favorites hide out in the SB to await the aliens' arrival. Again, short, but to the point. I don't know about you, but I wouldn't want to piss off that many people who have just been told they're about to die."

Thirty heartbeats passed during which she didn't know if he was going to punch her in the face or summon the MPs.

"There's something you haven't factored in, JD," he said, his voice oddly resigned.

"What's that, sir?"

"These aliens may possess the ability to detect human life through rock. If they're capable of interstellar space travel, that wouldn't be much of a stretch."

"Actually, I did think of that. All that means is the playing field will be level. The SB folks won't have an advantage over the Oxblood people."

"That's what this is about? Fairness? No one dies or everyone dies?"

"Yes," she said. "That's all this has ever been about. I'm responsible for every person in this colony, not just three hundred of them. And so are you. Now, what are you going to say in your speech?"

***

One of Khandar's most useful talents had been on full display during the improvised speech that came moments later. His hastily composed words managed, miraculously, to explain the aliens' impending arrival without inciting hysteria. Nobody lost their shite. Nobody panicked about aliens coming to Mars and quite possibly, in some dreadful alien manner, putting an end to their puny lives. The Colonel had a way of acknowledging problems so as to diminish their negative impact, but not their truth.

Whether it was a gift or a learned skill, she would never know.

Now, weeks later, everyone worked long days. Even the children in Omega pod helped out by transporting the red

Martian soil from the excavated trench where the tubing would lay to a nearby low area. People were cranky and exhausted, but they weren't terrified or despondent. Fourteen days out from the Arrival, and there was still much work to be done.

"JD, wait up." Corporal "Shroom" Eckland's voice called from the end of the corridor.

Jaeda had just finished a long shift at Oxblood. Workers had been going over every inch of the interior rock surface to make sure all the holes had been plugged with the beryllium panels and expanding foam. All she wanted to do now was shower and pass out on her bunk. Instead, she turned to face the stocky bull of a woman charging toward her.

"Inside," Shroom said, abandoning all pretense of proper military protocol and stepping into her superior officer's quarters without an invitation.

Jaeda followed, pressing the button to close the door. It seemed this was to be a private conversation.

"Have you heard the voices?" she demanded.

Shroom's ancestry was Nordic. Jaeda had done a thorough investigation of her personnel file after their talk weeks ago. The blood that ran through the young woman's veins was that of the Viking hordes that had invaded Britain in the first century. Jaeda could picture this twenty-five-year-old wearing a horned helmet and sporting a battle axe. The Zulu spear of her own warrior ancestors would have given that axe a run for its money.

"What voices? The thought-noise?"

"No, but it's coming through the HIVE communication center just like the thought-noise."

Something tugged at the inside of Jaeda's brain. She had been so busy and so tired lately that she had relegated the weird incident to the something-to-deal-with-later category. Now she brought it fully into the realm of conscious analysis. "The whispers."

The blond head nodded. "So you hear them, too."

"It's probably just a new twist on the thought-noise. Why are you so worked up about it?"

"Because it's different."

"How can you tell?"

"We'll get to that. I figured you had heard it too."

"We've been over this, Shroom. I'm not telepathic."

"You sure as hell are, and yours comes naturally. It wasn't programmed into your DNA. Let's establish this as fact so we can move forward."

Perhaps the young woman was right. Since the techies said it was impossible to hear what she heard, maybe she truly did sense it on some psychic level. "Fine."

"I've been taking notes, JD."

"Of the whispers?"

"Yes. At first it sounded like gibberish, but the more I tuned into it, the more it sounded like an actual language."

"Then it's just us, Shroom. More thought-noise coming from all these people in the biosphere, like I said."

"Really? Do you know anyone here on Mars who thinks in Sanskrit?"

"How do you know anything about Sanskrit? Isn't that an old Earth language?"

"Correct. The oldest. I know about it because I take excellent notes. I entered the gibberish into the HIVE's linguistics app. Guess what? It came back as Sanskrit. Not an exact match, of course. Language is fluid. But enough markers showed up that I was able to conclude an origin in Sanskrit. Kind of like Latin is the origin of English. Fecking *Sanskrit*. You have to ask yourself, who would know a dead Earth language these days?"

"Linguists? Historians? Ghosts?"

"Ghosts, exactly. But not the type you're thinking of. I already ruled out linguists and historians. Nobody on Mars has either of those backgrounds."

"There are different types of ghosts?"

"Yes. Traditional ghosts are the souls of the deceased who return from death to scare people and cause trouble. That's all nonsense, of course."

"We agree on that."

"I think these whispers are coming from living ghosts. Ghosts from our past. Our collective past, as in humanity."

"You lost me." Jaeda struggled to keep her eyelids from closing. She glanced at her comfy bed with the wrinkled sheets and the soft blanket.

"JD, pay attention. This is where it gets interesting."

"I'm listening. Just make it fast. I'm coming off a twelve-hour shift."

"There are two relevant questions. Number one: how are these whispers spoken in an ancient language not heard in more than two thousand years?"

"That's a superb question. I don't know the answer. What else?"

"The second question will help clarify the first. Why are we just now hearing them?"

"I don't know the answer to that either."

Shroom blew out an exasperated breath. "Think, JD. Think about all the work we've been doing lately and why we're doing it."

"Because of the Arrival."

"Right. Do you think it's a coincidence that we started hearing the whispers as the aliens are drawing near?"

"You think they're coming from the vessel?"

"Yes."

Jaeda pondered the notion for several heartbeats. She had to admit it was intriguing. "If that's true, why are their thought-whispers in Sanskrit?"

Jaeda had never seen such a big smile on the face of the bad-ass corporal. Her small, white teeth looked like a string of cultured pearls.

"Because I don't think they're aliens at all. I think they're just like us."

***

"You expect me to believe the two of you can hear the thoughts of the beings currently hurtling toward our location at a speed our technology can barely calculate?"

"I know it sounds crazy, sir," Jaeda replied.

She and Corporal Eckland stood at attention in the Colonel's quarters. He had turned on the hack block, of course. The buzzing sound made her feel as if she should be swatting at insects. Even though everyone knew about the Arrival, they weren't privy to the classified details. Jaeda herself didn't know everything, though she knew more than most. Khandar had taken her into his confidence since the day she had defied him. She could only assume her insubordination had somehow won his respect. Perhaps he too had secretly chafed at the thought of throwing seven hundred people to the proverbial wolves.

"It makes sense, sir," Eckland added.

"Really? It makes sense that these alien beings are human, just like us, because of a theory based on so-called telepathic whispers heard on the HIVE? That's preposterous."

Shroom was not easily intimidated, not even by the Kraken.

"Yep," she said. "I mean, yes, sir. It's only preposterous to think we could hear them audibly. It's plausible to hear them telepathically. You're aware of my Psi upgrade?"

He gave her a withering look. "If they can communicate in an Earth language, why wouldn't they have used it on the DSN instead of speaking in mathematics? The linguists at NASA would have been able to translate Sanskrit."

"For one very good reason. They don't want us to know they're human."

"Why not?"

"It might give us leverage, some kind of advantage."

Khandar shifted his fierce gaze from Shroom to Jaeda. "And you're buying into this?"

Jaeda reminded herself of those Zulu ancestors. "I think the theory has merit. I can substantiate the thought-noise. I've heard it myself for a decade, and it's actually gotten worse. Or maybe I've become more adept. I wanted to deny that this was some kind of Psi talent, but nothing else makes sense. Ask the techs. They'll have records of all the times I complained about it. And I can substantiate the thought-whispers as well, but I didn't give them the attention Corporal Eckland did. If she tells me she documented the sounds and it turned out to be Sanskrit, I believe her."

When Khandar looked away in disgust, Shroom gave her hand a quick squeeze. The two women waited in silence, watching him pace the short length of his quarters.

Minutes passed. The thunderous eyebrows never relented, but finally his expression turned thoughtful.

"How does this change anything? Assuming any of this is true, what would we do differently? Should we stay above ground and welcome them with a muffin basket? Do you remember their message? So what if their biology is human. They still want to kill us."

"I'm not so sure about that, sir," Shroom replied. "I think NASA might have that wrong. May I see the communication itself? Both the original and the translated version, specifically the subjective part about their intentions."

"You know that's not possible. Asking your commanding officer to give you unauthorized access to classified material well above your paygrade is an offense for which I could have you court-martialed. Allowing it is an offense for which *I* could be court-martialed."

"I know," she said, then nothing further. There must be ice water running through those Nordic veins.

The Colonel crossed his arms and narrowed his eyes. The next moment, he stalked toward his HIVE portal, swatted at the v-board several times, then waved the young woman over. "There," he said, thrusting a finger at the information scrolling across the hologram display.

Jaeda watched her gaze drift from left to right, up and down, then repeat the process several more times.

"You're neither a scientist, nor an engineer, nor even a tech specialist. I have no idea why I'm permitting this," Khandar said. The statement would have been offensive if not for the soft, almost indulgent tone he had injected. He needn't have bothered. Corporal Eckland seemed to be in some kind of trancelike state.

"You're permitting it because of her Psi, and also because you sense on some level that there may be something to this. What is it, Shroom?" Jaeda said. "What do you see?"

The blue eyes blinked several times, slid away from the holo-screen and settled, unfocused, on Jaeda's face.

The short, muscular body shuddered from head to toe.

"Corporal, snap out of it," Khandar's voice had the desired effect.

The dreamy look faded, quickly replaced with an unsettling combination of indignation and savagery.

"The NASA scientists were right," she said, finally. "They want to study our technology, but eliminate everything remotely homo-sapient. Those human feckers want to kill us all."

***

Khandar never admitted to believing that the aliens were human, but it didn't matter. He knew a threat existed and doubled down on the work schedules. It would be tight. Oxblood was almost ready, but the ductwork trench that would supply oxygen to the cavern was taking longer than expected. In addition, the colonists from Omega pod were relocated to Beta and Delta since their air tubing had been commandeered. The Meggies – all civilians down to the six-year-old who had charmed everyone with her willingness to work as hard as the grown-ups – surprised Jaeda in their stoic acceptance of the move. Normally they complained about everything. But not, it seemed, about being homeless when faced with the prospect of impending peril.

Finally she had discovered a way to shut them the hell up.

She was shuffling through the chow line in Theta pod after another long shift at the trench, when she felt a tugging on her sleeve. She turned, then looked down to the curly red hair of the six-year-old she had just been thinking about.

"Hi, Tana," she said, smiling and squatting down to the child's level. Serious green eyes stared back at her. "Are you after my cookie?"

Crimson curls swayed from left to right, then back again. Emerald eyes beseeched her, begging her to ask the correct question. As bright as the little girl was, Jaeda instinctively knew she didn't possess the vocabulary to explain what troubled her.

"You want to come sit with me for dinner?"

Another vigorous shake of the curls, but this time up and down.

"Okay, let me get my tray. Hey, Cluck, can I get extra for the little one?" She spoke to the exhausted man behind the silver thermal food bins. Cluck managed the meal commissary and everything that entailed. He had lost much of his staff to the work going on outside, so it fell to him to prepare and serve the chow.

"Yeah, yeah." A silicone-gloved hand placed three cookies in the dessert space of her segmented tray.

It was a shocking display of rebellion. All the non-indigenous food on Mars, down to the last chocolate chip, was ordered, inventoried, and appropriated from Earth for their tiny population. Those cookies had traveled 54.6 million kilometers so they could provide sustenance and minor comfort to the colonists. Jaeda didn't know who would have to sacrifice their desserts for this gesture, and she didn't care. They might be dead in another week anyway. When she made eye contact with Cluck, she could see he was thinking the same thing. She gave him a conspiratorial wink.

"Let's sit over here, Tana," she said, guiding the child to a corner table.

Everything in the dining space was made from aluminum. The combination of stark lighting and cold, uncomfortable furniture created a cheerless environment. The ambience was no accident. Folks ate their meals quickly and left, focused on heading to their jobs or the rec center or their beds rather than on the meager five to seven-hundred calories (depending on height, weight, and occupation) allotted at each meal.

Nobody came to Mars for the food.

"Here, sweetie." She handed all three cookies to the little girl, whose eyes opened wide in surprise at the unexpected bounty.

"Are you sure?" she whispered.

"Of course. Now, tell me how you're feeling. Are you worried about the ship that's coming here?"

"Yes." Both of her front baby teeth were missing, so the child took bites from the side of her mouth. The sight made Jaeda smile. She would never have children of her own – that option was not part of her career plan – but she enjoyed spending time with those born to the civilians...even the teenagers. There was something about their candor she found delightful.

"You know we'll all be hiding underground, right? That's why we've been working so hard to get everything ready."

"Yes, I know," Tana said between bites.

"Don't you think we'll be safe there?"

"Maybe. But maybe the aliens will find out where we're hiding and they'll just come there."

"That's true." She wouldn't insult the child's intelligence. "But Colonel Khandar..."

"The Kraken!" Tana injected with an impish grin.

Jaeda laughed. "Yes. The Kraken thinks they won't find us. He thinks they'll see the empty biosphere and go away."

"Is that what you think?" The green eyes bored into her. There would be no dissembling with this child.

"I don't know. The thing is, we don't have a lot of options, and this one seems like the best one. Does that make sense?"

"Yes. Actually, I'm not so worried about us."

"Then what are you worried about?"

A dimpled hand set the third cookie down on the table, uneaten.

"Grandma and Grandpa on Earth."

"Ah, I see."

"They might not have a place to hide in Texas."

Tana had been born on Mars and had never even met her grandparents in person. Like everyone else, her family would have been allocated bandwidth for vid exchanges on the Deep Space Network, but she had never had a live conversation with anyone on Earth. Yet she had developed affection, perhaps even love, for these relatives. Jaeda could see anxiety etched into every inch of the guileless face.

"The aliens might not go to Texas," she replied. "Earth is a big planet. And even if they do, I bet your grandparents are smart, just like your mommy and daddy, and they'll know where to go so the aliens can't find them."

"I think those aliens must be pretty smart too since they can travel through space so fast. Maybe they have special machines that can find people, no matter where they are."

"The people on Earth are also smart. They have a lot of weapons they can use if the aliens try to hurt them. They have thousands of soldiers on Earth. Hundreds of thousands. That's a lot, right?"

"Yes. But wouldn't it be better if those aliens never even got to Earth?"

"Of course, but I don't think they're going to change their minds about that. The message they sent was...clear."

"I know. That's why I think we should try to stop them when they come here to Mars instead of just hiding in the caverns. If we stop them here first, then everyone on the Moon and Earth will be safe."

Jaeda was stunned. In all her discussions with not only her superior officers as well as the enlisted, nobody had suggested their contingent of soldiers try to fight. Their plan was simply to keep everyone alive and hope that Earth with all its resources could handle the invasion. The notion of the Martian colonists engaging in battle with the aliens was ludicrous. Merely existing on a planet inherently hostile to human life took everything they had. But the baffling part was why had no one even pondered it out loud? Five-hundred-seventy military personnel on Mars and no one had said, *Maybe we should try to kill them before they kill us and everyone else?*

"Tana, how would we fight them? We have some weapons, of course, but we don't know if those would be effective against the aliens. We don't know how many will be coming, nor anything about their technology."

"Maybe we should try talking to them."

"But we already know they want to..." She had almost said *kill us,* but stopped short. That information had been kept from the children – there was nothing to be gained from terrifying the kids. "We know they aren't nice. We figured the best thing to do was just let them think nobody is home."

Tana rolled her eyes. "They're going to know we're hiding somewhere. They'll see the empty biosphere and come looking for us."

Jaeda stifled a snort. "We thought of that. That's why we're going to camouflage the entrances to both caverns. We hope it will appear as if we left months ago."

"That'll mean more work, I bet. Wouldn't it just be easier to talk to them? Get them to change their minds about killing us?"

"How do you know about that?"

"I hear everyone thinking it."

Just as with military files, she couldn't access certain parts of civilian personnel files, nor that of their offspring. Tana may have inherited some Psi talent from a parent. It was still a relatively new area of the explosive biogenetics industry, and Jaeda had no idea how many people possessed it. The geneticists on Earth were rather proprietary about their work, but Khandar could tell her.

"You can hear people's thoughts?"

A shrug of the small shoulders. "Sort of. Mostly if they're really happy or really mad. Or scared."

"I see. Those are strong emotions, so they make loud thoughts."

"Right." Tana reached for the third cookie.

"Do your mommy and daddy know about this?"

"Oh, sure. My mommy practices with me. Daddy can't do it, so he's the thinker when we do our exercises."

"The thinker?"

"Yep. He thinks of stuff, and I try to hear what he's thinking. Mommy is really good at it, but she says I'm going to be even better than her when I get bigger."

"I didn't know people could practice it."

"Hearing thoughts can be fun, but it can be scary too. Like now, when I hear about the aliens coming to kill us."

Jaeda sighed. What could she say? What reassurances could she impart to this child? If she had to guess their chances of surviving the Arrival, she would give them about one in five. And that was being generous.

"I'm sorry you have to hear all that."

"It's okay. And I know you hear stuff, too. I think yours is different, though."

"So I've been told."

"Did Shroom tell you? She's the only person I know besides you and me and my mommy who can do it."

Jaeda nodded.

"JD, what if the aliens can do it too? Shroom thinks they're not really aliens at all, but people just like us. If they can hear thoughts, they'll know we're here."

Feck.

"You just thought a bad word," Tana said, popping the last bite of cookie into her mouth.

***

"It makes sense, if these aliens are actually highly advanced human beings. Telepathy could have been part of their evolution, just as it appears to be a new facet to ours." Jaeda sat in Khandar's quarters with the hack block turned on. She was getting tired of that invisible honeybee swarm. It was distracting and annoying, but he insisted on using it during their private conversations.

"For any of this to be an issue, I would have to concede that I believe the human-alien theory." He slurped some of his sissy coffee. "Turns out, I do."

"You do? That's great. So all this work we're doing could be for nothing."

"All this work was your idea."

"I know," she said, irritated. The hack block was driving her crazy. It felt like those bees were trying to burrow into her brain. "You seem calm these days. Almost...fatalistic, if I may be so bold."

"That's how I feel. We're doing everything we can to survive. If it's not enough, so be it."

Jaeda was surprised. This attitude was quite un-Kraken-like.

"Again, if I may be so bold..."

"You're all about the boldness today."

"What has changed with you? Why the tranquility? It's not normal."

"I could tell you, but then I'd have to kill you."

"Very funny...sir."

He fixed his gaze on her face. The old fierceness returned. She didn't know whether to be relieved or alarmed.

"I won't be going below ground with everyone else."

"What? Why not?"

"JD, ask yourself this question: Why would I allow a known threat to proceed to Earth if I can stop it here on Mars?"

"I was just having a conversation on that subject with a six-year-old. It's what I wanted to talk to you about."

"How interesting. Tell me everything."

So she did.

"What a remarkable child," he said. "Of course I was aware of her mother's Psi upgrade, as well as that of

Captain Eckland. I had also been informed that the little girl...her name is Tana?"

Jaeda nodded.

"That Tana's talent is being nurtured. It's extraordinary the things scientists are accomplishing these days. But what does this have to do with our situation?"

She took a deep breath. "I think I should meet them when they arrive. I think I'll be able to communicate with them. Telepathically."

"Indeed? That happens to be my strategy as well. Not the telepathy part. Just the meeting them part. Then I will exterminate the feckers." He took another swig from the mug. Adding cinnamon and cream no longer seemed like a sissy way to drink coffee. "And now since I shared my diabolical plan, I definitely have to kill you."

He gave her a rare Kraken smile. She always forgot that he was only a few years older than her. The burden of leadership had a way of aging a person. The smile turned the clock back to its rightful position.

"How will you do it?" she asked.

"A deadly bio-contagion."

He might have said 'a fly swatter' or 'a slingshot,' so casually was the horrific term uttered. Biological weapons had been eradicated in the mid twenty-first century after the Russians launched an attack on China, their economic adversary. Operatives had released a weaponized pathogen onto the streets of Chongqing, Shanghai, and Beijing; the subsequent plague roared through the Asian continent like wildfire, decimating the population. The newly reenergized

United Nations had acted swiftly and decisively. Russia's military, dismantled. Its research labs, destroyed. The crushing sanctions leveled against the Russian oligarchy resulted in the fall of that nefarious empire three years later.

Jaeda believed, as most did, that bio-weapons no longer existed. As with nuclear weapons, humanity had finally gotten smart enough to decide Earth was better off without them.

"What are you talking about?" she said, after her mouth caught up with everything she had been thinking.

"The information resides above top-secret clearance. Not even the U.S. president knows we have it. This won't end well for you."

"Sir, what are we doing with a bio-weapon on Mars?"

"Does it matter? The point is, we have it, and I intend to use it. You gave me the idea, actually, when you said the aliens are human. A contagion that is deadly to us would likely be ineffective against a species radically different from us. But if their biological makeup is similar to ours, it's a good bet that Chimera-23B will affect them."

"What is Chimera-23B?"

"You've heard of the word chimera? In Greek mythology, it was a fire-breathing hybrid creature. Head of a lion, body of a goat, tail of a serpent. Akin to a Kraken in its monstrosity," he added with a wink. "Chimera-23B combines three of the deadliest agents known to humankind – anthrax, smallpox, and botulinum. The result is a nightmare concoction that would end all human life on Earth in a week if only ten grams of it were released into the stratosphere."

"Oh my god. What if it got out? On Earth, I mean."

"It's not on Earth. It's only here on Mars, where it would annihilate all one thousand and seventeen people if it somehow escaped the confines of its refrigerated prison. It won't escape, though. It will be utilized."

The shocking new knowledge took a moment to assimilate. "That's why it's here instead of there. It's too dangerous for Earth."

"Precisely. This colony serves many purposes. Deadly bio-contagion custodian is merely one of them."

Jaeda wondered what the others were she didn't know about.

"How will you deliver it to the aliens without getting infected?"

"There's the rub. I can't just wait for them in the commissary, pop the lid, and fling it at them when they show up for breakfast. Even if I were successful in transferring the virus to the invaders, it would still be present when you all return from the caverns." Slurp. "Plus, they'll likely be wearing some type of bio-suit, which it wouldn't penetrate."

"You've put some thought into this."

Golden eyes crinkled at the corners. "You could say that. All I have to do is get them to take me prisoner."

Jaeda felt the knots twist in her stomach. "So this is a suicide mission?"

"Since I'll be injecting the pathogen directly into my body as well as slathering it on before I don my bio-suit, the answer is yes. It must be timed perfectly. The pathology of the virus runs its course in about five hours. I'll begin to feel uncomfortable starting at about the second hour. It's all downhill from there."

"How will you get yourself taken prisoner?"

"I'm still working on that part. I'm considering several options."

"Sir, you can't do this," she said, moving toward him. She wanted to grab him and shake some sense into him. She stopped short of the shaking part. Inches from the face of her commanding officer, both hands gripping his shoulders, she added, "I won't let you do it."

His eyes looked into hers with infinite kindness. "You can't stop me, JD. My mind is made up. I'm only telling you because I need your help with my cover story. I don't want anyone questioning my decision. You and I have a...connection."

"Then I'm doing it with you."

"Absolutely not."

"Yes, I am. I can communicate with them telepathically. I know I can. I've been listening to their thought-whispers, and while I don't understand Sanskrit, I'm getting impressions and images. It's been a one-way process until now, but I think I can transmit as well as receive."

She saw hesitation in his resolve and pounced. "I'll project images of where to find us. I'll lure them to our location. Then when they arrive, we'll spring the trap."

He smiled. "You realize there's virtually no chance that my plan or yours, or any of this, will work. Too many variables. Too many factors. Too many unknowables." He sighed heavily.

Jaeda had an idea. "What if we conduct a reconnaissance operation? Find out everything we can about these invaders."

"Let me guess. A telepathic one?" His grin was intended to be indulgent, but she could see he found the notion provocative.

"Yes. We'll assemble everyone who has the Psi upgrade, as well as folks like me. We'll see what we can discover, then revisit your idea and at least tweak it, if not come up with something better."

"We have nothing to lose, I suppose," he replied. "Very well, JD. Just do it covertly. I can't officially sanction this insanity, but you have my unofficial support. Let me know what you find out. We only have four days until the Arrival."

"Yes, sir."

When she was back in the corridor, she realized how much clearer her thoughts were now than in Colonel Khandar's quarters. For the first time in all their recent secret discussions, she knew why: there was no hack block in the corridor.

***

"Focus, people." Corporal Eckland's ice-blue eyes flashed with annoyance. Six people sat elbow-to-elbow in a circular cluster of aluminum chairs. The stark lighting of Theta pod's commissary made them all look even more tired than they were. It was well past dinner time, and the entrance had been locked from the inside. Not even Cluck had access to the room at that moment.

Jaeda contemplated a period from American history: the stories about the Old West and the covered wagons rolling across the plains toward the Pacific Ocean. The indigenous population had posed a constant threat to the mixture of largely European settlers who had set their sights on making the wild continent their new home. When in danger, the unwieldy caravan would gather in a circle for more effective defense.

The ring of chairs and its diverse occupants felt like that.

"Is everyone plugged into the HIVE? JD, is your headset optimal?" Shroom demanded.

Jaeda nodded, stifling a grin. She had delegated supervision of the telepathic reconnaissance mission – the TRM – to the indomitable young woman. Military people loved their acronyms. If they all survived the Arrival, Corporal Eckland had a brilliant career ahead of her.

"Let's begin."

Everyone closed their eyes except for Jaeda. Her gaze fell in a mute procession upon each face, resting finally on the tiniest member of the group – Tana. The red curls didn't move; the brain within concentrated on whisper-thoughts. All the Psi folks heard them now. The alien beings sped closer every moment, thus their thoughts had become easier to detect. One of the techs had rigged up an overlay between the HIVE communication center and the Sanskrit translating program. Shroom would plug the whispers into the program, where they would be recorded and forwarded to Khandar.

"They're not wearing bio-suits," a woman with red hair said. It was Cara, Tana's mother.

"They're inside their ship," Shroom replied. "So, yeah."

Jaeda ignored the sarcastic tone and hoped Cara did as well.

"One of them is thinking about their home planet." The man who spoke was from the same deployment as Corporal Eckland, also a recipient of the Psi upgrade. Jaeda had had little interaction with the young lieutenant previously, but after a short conversation prior to their covert meeting in the commissary, she decided she liked him. His golden eyes reminded her of the Colonel's, but less intense. Nepotism was allowed in their branch of the military under the condition of anonymity. Rajish could be sharing DNA markers with the Kraken, but Jaeda would never know.

"What do you see, Raj?" Jaeda's primary role during the TRM was to facilitate any data they might collect. If she could also pick up anything with her own natural Psi, even better.

"I feel their planet is similar to Earth. I'm picking up oceans and large land masses. Whomever I'm tapping into misses home."

"So they have the capacity for homesickness."

"Yes. There's something else, too. Let me concentrate."

"I don't think they have any kids on that ship," Tana said, with a comically scrunched-up face.

"I'm feeling aggression," Cara, muttered. "I get the impression they're trying to ramp up their emotions. Does that make sense?"

"Yes." Again Jaeda pondered another piece of history: the Nordic berserkers who entered a state of animal-like frenzy before going into battle. The notion was terrifying. She glanced across the circle to a real-life ancestor of the race which had bred that violent sect. Shroom's expression was dreamy now, but Jaeda remembered the savagery she saw there recently. *Those human feckers want to kill us.*

"I feel it, too," Tana said. She and her mother practiced telepathy together. They may be traveling along the same channel to the alien vessel. "It's like they want to be mad about something. That's crazy. Why would anyone want to be mad?"

After a few moments, Shroom said, "I feel it too."

Raj frowned. "I'm not getting that. I think I'm tethered to an individual. I don't perceive a group or a collective. I think on some level, he's aware of me."

"Uh, oh. Better pull back, Raj."

"Not yet. This is important."

"Oh, my," said the tall, slender male sitting next to Shroom. It was the first time the man had spoken. His limbs were folded at odd angles to fit within the confines of the chair while avoiding inadvertent contact with straying elbows. He looked like a praying mantis, but Jaeda knew the civilian colonist possessed an astounding intellect.

"What is it, Doctor Marsden?"

"They're definitely human," he said in a voice slightly less acerbic than normal. Marsden did not suffer fools nor foolish questions.

"How can you tell?"

"I'm looking beyond the images to the source of what's projecting them. Their brains."

Shroom's eyes flew open, latched upon Jaeda's face, and saw the same look of astonishment.

"I don't understand," Jaeda said.

"Of course you don't. It's not your field of expertise. If we were quantifying water and food for space travel, I would expect you to supply the answer."

She had no response.

"I'm using an interesting combination of Psi and my vast neurological knowledge to slink past their subconscious output to the source of the output itself. I comprehend how the transmissions are working, but explaining it in terms you would understand would take days."

Jaeda didn't bother being offended. She knew he was right.

"I sense neurons firing, dendrites receiving data, axons carrying outgoing messages. This is how the brain communicates with its host. Its human host. No other organic brain works the way a human's does. There's no doubt we are dealing with carbon-based life identical to ourselves. Biologically, at least, if not evolutionarily."

"Excellent, Doctor," Jaeda replied. "Colonel Khandar is streaming our operation. I know he'll be happy this intel came from you."

"As well he should."

"I'm getting something else from that individual," Raj said. "Dismay, perhaps? I could be wrong, but I think this might be the entity charged with our...extermination." Eyelids fringed in thick, dark lashes fluttered open. Raj stared at Tana's cherubic face and frowned. Jaeda saw a flash of anger on the handsome features.

"Don't lose contact, Raj," Jaeda said, urgent now. She had an idea. "Let him know you're there. Announce yourself. Can you do that?"

"Yes, I think so. There. I'm sensing something like surprise now."

"Send him images of us, especially of Tana and the other children. Let him see them playing in the rec center and studying in the classroom. Everyone do the same."

"Okay. Working on it. I have no idea if they're going through."

Jaeda closed her eyes now too, increased the volume setting on the HIVE, and concentrated. She pictured Tana and the other children dancing, and singing, and reading.

Were the images being received on the other end? Unknown. All she could do was hope.

Everyone stayed silent for several minutes.

Finally, Raj said, "I think he got the picture, JD. I felt a vague emotional shift. I don't think there's anything else we can do."

She opened her eyes. "There's one more thing," she said, then stood and walked over to a device set up next to the door. She tapped a button. A faint insectile hum immediately filled the room. Jaeda had the sudden urge to scratch her head.

Everyone else did too, it seemed. She watched the others rub their foreheads and tug at their ears.

"What happened, JD?" Shroom snapped. "I lost the link to the vessel, damn it."

Jaeda smiled. "Me too."

"Same here," Marsden said, raising an eyebrow. "What did you do?"

"I activated a hack block, which I had tech-sergeant Landry install along with the other equipment."

"Fascinating. I believe it interfered with the Psi connection. Severed it, in fact," he said, without a trace of condescension. He looked at her with something like respect. "Well done, JD."

"What? Why is that a good thing?" Shroom said.

"Very simple, young lady," Marsden replied. "It means our ambient thoughts won't reveal our presence in the caverns when the galactic invaders arrive."

***

"We've done everything we can do. We're as ready as we'll ever be." Khandar wore the tranquil grin that had appeared even more frequently now that he was about to die. Jaeda thought she understood. Everyone dies. In some ways, he was fortunate. Not only was he in complete control of his own death, his sacrifice may result in a thousand – or perhaps eleven billion – saved lives.

That was his hope.

"I don't suppose I can talk you into a quick vacation to Oxblood Cavern," he continued through the communication system of their bio-suits. Chimera-23B coursed through his veins as he stood next to Jaeda on the colony's landing strip. This was where all the rockets had arrived and departed for the past two decades, bringing humans and supplies to Mars. It seemed the most likely location at which the invaders would arrive. In another hour, it might be that all this – humanity's exhaustive efforts to colonize planets other than Earth – may have been for nothing. All that work possibly brought to an abrupt end by these human-alien beings.

Their arrival was measurable in minutes now.

"No, sir. I'm staying right here with you, sending them images of the value in taking you prisoner."

Every time she said it out loud, it sounded even more ridiculous. The odds that they would be successful were astronomical. Fortunately, it didn't have to work in order for them to prevail in their primary mission: keeping the colonists alive. The hack blocks installed at both underground facilities were operational now, and the devices would impede stray thoughts and emotions from escaping the caverns. Armed soldiers were stationed inside the digitally camouflaged openings of the two locations in the event the invaders discovered their hiding places. If everything went according to plan, even partly, those soldiers wouldn't need to fire a single shot.

The remaining soldiers manned the landing strip. They would be the ones doing the firing.

Space on the supply rockets had always been limited. It was largely reserved for food and medicine and all the necessities of life which people required. Before people arrived, life on Mars had consisted of harmless frozen microbes. The colony was a military operation, though, so they had brought weapons.

Of course they had brought weapons.

The MAHEM system had been moved from one of the storage pods, then placed at the landing site, where Khandar believed the Arrival would occur. MAHEM utilized a magnetic flux generator rather than traditional chemical explosives, resulting in a vastly more efficient and precise launch of its molten projectiles. The fiery globs could penetrate all known metals within seconds. When the alien vessel landed, commandos would blast fifteen holes into its hull. The goal of MAHEM was twofold: disable the craft so it couldn't continue on to Earth, and breach the internal atmosphere of the ship, which was surely keeping the human-aliens alive as they traveled through space.

Khandar hoped the element of surprise and the invaders' overconfidence would help the colonists prevail.

"Imagine an arrogant human, walking around barefoot in the Australian outback," he said. "He's never been to that part of Earth before, so he doesn't think much about the insect he's about to tread upon. He has nothing to fear from something so obviously inferior to himself. The insect bites his big toe, injecting deadly venom into the foot along with a jolt of pain. All we have to do is make sure we get out of the way before the body comes crashing down on top of us."

He was downright giddy now, despite the effects of Chimera-23B. Or perhaps because of them. She could see a sheen of sweat on his face behind the visor and wondered if mania was one of the symptoms. How could anyone be so happy about dying?

"Right. With luck, at least one of our strategies will prove effective," she replied.

"Oh, do you feel that?" He pivoted on the red Martian soil. A bright light filled the sky behind them. It seemed to coalesce suddenly, then the source of the intense illumination streaked overhead.

The vessel landed precisely on the spot where the supply rockets set down, a turn of events that was the best they could have hoped for. The craft's occupants recognized the significance of the area. Would entities of non-human biology have done the same? Much was riding on the conclusions they had formed based upon Psi intel from a handful of people. If they were wrong, and the aliens were in fact lizard people or little green men, they may well be fecked.

The spaceship looked nothing like the rockets from Earth. Instead of a white carbon-composite shell, the alien craft was gun-metal gray. Instead of cylindrical, it was spherical. Instead of touching down in a thunderous cloud of red dust, it alighted upon the landing strip like a feather in a breeze, all elegance and effortless grace.

The colonists who came from engineering and astrophysics backgrounds would have been enthralled to witness it. Instead, they were hunkered down in the caverns. If any of them lived to see tomorrow, they could rewind the vids from the surveillance cameras, strategically placed throughout the colony in hopes of capturing the most monumental event in human history.

She thought her heart might pound out of her chest and splat against the interior of her bio-suit.

"Here they come," Khandar said. "Did you see that section near the bottom? It moved. That must be the vessel's point of egress."

When the human-aliens descended from the opening, it was almost anti-climactic. Their suits appeared eerily similar to those from Earth. The entities had two arms and walked on two legs. Some sort of breathing apparatus encased their heads; the section covering what would be their faces was opaque. Ten beings strode toward Jaeda and Khandar without hesitation. If she didn't die of a heart attack, she would be one of the first people to see an alien face-to-face. Or at least, visor-to-visor.

She fought a sudden urge to stop the MAHEM directive. These were humans. No question. But the commandos manning the weapons didn't answer to her.

"Sir, they're human. I can feel it," she said.

"That's wonderful news, Captain. What we already suspected." She watched him blink moisture from his left eye. The grin had turned maniacal now.

"Maybe they've had a change of heart."

"That seems unlikely."

Every step the invaders took was a step toward their demise.

She tapped her communication panel. "Shroom, Raj, get the hell over here now."

"Belay that order," Khandar bellowed.

"Please, sir. Trust me."

"You're pissing me off, JD." He sighed. "Very well. I shouldn't stop trusting you at this point."

Thirty seconds later, the two stood beside her. They had been stationed close by in case their Psi talents were needed.

"What do you feel?" she asked.

"It's him. The one in front," Raj said, his eyes closed. "The individual I connected with."

"Are you picking up anything, Shroom?"

"Yes." The savage expression had returned. "They're here to kill us."

"That's not what I'm sensing," Raj said, his eyes open now.

"The message is coming through to me loud and clear." The young woman reached for her weapon, an empty gesture since the standard-issue bio-suits didn't provide a holster for them.

"It's okay, Corporal," Khandar said. "We've got this."

The aliens were a stone's throw away now. Jaeda dreaded what would come next.

The colonel said, "Engage."

The next moment MAHEM unleashed fiery fury upon the vessel. White-hot balls of super-heated magnesium smashed against the gray sphere. At the same time, the colony's small contingent of Marines cast off their camouflage cloaks and fired at the ten figures. Jaeda resisted the urge to close her eyes and not bear witness to the carnage those .30-caliber recoilless machine guns would render.

But carnage didn't happen. Not to the alien vessel, nor to the aliens themselves. Molten globules slid harmlessly off the metal and sizzled in the red dust. The .30-caliber bullets slammed against the aliens' protective suits, then bounced off, leaving the occupants unscathed.

Even worse, none of the explosive drama even slowed them down. They continued walking toward Jaeda's group, which stood in mute horror a mere twenty paces away now.

"We knew this was a possibility. Time for the next phase." Khandar's voice trembled slightly, but not from fear. The effect of Chimera-23B was evident in the resolute grimace and oily perspiration. At this point, he would be running a high fever and experiencing acute joint pain. The muscle spasms could begin at any time. She hoped the involuntary convulsions would hold off long enough for him to infect the invaders before it was obvious there was something terribly wrong with the leader of the Martian colony.

"Is the syringe gun ready, JD?"

"Yes, sir." She covertly handed it to him. "I doubt it will pierce their suits if the Marines' RIP cartridges couldn't."

"Scalpel versus sledge hammer. Perhaps their suits' defense system is triggered by traditional attacks. We can only hope at this point."

Raj spoke. "Before that, sir, please let me try to communicate with them. Specifically, the one in front. I'm positive he's the one I connected with before." His face also glistened, but from anxiety and terror rather than a deadly contagion. As Jaeda's graze traveled from Raj's face to Khandar's, she knew she was looking at father and son.

Before Khandar could respond, the individual in front hand-signaled to the nine others behind him. It was a human gesture: *stay back.*

"That's him," Raj said. "He's their leader. I think I can communicate with him. He wishes he could be home, but that's not possible. His prime directive is to..."

"Kill us," Shroom finished the statement.

"Yes," Raj said, his voice a whisper. "But he doesn't want to."

"Doesn't matter, son," Khandar said. "He has his orders."

Four Earthlings stood on the red Martian soil, awaiting the lone figure who strode toward them now. When it finally reached them, light filled the inside of the helmet. Jaeda was one of the first humans to see the face of a sentient extraterrestrial life form.

And it...*he*...looked exactly like the eleven billion people on Earth.

She felt a wave of gratification and exchanged an excited look with Shroom, the one who had first suspected these aliens were just as human as everyone they knew.

A hand, wrapped in otherworldly material, was raised in Khandar's direction. The being must have identified the Kraken as the leader, and he stopped just short of the Colonel with the gloved hand still raised. Was it a greeting? An attempted handshake?

She watched the two in mute fascination. The colonel also raised a hand – the other hid the syringe gun. She saw the grim facial expression of the invader as he pointed toward the unraised hand.

He knew it was there.

In a swift motion, he removed the glove. The exposed hand was hairless but possessed four fingers and an opposable thumb, now laid bare to the frigid temperature of Mars. The naked fingers pointed toward the syringe in Khandar's hand again, followed by another gesture: *give it to me.*

Did he expect Khandar to just hand it over?

Another *give-it-to-me* motion, impatient now. Urgent. The bare fingers were splayed open. The palm faced downward, not upward to receive an object being given to him. The gloved hand now pointed to the bare hand.

Jaeda understood. And so did Khandar.

Chimera-23B shot into the exposed flesh. The face behind the visor winced, then the body turned to face Raj.

"He's sending me a message," Raj said, choking with emotion. "We won't make it out of this alive, but neither will they. He knows what's in the syringe. He plans to take it back with him to his ship. Our people – below ground and on Earth – will live. He is determined to make it so."

The leader replaced the glove, then signaled to the nine figures waiting behind. Before terror could consume her, Jaeda's life ended in a blazing, painless flash of light.

The In Between

Jaeda opened her eyes. The bright flash that preceded her arrival at the In Between still blinded her for a few seconds. Of course that wasn't physically possible since her presence here wasn't of a corporeal nature. Nevertheless, the eyes, quickly manifested, saw sparkles from the blast that had killed her on Mars. Then the sparkles faded, and she experienced the familiar sensation of being in the In Between. It was comforting. She knew Sarah would be along shortly, so she created an appropriate setting in which to have their discussion.

She closed her eyes and imagined Khandar's private quarters. She didn't turn on the hack block, though. It wouldn't be needed here. She actualized lips so she could smile to herself. Soon she had legs and arms covered in the soft bamboo cotton of the Martian colony's clothing. They couldn't have all the luxuries on Mars that people had on Earth, but at least their clothes were snuggly and warm. It was a pleasure to wear them again now. She sat in Khandar's small guest chair and waited for Sarah.

She didn't have to wait long.

"Hello, Jaeda," a voice said from the black void beyond. Soon a figure emerged. She immediately recognized the short, stocky form of Corporal Eckland.

"Hi, Sarah. I love that you look like Shroom. She was a pivotal part of my experience this time."

"Indeed," Shroom said in Sarah's voice. "How did it go, my dear?"

"I think it went quite well. My ears are still ringing a bit, though."

"I hope it didn't hurt too much."

"No. I didn't feel a thing. A good way to go. Much better than when I died of old age in Renaissance Italy."

Sarah's tinkling wind chime laughter filled her heart with joy.

"Are you ready to talk about it?"

Jaeda pictured her head from her previous life: tight, black curls surrounding an oval face and brown eyes twinkling within the mocha-skinned, heart-shaped face. She nodded the head now.

"Yes."

"Very well. Your lesson was Responsibility and Accountability with a Moral Restraint Rider. Explain how all that was learned, please."

"I think I was born with an inherent desire to take care of people. That seemed to make it easier to learn about Responsibility and Accountability. Don't you think?"

Sarah didn't answer.

Right. That's not how this works.

"Even as a child, I wanted to tend to people and animals...protect them, make them comfortable and happy. It was ingrained. I'm not sure if you were able to manage that before I incarnated this time, or if it was always part of me and surfaced more overtly this time. Anyway, when I got to Mars and everyone depended on me, I felt I was exactly where I should be, doing precisely what I was meant to. When something went wrong, I didn't shirk from the mistake, even when it wasn't my own. I suppose that's Accountability, right?"

"When you were told about the invaders...?" Sarah prompted.

"The officers wanted to screw over seven hundred people. I came up with the plan for the second cavern to try to save everyone. Once Khandar was on board, I continued to do everything in my power to keep people safe. In the end, it didn't work out so well for us and the marines on the surface, but those in the caverns should have been okay. They were, right?"

Shroom-Sarah smiled. "Yes. The contagion infected all the human-aliens on the invading vessel. They returned home, never reaching Earth."

Jaeda constructed lungs so she could breathe a sigh of relief.

"I'm so happy."

"What about the Moral Restraint Rider?" Sarah asked. The physical features that made her resemble Shroom dissolved, replaced now by the intense golden gaze of the Kraken. Jaeda's figurative heart skipped a beat.

"I think you already know," she said.

"Of course, but please express it in your own words."

She sighed. "I was in love with Colonel Khandar. And I think he was in love with me. But he was my commanding officer and fraternization was not allowed. Besides, he had a wife on Earth. Even though he would never see her again, I felt that he wanted to remain loyal to her. I knew if I had...pursued him, we would have been together. But I didn't. It was frustrating. There was quite an attraction."

"But you held back."

"I did."

"Anything else?"

She thought about her most recent life, specifically the end of it and the people who had played such a pivotal role in that final scene. "I think I got another bonus lesson."

"Clarify, please."

"Self-sacrifice," she said.

"How did you sacrifice yourself?"

"Not me. Khandar. He injected himself with a deadly pathogen, sacrificing his own life to save others. It didn't go as planned, but that doesn't matter. And you know what else?"

"No, what?"

"The human-alien leader did the same thing. He asked to be infected. He didn't want to kill eleven billion humans, so he took a bullet for all the inhabitants of our solar system. I think that's quite remarkable for someone who wasn't even part of our world."

"Agreed."

"They were human, right? Were they originally from Earth, as Corporal Eckland surmised?"

Sarah transitioned back to her original form – long blond hair and luminescent blue eyes – wearing that trademark mysterious smile. She said nothing.

"I guess that's not for me to know. So did I pass? Am I ready for the next lesson?" She knew what the response would be, but it made her smile when she heard the words.

"Do you think you're ready?"

"Yes."

"What will you tackle this time?"

"I want to do Curiosity and Sense of Humor with a side helping of Gratitude."

"Very well. Let's discuss the framework."

Chapter 6 – Curiosity and Sense of Humor with a side helping of Gratitude

Dakota Territory, American Frontier - 1862 CE

"You just gonna stand there and stare at me?" Jacob said. He was irritated as hell, partly because his back was killing him after a long day of cutting sod, but also because the injun was so tranquil. He didn't trust tranquil people. They were usually up to something sneaky.

"You speak English?" he said, after his first question went unanswered. A half-minute passed. He figured the silence was his answer, so he was surprised when the red-skinned heathen spoke.

"Yep," the injun replied.

"Well, I'll be damned." Hearing another human voice after being alone for so long was a comfort. That the injun could understand him and speak to him was even better. But perhaps the best part was that he hadn't tried to scalp him. At least not yet.

"That your horse?" Jacob said, standing and stretching. His knees popped in protest. Constructing a house out of sod was not slothful work. He'd built several log cabins in his life, but out here on the prairie, trees were scarce. Anyone who wanted to live through the winter without freezing to death built a soddy.

"Yep." The Appaloosa pony grazing next to its owner was an impressive specimen and clearly well-taken care of.

"Fine animal. Wanna trade for it?" It was a joke. He doubted he possessed anything the feller would want in exchange. Even if he did, these heathens wouldn't part with their horses if their lives depended on it. It was the injun way.

"Nope."

Jacob couldn't read the stoic expression. Might as well try to lasso the moon. "What the heck do you want, then?" He felt braver now that no other injuns had snuck up on him. He wondered how he would fare in a fight with this one. The man looked to be about thirty-five, Jacob's own age, but you never knew with these heathens. Could be thirty-five or fifty-five. Red-skinned folks didn't seem to age the same way as the whites.

The injun pointed to the smoldering campfire. "Needs more dung."

"Yeah, well, I don't have more dung. The bison roamed through last week, but I haven't had a chance to gather more."

The use of the English word was surprising. The Cheyenne's term for dung was hemahkase, or something like that. He only knew a handful of their words. He was glad he didn't have to talk in Cheyenne.

"I have some." The injun reached for the Cheyenne's version of a saddle bag.

"Much obliged," Jacob said, after the feller tossed some buffalo chips onto the fire.

"Hmmm." Eyes like obsidian marbles studied Jacob's labors with the sod.

The house was only half-finished. It would be a small miracle to get the roof on before the first dusting of snow.

"You will need help if you hope to get the roof on before the first winter storm." The injun mirrored Jacob's thoughts.

"There ain't another white man for thirty miles. Gotta do it myself."

"You will only accept help from a white man?" The mouth in the mahogany face twitched.

Was this feller laughing at him?

Jacob straightened again, leaned on the shovel, and then narrowed his eyes. "I reckon I'd accept help from a working man of just about any color. Yellow, black, white, green, purple. Even red." He waited to see if the injun would be offended by the last part. Injuns typically didn't enjoy being called red-skinned.

"I guess you are in luck then. Do you have another shovel?"

"'Course I do. But I gotta know something first. Actually, I gotta know two somethings first. How did you learn to speak English so good, and why the hell do you want to help a white man build his home in Cheyenne territory? I paid the United States government three-hundred and twenty dollars for this parcel. That's a dollar an acre. Took me eighteen years to save all that money. But I know you injuns don't recognize our government, our laws, or our money. You trade in furs and such instead. I reckon this little scrap of paper don't matter a hill of beans to the likes of you." He tapped an interior pocket of his coat.

The injun shrugged. "It matters to you, so what difference does it make whether it matters to me?"

Jacob opened his mouth only to find he had no response.

"As to your first question, I learned English from a white preacher who took up with my tribe when I was a ka'eskone about this tall." He made a flat-handed gesture at knee level. "He spoke proper English, not the slang one hears from most whites around these parts. He taught me how to read and write, too."

"Well, knock me over with a feather. Not only do I find myself in the company of an injun who doesn't seem to want to slice off the top of my head, but he also speaks proper English, and reads and writes to boot. Says he wants to help with my soddy, too. What's next? Pigs flying out of my butt?"

"I would trade my fine animal to see that."

Jacob laughed, then thrust his hand toward the man – after first wiping the dirt off on his dungarees. "I'm Jacob Payne. Pleasure to meet such an upstanding injun."

"I am Shoemowetochawcawe. That is Cheyenne for high-backed wolf." The feller returned his handshake. Dark-skinned fingers were calloused and warm in his own. A working man's hand. Or maybe a fighting man's hand. It was difficult to tell the difference.

"I'll never be able to say that. Why do you people have such stinkin' long names? I'll call you Shoe. How's that?"

"Hmmm. Very well. I will call you Jacob Payne."

"You don't have to say my last name once introductions have been made."

"It shows respect to address a man by his full name."

Was there a hint of annoyance in the tone? Too bad. He had no intention of trying to pronounce that lengthy name.

"And also, Jacob Payne, you should know my people find that word offensive."

"What? Stinkin'?"

"No, 'injun.' It is insulting."

"But that's what you are."

"No, it is an ignorant white man's term for my people. How would you like it if I called you Ignorant White Man in casual conversation?"

"I reckon I wouldn't like that at all."

"Exactly."

"Dang. You're a tough nut. Why do you want to help me, Shoe? And why are you out here alone? Why aren't you off with your tribe raiding the Sioux or the Arapaho?"

"You ask a lot of questions, Jacob Payne. Let us get to work. The answers can wait." Shoe walked around the half-built sod house to the back where the implements were stacked.

Hours later, the soddy – two-thirds finished now – was a dark, house-shaped silhouette against the starlit sky. Smoke from the campfire wafted into Jacob's nostrils, then continued heavenward. He had gotten used to the smell of burning buffalo chips instead of wood and had even begun to associate it with a sense of home – a sense of belonging.

If all went according to plan, this speck of prairie dirt would be where he ended his days on Earth.

His gaze kept drifting to the silhouette. With the help of the injun...Shoe, rather...he had made five days' progress in five hours' time. A second worker made the process much more efficient and faster. If he could get the inj...*Shoe*...to stay around a couple more days, he would be snug and dry when the first snowflakes fell.

"What is in this stew?" Shoe asked through the smoke. Dung fires didn't blaze and crackle like a wood fire, but they lasted a lot longer.

"Beef, potatoes, a few beans. Bacon fat gives it the flavor. I'm almost out of the spuds, so enjoy 'em while they last. Not bad, huh?"

"It is adequate."

"Adequate? You're eating it like it's the last meal you'll ever have."

Shoe chuckled but didn't respond.

"My momma taught me how to cook when I wouldn't stop asking questions about how she made her biscuits so fluffy, or why brown gravy went with beef steak and white gravy went with chicken, or why she added a pinch of salt to her apple pie crust before she rolled it out on the sideboard. She figured it was easier just to show me than to explain it all. Cooking ain't manly work, but I enjoy it. Besides, there ain't any womenfolk around to do it for me."

"That is a fine pot. The womenfolk in my tribe would probably scalp you for it." The braided head nodded in the direction of the caldron, suspended from a cast-iron tripod over the flames.

The set-up had cost a lot of money in Yankton, but it would be worth its weight in gold come winter, when it would be moved inside the house. He planned to keep a pottage simmering all the time. The ingredients would change – barley or corn meal, maybe some beans, and always some type of meat, bison or salt pork. But as long as he kept a fire under the cauldron, the pottage wouldn't spoil and he'd have a hot meal. He would eat the hardtack and jerky only as a last resort if he ran out of everything else. The barrels of flour, salt, coffee, and sugar, along with the sacks of cornmeal, barley, and beans were all wrapped in oil cloth and buried in caches placed strategically around his homestead. He had taken pains to disguise the locations and was relieved everything he needed for the evening meal was already above-ground.

He liked this Cheyenne feller, but that didn't mean he trusted him.

"Some bison liver would taste good in this," Shoe said.

"That sounds godawful. You don't put liver in stew. Here's what you do with liver. You fry it up in a skillet with onions and spuds. Get it nice and crispy. Bacon fat is good for that, or some butter, if you have it. If you got a few hot peppers, throw 'em in. Add a little salt, keep stirring so it don't get burnt. Then when everything is cooked through, you eat the onions and the spuds and the peppers, and you toss the liver in the hog pen."

Another chuckle. "Raw liver is a delicacy in my culture. We consume it fresh from the animal, along with the heart while it is still beating."

Jacob shuddered. He had eaten a lot of unusual things in his life. His curious nature had compelled him to sample bull testicles, fried grasshoppers, and stewed chicken feet. But never any uncooked organs, especially if they were still warm from being inside the animal.

"If God meant people to eat such nonsense as raw liver, he never would have invented the cooking fire."

"God did not invent it. Man did, and my people did it first."

It was true that the native tribes of the American frontier were ancient. Maybe they had invented the cooking fire. If so, he was thankful for them. He could never have gotten by on raw meat.

"You heathens don't believe in God, right?" he said.

"We heathens do not believe in the white man's god."

"What god do you believe in?"

"We believe in the spirit energy which resides in the mountains and prairies, in the trees and in the rivers, in the tall grasses and in the gentle breeze that blows through them, transforming their feathery tips into a golden sea. Spirit energy is in everything that is part of this world. We worship Mother Earth and Father Sky because we can see them and touch them, unlike an invisible white-bearded man who lives in the clouds."

Jacob pondered the words for several minutes. They reminded him of the poetry he had read at the schoolhouse back in Missouri.

"You sure talk purty for a heathen. That preacher must have been something."

"He was, indeed. He was an excellent instructor, and I was an eager student."

"What the heck was a white preacher doing living with heathens, anyways?"

"For the answer, consider the primary directive of evangelical Christians."

Jacob did just that. "I see. He was trying to convert you."

"You sure are smart for an ignorant white man."

"Thank you. I took my book learning serious, but I only got through the fifth grade. I don't have the words you do, but I can appreciate hearing them, at least."

Shoe nodded. "I am sorry for calling you ignorant."

"I'm sorry for calling you an injun. I'll probably do it again, though. By accident, of course."

"Of course."

"He must have been better at teaching than preaching. Seems to me you're still a heathen."

"That I am. I am a spiritual heathen. Does it bother you being in the presence of a non-Christian?"

"Nope, so long as you keep working that sod shovel like you did today."

"You want my help again tomorrow?"

Jacob realized how lonely he had been these past months since moving himself and all his worldly goods from Missouri to the remote, expansive plains of the Dakota Territory. He could use the man's physical labor, and would appreciate his company.

"I don't have much to trade for your work. I can feed you, though. If you like the stew, wait 'til you taste my breakfast biscuits. They melt in your mouth. I got a jar of gooseberry jam to spread on 'em, too."

"I will stay, then. At least for one more day."

He felt a rush of gratitude. In another day, they could well be close to getting the roof on. "Much obliged, Shoe. I'm ready to hit the sack. It's a little chilly out tonight. You can bunk inside the soddy, if you'd like. The walls keep the wind off."

"No thank you, Jacob Payne. If word got out that I slept in a white man's house, I would never be welcome in my tribe again."

"I reckon that makes sense. You'd be a kind of traitor? Is that it?"

"Something like that."

"I'll see you in the morning, then. You can put your pony in the corral with my geldings. She won't wander off that way."

"Waynoka will not wander off. She has decided her place is by my side."

"She told you that?"

"In her horsey words, yes," Shoe said, then disappeared into the night.

Jacob stood in the doorway of his unfinished home, barely able to keep his eyes open after the hard day's work.

"Hope he don't come back and scalp me in my sleep," he muttered to the darkness.

He slept with his Winchester by his side, as he had done every night since his arrival on the prairie. And like every night since his arrival on the prairie, he awoke in the morning with his noggin intact. He knew so because he reached up and felt the top of his head. Every morning while in injun country, he performed the same ritual.

Cheyenne country.

In a half-hour, the biscuits were made and baking nicely in the iron skillet he had purchased in Yankton along with the other cooking implements. He jumped a little when a voice came from just a few feet behind him.

"Smells good, Jacob Payne."

"Dang it, Shoe, don't do that. Nearly dropped the skillet."

"Sorry. I thought you heard me."

"No, I didn't hear you. You people are quiet as mice."

"Quieter. Mice can be loud."

"If you say so." He couldn't deny the intense relief he felt at the appearance of his new friend. Shoe had come back to help. Or maybe to scalp him, but probably just to help.

The sun had edged above the horizon now, and an unfamiliar chill tinged the air. The cold temperature would have sparked more panic if a second pair of work hands hadn't shown up.

"Reckon we can get the walls finished today?" Jacob said, placing hot biscuits on tin plates, then handing the jar of gooseberry jam to his breakfast companion. "Here's a butter knife. It's for spreading."

"Really? I'm not supposed to stick it up my nose?"

"Why would you...oh. Very funny."

"The preacher taught us white-man manners as well as white-man English."

"That preacher feller gets more impressive by the hour," Jacob said, biting into a hot biscuit. It was his mother's secret recipe. He hoped he would have enough flour and baking powder to last through the winter.

He eyed Shoe's enormous bites as the dark eyes half-closed with pleasure.

"Tasty, ain't they? I'll make something even more delicious for dinner. After we get those walls up."

"They are adequate."

"Uh-huh. Sure is a purty sunrise," Jacob said, admiring the pink, lavender, and orange sky. The gentle hills were bathed in the fragile, golden light of a new day. He would never get tired of that sight.

"Yes, it is a pretty sunrise."

"It ain't purty?"

"No. The word is pretty."

"I got an injun trying to teach me English?" He was embarrassed at his own ignorance. "That don't seem right."

"Doesn't seem right."

He blew out an exasperated breath. "I told you I only made it to the fifth grade."

"I know. Your grammar is not your fault. If you would like, I can teach you, like the preacher taught me."

"While we're working?"

"Of course."

Jacob nodded. "I think I'd like that. While we're at it, I'd like to know more Cheyenne words. They'll come in handy, I expect."

"True. You are less likely to be scalped if you can speak to your would-be scalper in their native tongue."

"Then I definitely want to learn. Where did you bunk last night, Shoe? It got purty...I mean pretty...cold."

"My people are camped a few miles from here."

"What? I got injuns living right next door?"

"No, you have an indigenous tribe living nearby. Don't fret, Jacob Payne. They will be moving to their winter lands today."

He felt a stab of alarm. "That mean you gotta go with them? I thought you were staying to work for a spell."

"I will stay today, since that is what I said I would do. I can always catch up to them."

"Whew. You got my heart a'pounding. If I only got you one more day, I'm gonna make the most of you."

"You *have* me for one more day. Not got."

"Was the first got right?"

"Yes, the first got was right."

"See? I'm learning already. Let's get to work."

Hours later, when the sun had risen mid-sky and Jacob's belly was telling him it was time for lunch, movement at the edge of his vision made him reach for his rifle.

"Do not do that," Shoe said, his voice low. "Just keep working. Pretend you have not noticed them."

Jacob shifted the movement of his hand and reached for his sweat-stained hat instead. He tugged at the brim, bringing more shade to his face, then stretched his back, trying to appear casual.

"Your people?" he asked, his eyes darting to the right where Shoe labored.

For the first time he studied the man's garb – the fringed sleeves and the feathers worked into the bison-hide tunic; the breechcloth and leggings; the moccasins also made from bison hide; the knife sheath attached to the beaded sash. A pipe tomahawk dangled from the sash on the other side. The multipurpose hatchet could be thrown at an attacker or stuffed with tobacco and herbs then smoked by a campfire.

Jacob was thankful for the presence of the tomahawk. He hoped his new friend knew as much about throwing the thing as he did about white man's English.

"No. My people went south at dawn." Shoe stretched now too, glancing casually in the opposite direction of the three motionless braves sitting astride their ponies, perhaps a mile away.

"What should we do?" He tried to ignore the Winchester that was, thankfully, within easy reach.

"Keep working," Shoe repeated, then made a soft whistling sound.

Waynoka emerged from behind the soddy where she had been grazing next to the corral. She stopped a few feet shy of her human and dipped her head, continuing to tug at the grass as if nothing at all unusual was happening. Out of the corner of his eye, Jacob could see the bow and arrow-filled quiver straddling her back in some kind of intricate blanket-pouch get-up. He had never seen the leather rigging this close up before. Injuns didn't use saddles, but they did have need to carry items on their horses. It looked ingenious. Later, if he survived the day, he would ask Shoe how it was made.

"You think they'll attack?"

"That is a possibility. How many bullets are in your firearm?"

"It's a Winchester New Model," he replied, unable to keep the pride from his voice. "That firearm can hold fifteen rounds."

"How accurate are you?"

"Ain't had much time to practice with it. I'm a decent shot with my old Burnside, but I traded it along with a few silver pieces for this here lever-action beauty. I bought one of the very first models 'fore I left Missouri. But I been so busy homesteading that I haven't had a chance to fire more than a few shots at that herd of bison that went through last week."

"Did you strike any?"

"Nope. They were pretty far away."

"When the Sioux start toward us, they will be riding at full gallop. Then they will spread out just before they are in range of your bullets. That makes it harder to take them down. You aim at the one on the left."

"They're gonna attack for sure, then?"

"They are doing it now." The braided head gestured in the direction of the three braves charging toward them.

"Dang it," Jacob yelled, dropping his shovel and grabbing the rifle.

Before he even had the walnut stock in his hands, Shoe had retrieved the bow and arrows from Waynoka's spotted side and was drawing a bead on the Sioux brave leading the charge.

"Not yet," Shoe said. His grip on the weapons was unwavering.

"Right. They'll be in range in a few seconds."

"Yes. Remember, aim for the one on the left."

Jacob located his target between the notched metal of the Winchester's sight. He took a deep breath, then blew out half the air in his lungs. He counted his heartbeats to steady his nerves. Horse hooves pounded against the ground like distant thunder, punctuated by high-pitched yells coming from the braves themselves.

He had wished never to hear the bloodcurdling sound of the Sioux war cry.

"Now." Shoe unleashed one of his arrows into the chest of the leading attacker.

Jacob fired a half-second later. Two of the three men toppled from their horses. The third kept coming without seeming to notice the absence of his companions. Shoe's second arrow stopped his progress the next moment.

All three had been hit, but they weren't down. They trotted alongside their ponies, using them for cover. Arrows arced toward the soddy now. Injuns could run and shoot at the same time, and one of them managed this feat with a feathered shaft sticking out of his chest.

He kept firing.

"Watch out for the tomahawks," Shoe said. "They will switch to those in a few seconds."

Sure enough, two of the attackers dropped their bows almost in unison and ran toward them now with tomahawks in hand. The third man was down. Shoe's second arrow had finally done its job.

"Keep firing, Jacob Payne. You should have five more rounds." The voice was utterly calm.

Jacob didn't have time to be amazed at his friend's composure, but it did register through the cacophony of noise and the disorienting gun smoke that Shoe had been keeping count of the bullets.

He sighted the brave on the left again and pulled the trigger. The bullet caught the man on the side of his head and brought him down for good. His pony ambled to a stop.

The leader zig-zagged toward them, tomahawk in hand, the keening Sioux war cry silent now. Jacob tried to target him through the smoke, but couldn't keep the darting figure in his sights.

Two tomahawks flew, released at the same moment, almost touching as they passed within a hair's breadth of each other.

Both weapons found their marks.

Shoe's tomahawk connected with the forehead of the leading attacker, whose tomahawk connected with Shoe's upper thigh. The man was dead before he hit the ground. Shoe merely collapsed, still breathing, still alive, his hand on the weapon wedged into the flesh of his leg.

Jacob dropped his rifle and ran toward him.

"We done it!" he said kneeling down to inspect the injury. "We got all of 'em."

"We did it. Not we *done* it," Shoe replied with a grimace.

"Right. How far in did it go?"

"Not quite to the bone."

"Good. You stay put. I'll go fetch some water and the stitchin' kit."

Thankfully he had hauled fresh water from the nearby stream that morning. What was in the bucket would be fairly clean, but he would still boil it along with the needle and thread from his sewing box, just to be safe. He didn't want the wound to putrefy, so he would also wash his hands with lye soap before he began.

"This is gonna sting a titch," he said a few minutes later.

Shoe's eyes were open. They studied Jacob's hands, as steady now as Shoe's had been with the bow and arrow. "You have done this before?"

"Yep. My ma taught me. The doc lived all the way in town, so whenever any of us kids or daddy got hurt, she tended to us. She got so good at it, neighbors came 'round to get stitched up, too."

"An impressive woman."

"She is. I learned a lot from her. Now be still. I'm gonna pull this out on the count of three. You ready?"

The braided head nodded.

"One..." Jacob said, then pulled out the blade. Blood quickly filled the gash. No white showed through, though. That was a blessing.

"You said you were counting to three."

"And you fell for it."

Shoe gasped as water splashed into the wound.

"I thought you injuns were supposed to be stoic."

"That is an excellent word, Jacob Payne."

"What, injun?" he said with a grin. "I do know a few words. Just not always the best way to string them together."

Shoe hissed as Jacob began stitching up the three-inch gash.

"Come on, sissy britches. This ain't more than a scratch. I don't see anything in there, like pieces from your tunic or such. That tomahawk must have been sharp, which is lucky. If you got any junk in a wound that's been stitched up, it'll putrefy. *Have* any," he added.

"You are a fast learner, Jacob Payne."

"That's what my ma used to say, when she wasn't scolding me for asking so many questions. All done. You'll be right as rain in a week or so. You should stay quiet for at least a couple of days, or you'll bust them stitches."

"*Those* stitches."

"Grammar ain't easy."

"No, it is not." Shoe's eyes were closed from the pain.

Jacob smiled, happy to be looking at a living Shoe instead of a dead one. The thought prompted another.

"You stay put. I'm gonna take the spade and bury those fellers. I know they're heathens, but they deserve a proper burial. Besides, they'll start stinking 'fore too long."

"Take your revolver."

"You think they might be playing possum? And how did you know I had a revolver?"

"It is a possibility they are not dead. And you are a white man homesteading in Cheyenne territory. Of course you have a revolver."

Shoe was right about both. The brave on the left was still breathing. When he was ten feet away, he could see the shallow rising and falling of the chest. He could also see a knife poking up from a dark-skinned fist.

He sighed. Even from that distance, he knew the head damage was too extensive to survive. He took a few more steps, then fired the revolver. The chest didn't rise again.

It took the rest of the afternoon to dig a hole deep and wide enough for three bodies. In between the laboring, he checked on Shoe, who lay on the western side of the soddy, enjoying the warmth of the sun's downward progression. It was floating just above the horizon by the time the burial work was finished.

He squatted next to his dozing friend, noted the paleness of his face, and felt the heartbeat in his wrist. It was strong and regular.

"Yes, I'm still alive."

"I didn't know what words were proper for a Sioux funeral. So I used the ones you said about spirit energy."

"What did you say?" Shoe's eyes were open now. He probably hadn't even been asleep.

"I said, 'Go young men into Mother Earth and Father Sky. Your bodies will soon become part of them just as your spirit already has. Let your energy now live in the breeze that turns the grass into a sea, in the clouds that float in the heavens, and the soil and rock of the prairie and the mountains. In this way, you will live forever.'"

Shoe's eyes were wide now. "That was beautiful, Jacob Payne."

"Surprised you, didn't I? Told you I was a good learner."

"I may have underestimated you."

He shrugged. "Most folks do. At least until they get to know me. Now it's time to start supper. You like chipped beef gravy?"

"I do not know. I have never eaten it."

"Well, you'll be eating it on top of the leftover breakfast biscuits."

"Then I will enjoy it immensely."

"I thought you said they were just adequate."

"'Adequate' is a good enough word."

"'Adequate' is only an adequate word. Especially when it comes to my biscuits."

"Very well. They were delectable."

"Wait 'til you taste my gravy."

***

"You can't keep sleeping outside," Jacob said. "You'll freeze. You feel that bite in the air? That's called winter, my friend. It's just around the bend."

He talked as he worked on the soddy. Tonight would be the first time since arriving at his homestead that he would be snoozing under a roof. Didn't matter that it was made of dirt and grass and moss. It was his, and it would keep him warm, unlike the stubborn injun sitting on the corral fence, sharpening his tomahawk blade.

Shoe had been convalescing for a week now, but he still refused to sleep in a white man's house. Instead, he slept next to Waynoka in the horse lean-to. Every morning Jacob would check on him, expecting to find a frozen, dead injun. But every morning, his friend was alive, in moderately high spirits, and a day further along in his recovery.

"I do not intend to keep sleeping outside," Shoe replied.

Jacob recognized the tone that said something was up, and thought he knew what it was. "Dang it. I ain't gonna lie. I've been dreading this day. You reckon you can still catch up to your people? They got a big head start on you."

"Nope."

"Then what do you mean?"

"I will go down to the stream and collect my belongings that I hid there before we became friends. I will stay in my own house tonight."

"You...what? Wait a minute. All this time you been sleeping outside when you got a tepee nearby?"

"We heathens are not as delicate as white folk. I enjoy sleeping under the stars, even when it is cold. But today I will put up my own house. Not too close to yours, but enough so as to smell the breakfast biscuits."

"I ain't never seen a tepee being put up. *Haven't* seen, I mean. This should be interesting."

While Jacob finished the roof on the soddy, Shoe took Waynoka down to the creek to gather the rest of his things. When he returned, the pony dragged a travois loaded with leather hides and satchels. The poles of the travois itself were part of the scaffolding that would support the bison-hide walls of Shoe's home.

Those Cheyenne were skilled at making items useful in multiple ways.

By the time Jacob placed the final section of sod, Shoe had assembled his home about a hundred yards away. Apparently, a hundred yards was close without being too close. Whatever that meant.

"That went mighty quick," he said when his friend approached the evening fire.

"My people are not sedentary. We can have an entire campsite packed and ready to go in an hour. Takes a bit longer to set it all up again somewhere else, though."

"You're walking better," Jacob said, stirring the contents of the cauldron. This time tomorrow, all the cooking apparatus would be moved to the interior hearth of his new home. He hoped the chimney would draw well. He expected the soddy to be a little smoky, but if he had constructed it correctly, it shouldn't be too bad.

"Thanks to your doctoring," Shoe said, accepting the tin plate covered with the steaming stew. He sniffed the aroma and smiled. Jacob suspected his friend had already become addicted to his cooking. Even though the supplies were going more quickly than he liked, he didn't begrudge feeding the heathen who had likely saved his life during the attack. He figured he owed him a few meals.

"We are going bison hunting in the morning," Shoe continued, between bites. "I heard them pass to the east late yesterday. We need to bring down two animals. Then we will be set for the winter."

"So that means you're staying?"

"Yes. I do not want to hear about a white man starving in Cheyenne country when my tribe returns in the spring."

"I don't plan on starving. I have more than you think."

"You mean the five caches?"

"Dang it. You know about those?"

"Of course."

"There's something I've been worrying about, Shoe. What happens if the locals find out we killed them Sioux? I know tribes fight each other, but they're still your kinfolk. More so than the whites."

"We cannot worry about what may happen, Jacob Payne. We can only address what is happening now and what we know will happen soon. Like the first snow. I think it will arrive within a week."

"You have a Farmer's Almanac in your gear?"

"No. No one can predict the weather from year to year. Only from day to day. I smell snow, though. Can you?"

"I believe so. There's a different quality to the air, like it's traveled through a blizzard in the mountains up north to get here. It meandered through pine and juniper on its way. I swear I'm breathing those scents even though the trees we have here are willow and cottonwood."

"Well said," Shoe nodded. "Have you butchered a bison before?"

"No. I'm eager to see how it's done."

"You will do more than see. You will be elbow-deep in raw organs."

"I don't have a problem with handling them. I just don't want to gobble 'em down, like some folks."

Shoe chuckled. "You did a fine job on your house. It is solid and well-constructed. Is it your first one?"

"Yep. I've built a few log cabins back home, but never a soddy."

"Then how did you know the correct method?"

"I met a feller who had built a couple. Asked him to explain it to me in detail. That was before I decided to come here. I was interested in how it was done, not knowing I would need to do it myself one day."

He felt Shoe's eyes on him. That was his appraising look.

"I definitely underestimated you, Jacob Payne. You are not a typical white man."

"And you're not a typical inj...indigenous tribesman."

"Do not strain yourself. How about using 'native' instead of 'injun?'"

He pondered it. "I think I like that. Native isn't offensive?"

"Not at all."

"All right. From now on you're either a native or a Cheyenne or Shoe."

"And you are just Jacob Payne. The meal was delicious, as usual. Tomorrow, I will make bison for supper."

"Cooked bison, right?"

Shoe's chuckle wafted behind him as he disappeared into the darkness.

***

"This hunt will be different from how my people do it. There are only the two of us, not the dozens of men normally taking part. We will leave the horses behind with the wagon and walk over that hill."

Shoe pointed at the highest slope within eyesight. This part of the Dakota Territory contained a few bluffs, but most of the topography consisted of gentle hills and sloping terrain, intersected by running streams and dry gulches. When Jacob had first arrived, he knew he was where he was meant to be. The wide-open spaces and unending sky of the plains felt like heaven on earth.

"Got it. I can hear 'em and smell 'em."

"They can hear us and smell us, too. That is why we will approach from the south, since the wind is blowing from the north."

"Right."

They crept up the incline on all fours as they neared the summit. Blue eyes and brown eyes peered over the final ridge a few seconds later.

"Sakes alive! This isn't the same herd that passed through a couple of weeks ago. Must be thousands down there."

"Yes, but all we need are two. Small ones would be best for transporting. No females. They are calfing. We need to get closer, but not so close that if they start running, we'll get trampled."

"If I shoot my gun, that'll spook 'em, won't it?"

"Yes, so save your bullets for when my arrows are gone."

With weapons attached to their backs and keeping a low profile, they continued down the hill. It was a magnificent sight, all those gigantic, shaggy brown beasts spread out over a vast expanse of land. The truly amazing thing was they would be gone in a day. When the herds arrived, they soon ate all the grass and sedge and moved on.

A male of average size yielded several hundred pounds of usable meat, plenty to feed a man over the winter. As with beef, there were many ways to utilize all the cuts from these impressive beasts. Jacob's mouth watered at the thought of tenderloin frying in his skillet.

"What's your range with those?" He indicated the quiver of arrows strapped to Shoe's back.

"In white-man terms, I am accurate up to about a hundred yards. I can shoot farther, but my precision suffers."

"Then we have a bit more to go. Dang this cactus." The bison had selected a location loaded with prickly pear and brittle cactus. His clothing had already collected a number of malicious, spiny needles.

"Do not curse it. You will be eating its fruit next year."

"I've never eaten it before. We didn't have much of it back home. Do you cook it or eat it like an apple?"

"As much as I would like to discuss the finer points of prickly pear as it applies to cuisine, we are on a hunt. Concentrate on the task."

Jacob snorted at the chastisement but did as he was told. As they scrambled, he kept his eyes on a small bull that had wandered off a ways.

"This spot will do." Shoe motioned for him to crouch. Of course it would be right next to a monstrous clump of jumping cactus.

"I've got mine picked out," Jacob said, eyeballing the herd.

"Do you have a backup?"

"No. You think I'm gonna miss?"

"Yes. You will miss the first one, and perhaps the next one, too. Plan three animals ahead. Then, when the first or second targets move in such a way that the shot is no longer optimal, go for the next one."

"You've done a lot of bison hunting?"

"Of course. I am an injun."

"Heeeyyy," Jacob began, but Shoe stood, releasing arrows in swift, fluid movements.

They were more than a hundred yards away, but the arrows hit their mark. It took three arrows to bring the first animal to its knees, then to the ground. Three more arrows in rapid procession toppled a second.

"My turn now?" The herd had noticed them and was getting agitated. Horned heads lifted from the grassy plain, and wide nostrils flared, scenting the human-tinged air.

"Yes. Just be ready for them to panic as soon as you shoot. Make it count. A running bison is much harder to hit than a grazing one."

He stood slowly, as Shoe had done, and sighted. He placed the animal's face between the notched metal, then pulled the trigger.

***

"It was your first time. There is no shame in failure. Shame is to be found in not trying."

"I'm just disappointed in myself. I should learn how to hunt like you do. It's quieter. Also, there's something elegant and graceful about the way the arrows fly."

"Agreed."

"Butchering is hard work. Reckon we'll get finished before dark?"

Both men were covered in blood from the shoulders down. The sun hovered half a hands-breadth above the horizon. Shoe glanced up at the sky, pausing the bloody knife mid-motion. The grisly carcass and the determined expression on Shoe's blood-spattered face created a striking contrast to the golden beauty of the late afternoon. If Jacob had possessed a talent for painting, he thought he would like to capture that image.

"Yes, if you stop asking questions and keep working," Shoe replied, returning to his labor.

In another hour, the two bison were ready for transport. The detail work would be done later. They tethered both geldings to the meat-laden wagon. Shoe rode Waynoka alongside with a travois dragging behind, also laden, but he didn't seem inclined to conversation. He was chattier than most of his kind, but he wasn't as chatty as Jacob himself. Not by a mile. It wasn't that Jacob loved talking, but rather that he loved listening. He had discovered years ago that listening was the best way to learn new and fascinating things. So it was a hardship to let all his questions go unasked on the way home. Something new he had learned recently in addition to building a sod house: how to sense when people needed quiet time.

After leaving Shoe at his tepee, Jacob went home. He unhitched the horses and put them in the corral, the first thing he had built when arriving at his homestead in the Dakota Territory. Unlike Waynoka, the geldings would wander off in a heartbeat if they thought there was better grass somewhere else.

He stifled a yawn and stoked up the campfire, tossing in a few willow branches they had found near the stream. Then he waited for his friend to appear and tell him what to do with their bounty. Soon, storing it outdoors wouldn't be a problem because the temperature would remain below freezing for a long time. But now, in September, it wasn't cold enough to dig a hole and bury it in the chilly soil. Amongst his supplies were two small barrels of salt. It would preserve the meat just fine, but a man could get awful tired of salted meat. He knew a little about native peoples' food preservation and was eager to see how Shoe would do it. Would he smoke it? Would he slice it thin and hang it on racks to dry? Would he grind it up with berries, fat, and herbs to make pemmican?

The answer was: all of the above. They did so between return trips to the grazing site to gather dung. But first, on the evening of the hunt, they enjoyed a delicious dinner of fried liver and tenderloin.

***

The bison had been a godsend, and processing all the inedible parts served to keep them busy during the winter months – a double blessing. He spent long evenings by the fire in his soddy or in Shoe's tepee, cleaning, drying, and stretching the hides. The horns were converted into soup spoons and ladles. The extra thick hide on top of the animal's head became a bowl. The heart was turned into a pouch. Nothing went to waste, a concept that resonated deeply with Jacob. And since lessons in English grammar and Cheyenne vocabulary were conducted simultaneously, their evening hours during that long winter were fully utilized.

"Who would have known that housed within that rough exterior lay the soul of a poet?" Shoe said one night while they worked.

Jacob had been thinking about getting back to his soddy, adding more grain to the horses' feed bags in the lean-to, and hitting the sack.

"You think I'm a poet?"

"I said you have the soul of a poet. And now that you have an improved understanding of how to string words together properly, perhaps you should write down these things that spill out of your mouth. Sometimes they are quite beautiful."

"Better than adequate?"

"Indeed. And you know who likes poetry?"

"Sissy men?" Jacob didn't want to admit he had been flattered by Shoe's words.

"Women."

"You may be on to something. If I sit outside my soddy, spouting original poems all day, maybe they will flock to my doorstep."

"Maybe. Not until spring, though."

"Right. Ladies don't like the cold."

"Native females do."

"Do you have one hidden under your blanket?"

"Not here, but maybe somewhere else."

"What are you suggesting, Shoe?"

"Nothing. I am just making conversation."

"Uh-huh. That reminds me, will I be losing my favorite neighbor soon? If I've been counting my days correctly, tomorrow is the first of March."

"Yes. My people will soon return, and I will go to them."

"Dang. I'll miss you. You've been a good friend."

"I will come back to visit. Remember, my tribe camps just a few miles from here."

"That doesn't make me feel better. I'll have to worry about keeping my scalp intact again."

"Perhaps I can put in a good word for you."

"I'd be much obliged."

"Why are you not married, Jacob Payne? You are a competent, decent man, and not too hideous to look upon. I thought you white folks have a societal imperative to find a mate and produce blue-eyed offspring."

He laughed. "It's true. There's a lot of pressure to get hitched. Females who don't are pitied, and men who don't are eyed with suspicion. To be honest, I just never found the right lady."

"So of course you came to this largely unpopulated land where white women are in even shorter supply than elsewhere. What requirements would you have for a wife?"

"Let's see. First, I'd have to say a sense of humor. That's very important. She'd need to be smart and kind and...capable. I don't mean at women's work, like cooking and cleaning house. I mean willing to tackle just about anything with a steady hand. She'd need to be patient to put up with all my questions."

"True. That may be more important than anything. So many questions..." Shoe smirked. "What about beauty?"

Jacob shrugged. "I think beauty comes more from within than without. Who's to say what's beautiful, anyway? I think it's subjective."

"That is a fine word."

"I learned it from you. What about you, Shoe? Why aren't you married to some Cheyenne princess with strong teeth and child-bearing hips?"

His friend chuckled. "I suppose my story is the same. I have not found the right woman yet. Or perhaps the right one is not one I can have."

"Some other brave's woman caught your eye?"

Shoe shook his head and refused to answer.

It was time to change the subject. "By the way, I never did ask you how you got that ridiculously long name."

"I told you when we first met that Shoemowetochawcawe is Cheyenne for high-backed wolf."

"You did. But why? There are no wolves here. And why *high-backed*?"

"As with dogs, when wolves are tense or unsettled, their hackles rise, giving them the appearance of having a high back."

"That makes sense."

"But you are wrong about them not being here."

"Then why haven't I seen any?"

"Because you do not roam about at night. Wolves are nocturnal, although they do occasionally hunt during the day. And while they prefer timberland, they will follow their prey even onto the prairie."

With preternatural timing, the wind carried a howl into the tepee, passing smoke on its journey down through the vent. Two pairs of human eyes widened in surprise.

"I better get going. Need to check on the horses." Jacob gathered his rifle and other things.

"Be careful. That wolf is not far."

"Are you worried about Waynoka?"

Shoe shook his head. "She will tell me if she smells a predator."

Jacob nodded, then opened the leather flap. A gust of frigid air washed over him. Spring was around the corner, but it hadn't arrived quite yet.

The night was cloudless. A luminous gibbous moon hung heavy in the starlit sky, casting enough light to see his way home without stumbling. A well-trod path had developed on the snowy ground between the two homes. He was only twenty paces from his front door when he heard a commotion in the lean-to. The horses whinnied and stamped their hooves in alarm, letting their human know a killer was in their midst.

He dropped the pouch he had been working on that evening, and hoisted the Winchester's stock up to his shoulder. He sprinted the remaining distance to the corral.

As he rounded the corner, he saw a shadowy blur to the right of his vision. It moved so fast that he didn't have time to swivel the rifle barrel toward the wolf. Instead, the animal knocked him to the ground, the impact forcing the Winchester out of his hands. As he reached for the knife wedged into a sheath on his belt, the creature lunged again. He felt the crushing force of the jaws on his forearm and the fangs sinking into his flesh. He had seen a few wolves back home, but never one this massive. It must weigh at least one-twenty, the size of a very large dog. But this was no domesticated pet. It was an apex predator used to getting what it wanted and prepared to kill a full-grown man to get it.

If it had been a solitary wolf, he might have prevailed in the attack. But this pack contained five, and their movements were orchestrated. Later he would learn there was no deadlier, more effective hunting unit on the frontier than a wolf pack half-starved from winter.

He blacked out after one began gnawing on his leg. The last sound he heard were the screams of his geldings.

Or perhaps those screams escaped from his own throat.

***

"Meseestse," a voice said. *Eat.*

When Jacob tried to open his eyes, he realized they were glued shut by a crusty build-up between his top and bottom eyelashes. He wondered how long a man would have to sleep to build up such a monumental crust. He had been having a lovely dream about a woman with fierce golden eyes. When she smiled, he could see that one of her front teeth was broken, yet it did not diminish her allure. He didn't want to wake up. He wanted to go back to sleep and finish the dream.

"I don't feel like eating," he said. His words sounded like the croaking of a frog.

"I guess you want to die, then," the voice replied, in English now. He recognized the feel of his own bed, but the revolting smell in his soddy was different than it had been before. It smelled like an unwashed body and the putrefaction of a wound. The memory of the wolf attack came flooding back into his consciousness.

That got him moving. He lifted an unsteady hand and rubbed at his lashes, then peered at the woman's face hovering above him. She was blurry, but he could make out almond-shaped eyes, skin the reddish brown of a cottonwood sapling, and a wise smile that reminded him of...

"Shoe! Where's Shoe?" he said, scrambling to sit up in bed. His head began to spin, and he flopped back down against the pallet a second later.

"He is grazing the horses. Do not worry, Jacob Payne. He will be home for dinner."

"Who are you?"

"I am Asha, Shoemowetochawcawe's sister."

"You can't be related. Your name is too easy to say."

The laughter was deep and rich, not the giggling of prim white ladies, nor the tittering of shy native women. He liked it instantly.

"Shoemowetochawcawe's outsized name is a reflection of his ego. I prefer your version of it. I have been calling him Shoe since I have been here. I do not think he likes that, which makes me quite happy."

"How long have I been out?" Judging by his feeble limbs, it must have been several days.

"Three weeks."

"Three weeks! What happened to my geldings? Did the wolves get them?"

He saw sadness drift into the amber eyes. His own began to water in response.

"Only the gray. The chestnut is fine now that his wounds have mostly healed. Just like you. Your injuries were quite serious and became corrupt at one point, but in the end, your body and my honey poultices triumphed. But you will die if you do not eat. Open up," she said, forcing a spoonful of bitter liquid down his throat.

"That tastes horrible. What kind of food is that?"

"It is medicine. Willow bark for your discomfort and Echinacea to speed healing. Now that you have had that, we will move on to the bone broth. Small sips until you get your strength back. We do not want you vomiting up all my work."

"You tricked me. I thought you were giving me food."

"Yes, but it was only a little trick due to your weakened state. My trickery knows no limits when I am dealing with a healthy, robust white man." She tugged on a lock of his hair as she said the words.

He reached a weak hand up to feel his scalp. "Did the preacher teach you English as well?"

"Yes. I was the same age as his daughter when they came to our people. He taught my brother and me, along with Miriam and a few of the other children."

"That's something I don't get. Why would the Cheyenne accept a white man into their tribe?"

"When he came to us and spoke about the Bible and tried to deliver his sermons, we thought he was masaha. A *crazy person*. We believe insane people are touched by the gods, and they are therefore considered sacred."

"Ah, I see."

"By the time we understood he was merely a Christian preacher, he had proven himself useful for his patience with the children's lessons. The elders were farsighted. They wanted us to learn the white man's language, and Shoemowetochawcawe and I learned it the best. I think that is because we are competitive. It makes him grumpy to see his little sister do something better than him, and of course I always try to do everything better than him."

Jacob smiled. He loved the sing-song cadence of her speech. He thought he would like to listen to that voice for a long while, if he didn't get too sleepy from the medicine.

"I have a lot more questions," he said, his eyelids beginning to droop.

"Shoemowetochawcawe said you would. Go ahead. I am ready."

"How bad do I smell?"

"I have smelled worse. But I will not lie, you are no field of yarrow flower. Do you know the scent of a bison carcass after it has rotted in the sun for a few days? Anyway, do not worry. I will give you a bath later, if you behave yourself." The grin was now more playful than wise. It was the last thing he saw before his eyelids shut of their own accord.

When they opened again the next morning, he sensed the house was empty, even before he could see that it was. Panic flowed through him. He was still too feeble to care for himself and he knew it. He sat up, then struggled to stand, realizing then the depth of his physical weakness. He looked down at his bandaged limbs, noting their thinness. His mouth felt as if it was stuffed with cotton, so when he saw the bucket of clean water by his bed, he collapsed with relief onto his pallet. Once his head stopped spinning, he filled the nearby tin cup three times and gulped down the water. He could almost feel it plumping out his insides, like Shoe's bison bladder when he replenished it at the stream.

Just then the door opened. Asha stood on the threshold, framed by a sky the color of the glass jars he had seen in Yankton's apothecary shop. He thought the color was called cobalt. He wasn't sure, though. He'd have to ask the next time he went to town for supplies. He was glad there would be a next time.

"Hello, Jacob Payne. How are you feeling?" she said, bustling into the house.

He had never been so happy to see a person in his life.

"Much better. Thank you." For some reason, he suddenly felt bashful. Her mischievous grin told him she had noticed.

"Very good. Every day from now on will be an improvement from the one before. Do you think you can walk? It is a beautiful day, and some fresh air will do you good. Also, I need to do some cleaning in here," she added with a delicate sniff.

"Yes, ma'am. I think I can manage that."

"My brother brought a stump from the creek for you to sit on and soak up the sunshine. While you were convalescing, spring arrived."

She was right. When he stepped outside, the snow had melted. The breeze was cool, but when he held his face up to the sun, it seemed to warm his soul. He breathed deeply of the crisp air, identifying the scents of new grass and budding trees. He would need to till the ground for planting as soon as it thawed. He pictured himself hitching the plow up to just the one horse, felt a stab of grief, and then pondered the prospect of trading something for a Cheyenne pony. Two horses could get the job done much faster than one. What did he have to trade that the natives would want?

"How are you doing out here, Jacob Payne?" asked Asha, emerging through the soddy's door with an armful of smelly bedding. The bundle went into his cauldron, filled now with boiling water and suspended above a smoky fire. He wondered how much of the dried dung was still left. He would need to gather more soon.

"I'm doing just fine. I'm feeling mighty grateful, too. How can I ever repay what you've done for me?"

"Perhaps you will come up with an idea," she said, reaching into a pouch and tossing a handful of herbs into the water. With a hand raised to shield her eyes from the sun, she looked out to the rolling prairie beyond Shoe's tepee. "There is our Cheyenne brave with the long name, returning home at last. Your chestnut has become close friends with Waynoka these past weeks. My brother will be happy to see you awake and sitting up. He has been worried about you." She patted him on the shoulder, then went back inside. He listened to her humming a tune as she tidied up.

He thought his heart might burst from the gratitude he felt for these two people. If it took the rest of his life, he would figure out a way to settle up.

***

Five months later...

"I am well rid of her. She is a thorn in my side," Shoe said as he finished dismantling his tepee. He had left it up over the summer to make his visits easier, he had said. Jacob knew the truth, though. After all they had been through, it would still be frowned upon by his people to stay in the house of a white man.

Even if that white man was married to his sister.

"Your loss is my gain." Jacob smiled as he watched Asha from a distance working in their vegetable garden. He caught little notes of her song on the late summer breeze. She had the prettiest singing voice he had ever heard, but it was her laughter he had fallen in love with. That and about a million other things. He would miss Shoe over the winter, but he wouldn't be lonely. "Are the elders any closer to accepting the marriage?"

"They seem to be warming to it. As with learning the white man's language, they see wisdom in establishing bonds between our people. They understand your kind is here to stay. Now that my sister is with you, you will probably not lose your scalp, unless it is her knife doing the job."

Jacob laughed. "I'd best keep her happy then."

"Indeed," Shoe grinned. "When I return, I may not be alone. You have inspired me."

"Thinking about getting hitched?"

"We will see."

When the travois was assembled and Shoe's belongings properly stowed, the two men stood facing each other, both at a loss for words, a situation in which Jacob rarely found himself. Finally, he reached out to his friend and pulled him into a hug. He was fairly certain Cheyenne braves didn't engage in hugging, but he didn't care.

"Shoe, you are the best friend a man could have. Not only did you save my life, you brought Asha to me."

"You may curse me for that later."

"Perhaps. But for now I just feel grateful. I wish I could think of a way to repay you. It weighs on me."

Shoe looked at him with those wise eyes, and said, "Gratitude should not feel like a burden. It should feel like a gift. It opens one's eyes to the endless opportunities for treating one another with compassion and love. That is how I felt when you tended my leg. No burden, just mindfulness. In this way, our gratitude is like a pebble thrown into a pond, creating ripples of kindness that will travel far and wide."

"I thought I was supposed to be the poet."

"You are the poet. I am the philosopher. Farewell, Jacob Payne. May your heart remain light and your scalp intact. Do not let Asha boss you too much. She will try, believe me."

***

The frigid months passed more quickly than seemed possible, thanks to Asha. It wouldn't be accurate to say she completed him, since human beings were born complete from the moment they wriggled out of their momma's wombs, squalling and gooey, and into the world. But her gifts – her intellect, her sense of humor, her sound judgment – were the perfect complement to his in every way.

And perhaps most importantly, she didn't mind all his questions.

Shoe returned in the spring, as promised, and he was not alone, just as he had intimated. When Asha saw the blond-haired woman riding next to her brother, she squealed in delight and ran toward the two. It seemed that Miriam, the preacher's daughter, had carried a torch for Shoe as big as the one he had carried for her. They were married and expecting their first child in two months.

Their tepee, larger than the one from last year, was soon assembled. That fall, the couple decided not to return to the tribe for winter. They would stay on the homestead with Jacob and Asha.

In the years that followed, more tepees were erected and a second soddy was built. Eventually, there would be a sprawling two-story home constructed with lumber from Yankton and large enough to accommodate current and future generations of Paynes.

All except one tepee would disappear in later years. Shoe's progeny all moved away, but never Shoe himself.

More years passed, quicker than Jacob could fathom. It was odd how the hands on the mantle clock seemed to move at a faster pace than they used to. Maybe one of the grandkids had tinkered with the inner mechanism.

He sighed, and pushed himself out of his favorite porch chair. He meandered – carefully, as is prudent for old people – out to the prairie. He walked past the neat crops, the horse-filled corral, and the handful of homes that belonged to his grown children and grown grandchildren.

It was mid-summer. The sky was the same shade of blue that he had seen through the doorway of his old soddy all those years ago, framing his beloved Asha. The color was called cobalt. He had confirmed that with the apothecary on his next trip into town that year.

The thought made him glance down at the gravestone, where he now stood, at the foot of the tallest cottonwood tree for miles. His gaze shifted a few feet, resting on a new marker and the fresh mound of soil below it.

"You wouldn't think so much happiness could fit into such a shriveled old body," he said to the soil. "Somehow I find room for infinite joy. I wonder where I store it. Maybe between my liver and my gall bladder. When I look at the newest baby, I realize there's always a space to squeeze in some more. You were right, Shoe. We white folks have a societal imperative to produce blue-eyed offspring, although there seem to be a few brown-eyed ones in the mix as well. I credit your people for that development." Jacob smiled, lifting his face to the sun so it could warm his soul.

He took a deep breath of the sweet air, then let it out slowly.

"I'll miss you, my friend. I know you don't believe in white man's heaven, and frankly, I don't think I do either. I don't know what happens next, but I sure hope I get to cook biscuits for you again someday."

His memory traveled back to another burial, the one from his first summer on the homestead.

"Go, young man, into Mother Earth and Father Sky. Your body will soon become part of them, just as your spirit already has. Let your energy flow with the wind that turns the tall grass into a sea. Let it dance with the clouds that float in the heavens. Let it reside in the soil and rock of the prairie and the mountains. In this way, you will live forever."

Jacob dabbed at his eyes with the handkerchief he always carried these days in the back pocket of his trousers. It was interesting how emotional a person became when they got old. The sight of a new great-grandbaby or Asha's grave set him off every time. Now that Miriam and Shoe's markers had joined hers, he reckoned he'd have to start bringing a backup hanky.

"I wonder how soon it'll be until I join you all," he whispered. "Everybody above ground is getting mighty tired of my questions."

The In Between

When Jacob opened his eyes in the black void, it reminded him of the day he pried open his crusty eyelids three weeks after the wolf attack. Unlike back in his soddy in the Dakota Territory when he was healing from half a dozen bite wounds, here in the In Between, he felt no pain. Just a satisfying lightness and a profound sense of well-being. He remembered his first time here after dying in that convenience store robbery in Kansas, and he was happy to be well past all that. In hindsight, he must have seemed naïve to Sarah then. All the souls she mentored probably were in the beginning.

When he thought of his Spiritual Guide, he closed his eyes again and pictured Asha sitting next to the fire pit on a starlit summer night. The soddy had felt stuffy and cramped those first few years before they built a bigger one, so often they would spend their evenings outside, under a canopy of black velvet punched with millions of pinholes for the light to shine through. He always wondered how many stars there were in the night sky, and whether there were people living on the planets which orbited those distant suns.

It was just one of countless questions he had ruminated on during the ninety-two years of his past life. He had been given answers to many of them, but not all. He supposed that was as it should be. If a person knew all the answers to every question, what would then occupy his mind?

He sat on the old willow stump in the In Between, stoking a dung fire with the special charred stick used only for that purpose – no other was the perfect length. Asha had decided early on that his Indian name would be Sits With Stick. It always made him laugh when she called him that.

So he wasn't surprised to see Sarah appear in the form of Asha, with her dark braids and her mischievous grin.

"Jacob, it's lovely to see you," Asha-Sarah said.

"Hi, Sarah. It's wonderful to see you, too. I have to admit, I was ready this time. I lived longer than most folks do. Sometimes a life can go on too long."

"Do you think yours did?"

"No. I think I learned a bonus lesson because of it."

"What was that?"

"Grief. Loss. You can't fully experience joy and all the other pleasurable emotions if you don't endure their dark opposites."

"Excellent," she said, smiling. It was Sarah's smile on Asha's face. "What about the other lessons? Curiosity? A Sense of Humor? Did you receive a side helping of Gratitude?"

"I realized how crucial being curious was to learning. Not just about the big stuff, but trivial stuff too. The more questions you ask, the more you learn and the more you know. The more you know, the more enlightened you become. And that's what this," he gestured to the void beyond the campfire, "is all about. Enlightenment."

"It is indeed. What about Sense of Humor? How significant was it in your journey? Did you come to grasp it fully?"

Jacob pondered both parts of the question for a long time before answering. In the In Between, time meant nothing, so he might have contemplated for hours or days.

"It might just be one of the most important aspects of being human. I don't think I realized that when I created my list. Hilarity and merriment have a way of sweeping away negativity, if only for a while. I think having a sense of humor is what keeps us sane. Laughter is like the steam valve on a pressure cooker. Life can be bleak and depressing much of the time, so having a sense of humor helps us get through it. And yes, thanks to Shoe and Asha and my blue and brown-eyed offspring, I laughed a lot. Certainly more than during any of my other lifetimes."

"So we can mark that off?"

Jacob nodded. "Yes, definitely."

"What about Gratitude?"

"As you knew beforehand, Gratitude could easily have fit into a life all by itself. For me to just tack it onto two other lessons was arrogant. I understand that now."

Sarah merely smiled. Her blond hair was back, but her skin was still the reddish-brown color of a cottonwood sapling.

"As with a sense of humor, Gratitude is vital. Without being thankful for the kindness others show us, or appreciating when we have good health or enough money in the bank to pay bills or a warm coat to wear when it's cold outside, what are we left with? A feeling of entitlement. Like the universe owes us something. Well, it doesn't owe us a damn thing, so we must be grateful for every positive thing in our lives, no matter how small – the handmade quilt on our bed, the headache that finally went away, the batch of biscuits that came out light as a feather."

"Shoe loved your biscuits," Sarah said.

Jacob nodded. "That he did. He was happy to get them most mornings. Being thankful is what keeps us from being jerks. And we can well do with fewer jerks in the world. When Shoe and Asha saved my life after the wolf attack, I felt a burden to repay them. But when Shoe explained that Gratitude is about mindfulness rather than a debt, it made sense. I spent the rest of my life applying that philosophy to the way I lived. Gratitude gave my life more joy and meaning than it would have had otherwise. I hope I was able to pass it on to others, like Shoe's water ripples. I wonder if I'll ever know how many lives we touch indirectly because of it. The number must be colossal."

"Larger than we can imagine," Sarah replied.

"So did I get everything right?" Jacob anticipated, as he always did, the familiar words he knew would follow.

"Do you think you got everything right?"

"Yes. I know I did."

"Onward and upward, then."

"You realize the next life will be the final of my Sublime Seven."

"I do."

"Let's work out the details."

Chapter 7 – Kindness with Compassion and Empathy, and Patience, Benevolence, and Tolerance too...they all seem to go together.

Proxima Centauri – 37962 PC-CE (2657 CE)

"Are you dreading the meeting this morning?" Jox's favorite husband asked at the morning meal. She had never told him he was her favorite for two reasons: it might hurt the feelings of her other two husbands, plus it might make him insufferable. He was already full of himself because of his beautiful face and body. Thankfully, his intellect was only average. Otherwise, he might have contemplated world domination, not an impossible notion on their tiny planet.

"Yes, these meetings are like juggling flaming torches and venom spitters," she replied. "They don't appreciate how fortunate we are. They always want more. More land, more water, more everything, even if it means taking it from someone else. It's infuriating."

Durbin kissed her good cheek, then whisked away the dirty dishes. "You're too kind. They'll take advantage of you if you let them."

"Hardly. They're terrified of me for reasons that are self-evident. And putting those haughty she-devils in their place is the highlight of my day."

"I'm surprised to hear that from you. You're the sweetest person I know."

"If you believe that, I've failed miserably in my intimidation campaign. Besides, you're seeing a façade. Lurking beneath this regrettable face is the soul of a depraved fiend."

"Not true. You're kind to everyone."

"You wouldn't say that if you saw me speak at the Table."

"There's no fear of that happening, since I was born with a penis. Speaking of, it's been a while since you've visited Little Durbin." He batted his eyelashes and licked his full lips. Coming from most men, those affectations would have looked ludicrous, but a beauty like Durbin could make it work.

For a half-second, she considered taking him to her bed, but she decided there wasn't time before the meeting. "We'll remedy that tonight, darling."

"I'll be counting the minutes. When you come home, don't let Vyg distract you with his attempts at clever conversation, nor allow Sawl's dinner to seduce you away from me. We have a date."

Her other two husbands were as jealous of each other as Durbin was of them both. It was a pity, too, because she enjoyed them all for their individual talents and company. Why couldn't they just be satisfied with being married to the One Who Sat in the Tallest Chair? That she had only three husbands should flatter them. Some members of the Table had dozens. She certainly could have afforded more, but she felt no need to grandstand. She barely had enough time to give the three the attention they deserved. Why would she accumulate more just to impress her peers? She wouldn't do it, even if her status and wealth practically demanded it of her.

All those unmarried men could work or enter into legal unions with other men, an acceptable option in a world where men outnumbered women fifty to one.

Besides, the men had brought it upon themselves.

"Don't kill each other while I'm gone," she said.

"Very well. Vyg has been pestering me to play Strategy with him. Maybe I will accept, although I think he only asks me because he knows he'll win, and then he can feel smart."

"Is that such a bad thing?" She kissed him, then reached for her wrap. "People who aren't born beautiful need to feel good about themselves too. I should know."

"No, I suppose not. He is smart, but I am handsome."

"That you are. Goodbye, love."

Before opening the door, she strapped the green-tinted goggles over her eyes, then draped one of her woven wraps around her dark hair and most of her face. When she stepped out into the wind, only partially blocked by the massive walls of her compound, she was happy to note the gusts weren't as strong as they had been the day before.

She tried to be grateful for every gift the planet gave her, no matter how small. They weren't abundant.

She trod along the rock pathway to the nearby underground terminal, then headed for the tunnel marked TR1. Additional tunnels ran spoke-like from the station positioned just beyond her compound. They led to various locations – the markets, the libraries, the hospitals, the services quarter – but the most important was TR1 because it connected to her seat of power: the Table Room.

The security was necessarily severe at its entrance. Even though the Guards recognized her, she was still required to provide a blood sample and to correctly answer the questions asked – only a member of the Table could accurately do so. The answers were given out at the previous meeting, so they were always unique and fresh. It was a simple yet elegant solution to ensure no one entered TR1 who shouldn't. The blood sample was to make sure the civil servants who traveled it hadn't been infected with chime-Ra. A concentration of the most valuable people in the world – women – populated the tunnel daily. Since they were particularly susceptible to the virus that had nearly ended humankind half a millennia ago, everyone had to be screened every single time, despite there being no cases of the disease in more than a hundred years.

"Greetings, Guard Ralork. I hope your evening was pleasant," she said to the man with the stern expression and the scar spanning from temple to angular jawline. His arms were folded in an unfriendly manner, but that wasn't unusual. He always exuded disdain, even though she made a point to be polite to him. Being on the receiving end of disdain was a familiar facet of her world. She had come to terms with it a long time ago.

"Sample, please." He grabbed her offered index finger and shoved it into the open end of the med kit. She blinked when she felt the stab but didn't register the pain. She was conditioned to it. Even though she had done this countless times, it was always a relief to see the little purple button light up. He waved her toward the next man.

"Guard Scordin, how is your partner? Better than last week, I hope."

"Yes ma'am." The young man gave her a shy smile. "The cough is almost gone. That soup recipe you gave me seems to be doing the trick. Thank you."

"You're quite welcome. I'll pass that on to Sawl. It'll make his day."

"Are you ready for the question?"

"Yes. Go ahead."

"If a worm can turn, then it can also..."

"Spiral out of control and explode in a blaze of fire," she replied without hesitation. These questions were always nonsensical, thus unanswerable using logic. A person had to know the correct response beforehand. Simple. Elegant. And frequently entertaining. The more gruesome, the better. She loved when explosions or decapitations were part of the riddles.

"Very good. Have a lovely day, ma'am."

It took fifteen minutes to walk from the terminal to the Table Room. Another man, older and balding, was posted outside the towering carved doors. He recognized her immediately, opened a door, and motioned her inside.

"Thanks, Brutin." Since he was a civil servant and didn't work directly for the Guards, no formalities were necessary.

He said in a low voice, "Watch out for the little one. She's in a mood today."

She snickered, nodded, and entered the cavernous room.

"Ladies, what a pleasure to see you all." The women sat in ornate chairs positioned around a circular stone table. The Table was even more ancient than the doors; they had yet to decipher all the runes on its surface.

"You're late," said a petite middle-aged woman with yellow hair.

"Only a minute or two. Shall we get right to business, then?" Jox folded her wrap and placed it – pointedly – upon the back of her chair. It was the tallest at the Table.

Falsten sighed dramatically, coiled a saffron tendril onto a bony finger, and commenced the hair-twirling. It was one of her tells. Brutin was right. She was definitely in a mood today.

"We need to consider annexing twenty thousand acres within the Western Quadrant," said the dulcet, soprano voice. It was easy on the ears. The statement, however, was shocking, even for Falsten.

"You must be joking," Jox replied. "You'd be sentencing thousands of people to slow starvation by taking away their primary source of income."

"I doubt that. I was just there last week and noticed the residents looked especially healthy. A few were almost plump." Falsten herself took care to remain thin. It was the current fashion.

"That's a ghoulish thing to say. Under different circumstances, I would have found it delightful. Did you skip your morning meal, dear? You seem grumpy. Knick, please fetch some nibbles from the kitchen. And coffee. Lots of coffee," Jox said to the servant standing nearby. A tall, grim-faced woman nodded and disappeared through one of the pocket doors hidden within the walls of the room. "We can't do that, Falsten. You know we can't. It would be seen as an act of aggression."

"Why do we care about the optics?"

"Because we're not an authoritarian nation."

"We are in all but name. Palantine suggests the rules of the game, and the other nations pretend they don't have to follow them, but they do. They have no other choice. That's how it's been for hundreds of years. Our superior technology, our resources, our military...all that buys us status. With it comes entitlements. The taxes we collect from our own people help feed those in the Western and Eastern quadrants. We might as well appropriate some of their land to offset it. We need that meager revenue from their acreage, or we'll be forced to raise taxes here. How do you think our citizens will like that? I'll choose bad optics over angering our constituents every time."

It was classic Falsten, pretending that Jox was overreacting. It didn't help that several heads nodded in agreement.

"*Annexing* is just a diplomatic way of saying we're taking over. *Appropriating* is another word for stealing.

This is how crime bosses, thieves, and self-aggrandizing bitches talk."

Falsten shrugged. "So be it."

Titters came from some of the women. Falsten sycophants sat at the Table, but Jox had loyal followers of her own. You didn't get to the Tallest Chair with a face like Jox's unless you had a brain that worked better than most.

"You want to gain the reputation of Dictator? That is what they will call this council."

"*Our* people won't. Only the Westerners."

She wouldn't convince Falsten of anything, today. The woman's mind was made up.

Jox had known for some time that something like this was coming. Palantine had experienced a revenue shortfall for the last two years. Something had to give. The conversation playing out at the Table now was for the benefit of the other twenty-three members. She studied those assembled faces now, noting the various expressions: trepidation, glee, fear, reflection. And resignation. That last one bothered her the most.

Jox narrowed her eyes and curled up the side of her mouth that worked properly. She was going for ghastly. "We have options. We can trim our Commons Budget."

"Really? Haven't we been doing that for two years now? Our people like their services. Our people enjoy the fruits of their labors, and why shouldn't they? What they don't like is cutting back on their own benefits to fill the bellies of others. It's not fair, and you know it."

"None of our citizenry goes without food, shelter, or medical care. They have nothing to complain about."

"Some of our people spend more time at their jobs than at their homes just so they can pay their taxes. Do you think it's reasonable to ask them to work even harder to compensate for Westerners who don't work at all?"

"Many of the Westerners can't work because of their climate. During those times of the year when it's hot enough to fry the skin off their bones, how can they labor outside? Since we don't allow them to emigrate here, what do you expect them to do? Resort to cannibalism? It's an intriguing notion, but not one I'm inclined to embrace. Despite my appearance, I'm not an actual monster."

"Is that the mantra you say to your mirror every morning, Jox? It's their bad luck that they weren't born in the Zone. Besides, they have mountains they could go to. It's cooler there."

Jox wouldn't allow amusement to show on her face. Falsten had gotten in a clever shot. "Their mountainous regions are uninhabitable for reasons beyond climate issues, and you know it. Chime-Ra levels still register in the danger zone on the bio-meters. Why are you being so willfully obtuse?"

"I'm not being obtuse. I'm saying it's not our problem. We cannot untangle every knotted issue on Proxima Centauri. We are only responsible for the citizens of Palantine. Right, ladies?"

More than half of the Table applauded. Jox's heart sank, but her voice was firm and steady.

"I won't agree to the annexation, period."

"If twenty Table members want it, you don't have to agree, despite the chair in which you sit. But rather than forcing a vote and risk humiliating you, let me offer another option: cut the Altruism Budget by half. That solves all our problems without raising our taxes or appropriating land from other nations."

Jox gasped. No one else in the room seemed surprised, though. When she realized that, she knew she had been played. Falsten had never wanted to annex acreage. It had been her plan all along to cut the budget which fed and clothed people living in the fiery Western Quadrant and the frozen Eastern Quadrant – the people who couldn't do so for themselves.

On a tidally locked planet where one hemisphere permanently endured the unrelenting sun, and the other the frigid vacuum of space, there remained only one tenable place to live. The terminator line between fire and ice, that swath of paradise longitudinally encircling the globe. The Zone.

Palantine.

***

"At least it didn't end in a coup d'état," Vyg said after dinner. The two lounged on plump cushions in the parlor. He was the most intelligent of her husbands and the one she sought out for political advice. If he'd been born a woman, he would likely have a place at the Table, too.

"I know, I know. That skinny twat out-maneuvered me. I'm fortunate to still be sitting in the Tallest Chair. I should have seen it coming, but I refused to believe that otherwise kind people would turn their backs on those in need. Cutting the Alt Budget by fifty percent will literally take food out of the mouths of children. How can they be so uncaring?"

"Did you consider that perhaps they don't enjoy what they're doing? Difficult decisions must be made, Jox. You're so tender-hearted that Falsten might have decided to take matters into her own hands."

"Falsten? I doubt that. She's a self-absorbed narcissist. And I'm not tender-hearted. I'm a hobgoblin. Everyone fears me."

Vyg chuckled. "Could it be that she's also correct in her assessment?"

"There are no easy answers."

"I understand, so you must select from answers that are not easy, or fair, or popular. Problems have a way of demanding solutions. They won't go away on their own."

She smiled, crookedly. "Is that your delicate way of suggesting I've been hedging?"

"Yes," he said without hesitation.

"Ahem," came a voice from the doorway. A shirtless Durbin stood there, crooking his finger.

Jox sighed. She was still no closer to knowing what to do. Falsten needed twenty votes to offset an opposing vote from The One Who Sits in the Tallest Chair. By Jox's count, she didn't quite have them, but it was close. And Vyg was right. A decision of some kind had to be made – and soon. Palantine couldn't continue to operate on a budget shortfall. It would decimate morale and rob future generations of fiscal security.

"I'm coming, dear," she replied, then turned to Vyg. "Thank you for your wise counsel, clever husband. Good night. Look for me in your nightmares."

She followed Durbin down the hall to his bedroom. The sex was incredible, as usual, and it helped her sleep that night. When she awoke, she knew what she would do.

***

"Greetings, Guard Ralork. I trust you are well today." She stood at the entrance to TR1. For once, the man wasn't scowling.

"I'm quite well, thank you. It's a lovely day. Sample, please."

Jox barely kept her jaw from dropping. She offered her finger, which he placed gently into the med kit rather than shoving it in.

Maybe he had great sex last night, too.

When the purple button lit up, she stepped to the next man, a stranger.

"Where is Guard Scordin today?"

"He's ill, ma'am. It's that cough that's been going around. Are you ready for the question?"

She frowned, wondering if his partner was well enough to care for him. "Yes, go ahead."

"If the cat chases the rat..."

"The rat will hide under the cheese bowl and bide his time." She smiled. The riddle was not one of the amusing ones, but nonsensical nevertheless.

"Very good, ma'am. Go ahead."

"Brutin," she said to the doorman a few minutes later. "You look pale. Do you feel well?"

He gave her a tight smile. "Just a bit of a headache, is all. I'm sure it will soon pass." He waved her in with a hand that trembled.

"Greetings, ladies," Jox said, noting the tension in the room. She was early today, yet everyone had arrived before her. Flutterbugs hatched in her stomach.

Maybe a coup d'état had been scheduled for that morning after all.

"Hello, dear," said one of her loyalists, giving her a smile.

"We have much work to do," came the soprano voice she had been dreading.

Jox sighed. "Knick," she said to the servant standing stiffly against the wall. "I think we'll be needing copious amounts of coffee this morning. And some of those little puff pastries, if there are any in the kitchen. Perhaps also something sharp to slit my wrists and thus spare me the imminent drama."

She was expecting the usual curt nod in return, but instead, the woman turned and disappeared through a pocket door – one that Jox didn't know existed.

"What a strange day," she said, mostly to herself, but her friend sitting to the left of the Tallest Chair nodded.

"I agree," the silver-haired woman whispered. "Something seems amiss. And I'm not referring to you-know-who," she added with a nod in Falsten's direction.

"I hope you wore your big girl panties, Agathe. I think we're in for a brawl."

She was about to call the meeting to order when one of the hidden doors crashed open with a loud bang. All heads turned toward the armed figures bursting through the opening and flooding into the room.

"What is this?" Jox yelled, jumping to her feet and knocking over The Tall Chair.

"This is a rebellion." The figure in front wore a scarf that covered most of his face. She thought the voice sounded familiar. "You women will be our guests for a while. Come with us quietly, and no one will get hurt."

"Nonsense." Falsten stood now too. "Nobody is going anywhere." Her response would have seemed more forceful if she had perched on her nearby footstool. Only the saffron hair and a pair of bony shoulders were visible above the faded runes of the stone table. Still, the petite woman exuded a ferocity Jox lacked.

The man, presumably their leader, spoke again. "You get no additional warnings." A silent gesture to his

followers prompted the five shrouded assailants to encircle
the chairs. Six blasters targeted the members of the Table.

"How dare..." Falsten began. She was silenced when the
top of her head exploded.

Jox looked in horror at the blood-soaked yellow mass
on the marble floor.

She pressed her lips together in a tight frown, then
said, "Come ladies. Do what he says. Come, come." Her
voice was surprisingly calm.

She ushered the most powerful people on the planet
toward the open door, like hens being shooed into a
narrow, menacing chicken coop. The corridors fanning out
from the Table Room were nearly as elegant as the Room
itself, but not this one. It must have been a service
entrance; the rough floor and oppressive stone walls
looked almost as ancient as the engraved runes. Spider silk
decorated the crease between the craggy sides and the
cracked wooden beams of the ceiling.

With every molecule of her body, she hoped the spiders
themselves were long gone.

"Single file, no talking," she said. "Just do what they tell
us."

The order was unnecessary. No one wanted to end up
like Falsten.

"You in the front, keep walking," a man's voice said
from behind.

She took Agathe's fragile hand into her own misshapen
one. The lighting system was triggered by movement. Each
sconce positioned along the walls at regular intervals

flickered on just before they came to it. Under other circumstances, the effect would have been charming. Here, it obscured whatever was at the end of the corridor. She took the opportunity to analyze their dismaying circumstances.

The leader of the armed group said it was a rebellion, but who was rebelling and against what? She knew of no abnormal unrest. Yes, the citizens grumbled about taxes and complained when the selection at the food markets wasn't optimal, but otherwise the nation had been experiencing a long period of peace. Had word gotten out that the Council was considering cutting services or raising taxes again? Everything at their meetings was supposed to be confidential.

The thought prompted another: secret tunnels like this rendered all that security at the terminal laughable. She had believed that the only tunnel leading to and from the Table Room was TR1. The tunnels behind the pocket doors were supposed to connect to support rooms within the complex. They had been walking long enough in a straight line now to place them well past the government offices. She had no idea where they would end up.

After another half-hour, she understood the depth of their peril. They had traveled beyond the city center by now.

"How are you doing, Agathe?" she whispered to the older woman behind her.

"Hush. I don't want to see your head blasted off. I'm fine."

Jox nodded. She knew pain raged throughout Agathe's frail body, but there was nothing to be done for her now. She took comfort in the strength of the woman's admonishment.

Finally, one of the men spoke.

"Stop there," the male voice said.

She obeyed just as one of the sconces lit up before her, revealing a corroded metal door.

"I'll be handing out blindfolds," the voice continued. "Put them on and tie them securely. No peeking. No second warning."

She watched the shrouded man who belonged to the voice pass out black lengths of fabric as he walked along the line of women. When he reached her, ice-blue eyes rested on her face before the final blindfold was placed in her hands. She tied it over her eyes, plunging herself into a pitch-black world.

She felt him brush past her, heard him fiddle with a latch or a keyhole, sensed the vibration of his body heaving against the door, and then the screech of rusted hinges. A cool gust of air washed over her.

"Hold hands and make a chain. Once you step through the opening, there will be a short walk to a transport. Climb into the carriage and find a seat along either of the two rows of benches running the length of it. You're lucky the winds aren't bad today," he added, guiding her through the doorway.

She tried to gauge the time as it passed in the swaying, bumpy transport. She counted the seconds, then the minutes, then the quarter hours. She gave up after the first two hours. The ride seemed endless, and at one point she might have fallen asleep.

She was awake when they came to an abrupt, jerky stop. The voice of the man with the blue eyes spoke from just a few feet away. Had he been there the entire time?

"You may remove your blindfolds. We've arrived at our destination."

She tugged the fabric over her head, then did a quick assessment of the women.

Agathe's skin looked gray rather than its usual mahogany shade, but resolve was etched into the lines of her face.

The others appeared subdued but not beaten down. They all had surely been contemplating the situation and how they would address it. Had they come to the same conclusions she had? They may well be facing the fight of their lives.

Blue Eyes waved them off the carriage and onto an unfamiliar concrete landing. She had never been there because she had never before been to the chilly world of the Eastern Quadrant. They must be near its border; beyond the twilight where they now stood lay perpetual darkness and never-melting ice.

She almost said something to Blue Eyes about the cold air and their bare arms but decided not to. She would be no help to anyone with her head blown off.

Instead, she stood with her council as they clutched at their thin clothes and shivered in the half-light. She wrapped a protective arm around Agathe and waited.

When the man with the familiar voice emerged, she recognized something in his movements. Coupled together, the voice and the movements revealed his identity at last. She now knew who the leader of this nefarious band was.

A respected member of the Guards was leading the insurrection which involved kidnapping the entire membership of the Table and taking them to the border of the Eastern Quadrant. It wasn't some hastily devised scheme. This was a well-planned and meticulously orchestrated uprising, possibly in the works for years.

She knew this because Ralork had been stationed at TR1 for a decade. Had he been subverted recently? Or had he been planted into the Guard ranks years ago by the rebels? Thinking back on the man's pervasive hostility, she surmised it was the latter.

At that moment her knees almost gave out.

"This way. Don't speak to anyone who happens to be out. We don't have far to go." Ralork stared at her with the usual disdain, then shifted his focus to Agathe. He removed his coat. Then, after brushing away Jox's arm, he draped the garment around the older woman's shoulders.

Agathe didn't thank him. She didn't say a word, returning his gaze with narrowed eyes and an imperious toss of her silver hair.

Ralork shrugged, then walked toward a dilapidated terminal. No busy commuters exited from it; no one but their group traveled toward it.

Were they in some kind of ghost town? The wind whipped about as it did everywhere on Proxima Centauri. It was an inherently windy planet, thus the tall windbreaks and the reason most of the machinery of civilization abided underground.

She had the sudden urge to flee. Something told her if they went into that building, they would never come out. She glanced behind her to the women and their masked abductors, blasters at the ready. They held those weapons with the casual competence of frequent use.

This was not the right time to wage a resistance. She must let things play out.

"Through here," Ralork said, at the terminal's entrance. The building's interior was in a state of complete disrepair. The walls of the circular space were crumbling. The entrances to a few of the tunnels had collapsed entirely, blocking access to their unknown destinations. The accessible ones were ominous unlit half-circles. She couldn't imagine where they might lead. She didn't have to wonder about spiders; she could see their webs.

Her shoulders gave an involuntary shudder.

Ralork approached the only light source within the space, removed the ethane torch from its rusted holder, and turned to face the women gathered in a tight cluster next to a gas heater and its welcome warmth.

He pushed back the shroud, then uncoiled the wrap from his face. She wasn't surprised when she saw the familiar scowl, but some of the women gasped. Still, no one spoke. They remembered the bloody mound of yellow hair.

"This will be your home for the foreseeable future. Supplies will be here shortly – food, water, sleeping pallets, implements for hygiene and lighting, and so forth. Does anyone have any critical requirements? Medicine? Allergies? Tell me now. Special requests will not be considered later."

Jox raised her hand.

"Yes, what is it? You may speak freely."

"Agathe has arthritis. She'll need her pills."

Ralork slipped a hand inside his shirt, pulling forth a delicate embroidered pouch. He handed it her friend. "Anything else?"

"I can't eat nuts. If I consume them, I'll die within minutes," said a tall woman with red curls spiraling down to her waist. Nodine was an adversary on the council. Hers was one of the oldest families in Palantine, and she never let anyone forget it.

"Yes, we're aware of your nut issue. It's been noted."

"Then why ask?" Nodine snapped.

Ralork gave her a cold smile. "You tell me."

"They're testing us," Jox replied. "Seeing if we intend to be truthful."

Nodine gave him a withering look. "Barbarians."

"Careful, " Ralork said. "It's not prudent to insult your captors."

"Guard Ralork, please tell us what this is all about." Jox used her most diplomatic, reasonable tone. It had served her well throughout her career.

"Ralork will do. I'm no Guard here. I'm your warden. I'm also a dispenser of death if anyone tries to escape. Or if anyone angers me." His insolent glance took in Nodine's lustrous hair, then slowly meandered down to the elegant leather boots in a show of scathing disrespect. Nodine's hand twitched as if it desperately wanted to slap the scarred face.

Jox breathed a sigh of relief when the slap failed to materialize.

Ralork's smirk said he had seen it too.

"To answer your question, this isn't just a rebellion. It's a reckoning."

She waited for him to continue, but no further words followed.

She took a leap of faith. "The very meeting you...interrupted...was going to be about the Altruism Budget. I had planned to propose a number of positive changes, including an innovative immigration policy and a worker exchange program. Amendments will be made to the Sacred Scrolls to create more freedoms and benefits for the people in both the Western and Eastern Quadrants. Let us get back and do our job, and I promise we can make our world a better place for everyone."

Ralork laughed out loud. "You think this is about geography? Borders and budgets?"

"Well, yes. What else could it be about?"

"My gods, woman. I thought you were smarter."

She cringed at the derision in the voice. Having her intellect questioned was particularly insulting, as it was the only jewel in her metaphorical crown.

"This is about oppression. This is about subjugation. This is about a profoundly dysfunctional system that advances a fragment of the population merely because of their genitalia."

"Oh, my. You're a Classicist, then. I thought you were more intelligent, Ralork." This time she didn't bother with the diplomatic tone.

Now she remembered the vague rumors of a shadow movement...a secret insurrection of men who chafed at the progress of the past five hundred years. But nothing had ever come of the rumors. What kind of fools would intentionally revert to an archaic society whose inherent aggression had nearly annihilated their race?

"I don't much care for that word," Ralork replied. "Step lightly, woman."

She took note of the menace in his voice and the steely gaze.

She persisted. "Men held power for millennia. You brought your diminished status upon yourselves because of your recklessness and impulsiveness. If not for your hostile overreach in space, our population would number in the billions instead of a few hundred thousand. Chime-Ra almost decimated our world when you carried it back from that nearby galaxy, and it *did* decimate the female populace. That is on you and your kind."

Was she being too aggressive? She didn't care. "Our female ancestors seized the reins and have governed with prudence and wisdom since. They were the ones who saved humankind from extinction, and we, their offspring, continue that mission. Men with their Y chromosome and their warlike natures couldn't be trusted with authority over the fate of our world, and you still can't. What's happening in this terminal underscores that perfectly. What happened to Falsten in the Table Room exemplifies it."

Ralork narrowed his eyes. "The days of enjoying power because of your anomalous biology are over. Starting now. That's the problem with ceding it to a minority. The majority, because of its superior numbers, will ultimately prevail."

"Only if it's stupid and nearsighted." She took a deep breath. "Ralork, this is ancient history. The Table and its members have guided our people with a steady hand. We have done the impossible by bringing the fertility rate back to almost ninety percent. This past decade, for the first time in five hundred years, there is a girl born for every four boys. Did you know that? It's a vast improvement from even the last century. Do you understand the significance? We're finally coming back. At this rate, in a few more generations, the male-to-female ratio will return to pre-space travel numbers. Perhaps then there will be a place for men at the Table. Until that happens, your aggressive dispositions forbid it. We can't take a chance on you yet."

Anyone who had attended lower school knew these things. And since all children were required to attend, of course Ralork and his fellow insurgents knew them. She couldn't fathom the mindset of people who would jeopardize everything gained since their near extermination merely to gain power.

"You don't have a choice, Jox. That's what you don't seem to understand. Do you think I can call it off on a whim? This has been in the works for a long time. I'm just a cog in the wheel."

The words felt like a punch to her belly.

"You women will stay here until everything settles down. As I said before, no harm will come to you if you don't cause any trouble. Don't attempt to escape. You're in the Eastern Quadrant now. I promise it won't end well for you." He gestured to one of the black tunnel openings. "The heater will keep you from freezing in here, but not out there."

He turned his back, replaced the torch, and strode out, followed by the other gunmen. The sound of the outside doors being shut and bolted echoed down the corridor.

"We should have anticipated this." Nodine eased her slender backside down to the cracked stone floor of the terminal as close to the heater as she could get without igniting her silk pashmina.

It was not frigid in the room, but neither was it toasty. Jox hoped that when the provisions came they would include blankets and pillows. Finding herself at the mercy of men felt like parting her hair on the opposite side – uncomfortable and unwelcome.

"What do you make of all this?" Agathe sat on the floor now too. The wrinkled face grimaced at the discomfort, but she still wore Ralork's jacket. She was warm, at least.

"I need time to analyze the situation. I had a plan to address the fiscal and welfare disparities in our world, but not this."

"Idiots," Nodine said. "This malfeasance exemplifies why they can't be trusted to govern. You were right about that, if nothing else, Jox."

Jox found the grudging compliment off-putting. Like Falsten, Nodine was a haughty, callous ruler, but her intellect didn't come close to Falsten's, and her world views usually ran counter to her own. If she and Nodine were in accord on a subject, she should revisit her position on that subject. Immediately.

"I wonder how they're going to do it." Agathe gazed into the simulated flames of the ethane heater. "Do you think they've abducted all the women or just those of us in government?"

"If this has been in the works for years, I would assume they've taken us all. It wouldn't be that difficult since they so heavily outnumber us. Any female who hadn't been taken hostage would impose martial law through the authority of her birthright. The men would have foreseen that."

"I wonder how many of them are in on this." Zania spoke for the first time. The athletic, middle-aged woman was new to the Table and Jox had yet to decide how she felt about her.

"Who knows? Probably all the bastards," Nodine replied. "Except for my husbands. They're utterly loyal to me, as well they should be. They're spoiled rotten."

She thought about Zania's question, then about Nodine's offensive reply. Men weren't chattels to be accumulated and displayed, nor were they pets to be pampered. Even though they enjoyed the same rights and privileges as women in all areas but one, she could understand that their lack of legislative control might make them feel like second-class citizens. In some ways, her appearance had delegated her to a similar ignoble realm. It wasn't a pleasant place to be.

Still, it was their own fault.

"There are too many unknowns at this point. I suggest we bide our time, try to coerce information from our captors when they bring the supplies, and go from there. Thoughts, ladies?" It felt proper for Jox to take the lead in this situation as she had done from the Tallest Chair for the past five years.

"Agreed," Agathe said. "As the Guard said, we're in the EQ. If those tunnels extend farther into the tundra, we'd freeze out there in no time."

"Or they could lead back to Palantine," Zania said.

"We were on that carriage for hours. We must be far from home."

"Who knows what direction we were going? The twilight suggests we're barely into the EQ. Or perhaps we're still in Palantine and it's dusk. Maybe the purpose of the transport was to confuse our sense of distance and orientation."

Jox raised her eyebrows in surprise. The idea hadn't occurred to her. "Very good, Zania. That's something to consider."

Noises came from the terminal's entrance, then flat-bed wagons rolled into the circular room, pulled by two men.

Ralork was not among them this time. She knew this because their faces were uncovered. It was worrisome that they no longer bothered to hide their identities.

She stood, adopting a demeanor of placid confidence, though her instinct urged her to rush the man in front and wrestle the blaster from his hand.

"Gentlemen, thank you. We appreciate the food and water, and are grateful for the blankets. It's chilly here in the Eastern Quadrant." When she said the last part, she watched for micro expressions on the face of the closest man. His pale eyes darted toward her, then an inscrutable veil slid back into place. It was Blue Eyes, the one who had passed out the blindfolds. Something in his demeanor spoke to her; subtle body language hinted at compassion.

She would exploit it if possible.

Careful to keep her distance from the one with the blaster, she moved toward Blue Eyes, affecting docile, compliant movements. She despised herself for them, but continued.

"Guard, is there anything you can tell us? I'm sorry I can't address you properly. I don't know your name."

Blue Eyes set down a heavy package, then turned to face her. She scrutinized his features. Had she seen him somewhere before? The markets? The libraries? He looked familiar.

"There's no need for names here, ma'am. We'll return with more food and water tomorrow."

He began to turn, then seemed to remember something. "Please don't forget what you were told. An attempted escape will not end well for you. It may not seem like it, but we'd prefer that everyone get out of this alive."

"Except for Falsten," Agathe said from a few inches behind. The antagonism in the older woman's voice was not helping their cause.

Blue Eyes glanced toward Agathe, careful to keep his expression neutral, but Jox saw a flash of remorse. There was no mistaking it.

"I've included a burner to heat your meals. Please don't repurpose it for anything hazardous."

"Repurpose it for what? We're going to turn a food burner into a blaster? Idiot." Nodine's words and tone made Jox cringe. So much for any progress she might have been making.

"Good night, ma'am," Blue Eyes said to her, ignoring the other women. Then, as he turned to catch up to the men, she felt something pressed into her right hand – the serviceable one.

She watched him file down the corridor toward the entrance without looking back. Once she heard the clanging of the door being shut and locked, she uncurled her fingers.

In the palm lay a flawless obsidian sphere.

The volcanic glass was rare on Centauri Proxima and highly sought after for that reason, as well as for its beauty. This marble was even more special – its surface had been engraved with the letters J and V.

Jox and Vyg. It had been a gift from her first husband on their wedding night.

***

"What does it mean?" Agathe asked moments later.

"I don't know, but I will analyze it. In the meantime, let's get everything unpacked and sorted. The portable privy should be placed down one of the tunnels, preferably one without spider webs. Tova, you're in charge of dinner since you know your way around a kitchen. Agathe, you have a head for numbers, so you'll be inventorying our supplies and calculating what everyone can have. We can't count on the men to return tomorrow just because they said they would, so we should ration. The rest of you, get your sleep pallets and blankets. Older ladies closest to the heater. Let's get started."

The simple work of organizing and delegating tasks allowed her mind to wrangle with their predicament as well as ponder the significance of the marble. What if they really weren't in the Eastern Quadrant? If they ventured down one of those black shafts, would they emerge in Palantine or onto the frozen tundra? There were a dozen passageways with entrances that had not collapsed. Surely there weren't armed men waiting on the other end of each of them. Did the marble mean her husband Vyg was part of this? Or was he fighting against it? Could he be a mole, inducted into the rebellion but subverting it from within?

"Jox, here's your meal," said the portly Tova, handing her a compartmented tray containing food that reminded her of the meals from lower school. Upon closer inspection, she realized that's exactly what it was. The men must have raided a distribution facility. If the children were going without lunches as a result, she would personally refashion all the rebels into eunuchs.

The room quieted as dinner was eaten. The sudden silence provided fertile ground for anxiety and fear to flourish.

"Agathe, did you take your pill?" said Jox, breaking into the gloomy thoughts she sensed were filling everyone's heads.

"Yes, dear. I'm not too uncomfortable. Don't worry about me. Have you come up with a plan?"

"I think so. Ladies," she continued, "the way I see it, we have two choices. We can sit here, dependent upon the charity and whims of others, or we can take our fate into our own hands and send a scouting mission down those tunnels."

"*Dependent upon the charity and whims of others*...perhaps that's how the citizens of the Western and Eastern Quadrants feel," Zania said. "We're lucky the rebellion has come from the men and not those people. Their grievances are valid and speak of existential distress rather than injured masculine feelings."

Jox pondered the sentiment. She had always focused on keeping everyone's bellies full, but she hadn't given much thought to how Palantine's largess might impact the self-esteem of its recipients.

She nodded. "Thanks to your clever observation, Zania, we cannot assume we are in the EQ. Terminals are chilly because they're underground. Our salvation may well lie at the end of one of these passages."

Most of the women agreed, but there were a few holdouts. There always were.

Zania was one of them. "Why do you suppose they didn't post a guard here to ensure that we didn't do the very thing we're contemplating? Maybe they've set a trap for us."

"Why would they do that?" Jox felt herself getting impatient now. "If they were going to kill us, they would have done so already."

"Not if they didn't want to turn us into martyrs."

The woman was right. She promised herself never to lose patience with someone who so clearly deserved it.

"I'm at a loss then. What should we do? You seem to have all the answers."

"No, I only have all the questions." Zania gave her a shy smile. "You're the answer woman. But I think the worst thing we could do is to rush into something. Perhaps we should sleep on it. We've been through a lot today."

Jox took a deep breath. "You're right. Again. You may have just saved us from making matters worse." She reached over to pat the woman's hand, trying to summon what she knew of her personal history. She drew a blank.

"Dirty trays go in that tunnel," said Tova with her mouth full. "I'll prepare the food, but I won't clean up after you all."

Jox smiled. "No one would expect you to."

Tova snorted. "That one would." She pointed to Nodine who sat alone, barely touching her meal.

Jox sighed, discarded her tray, and then approached her adversary.

"What's wrong, dear?" she said in the kindest voice she could muster.

"What's wrong? What do you think is wrong? We've been abducted. We'll probably be tortured and killed. My husbands must be worried sick about me. And I'm missing a hair appointment!" The last words came out in a sob.

If there was one thing Nodine hated, it was displaying weakness. Jox knew she wasn't concerned about spouses or hair appointments. Well...not overly concerned. She was just frightened to death and didn't want to show it.

She lowered her voice so no one would hear. "You're going to make it out of this."

"How do you know that? You can't know that, stupid woman." Unshed tears glittered in the violet eyes.

It wasn't easy showing love to someone so thoroughly unlovable. Jox did it anyway, wrapping her arm around the slender shoulders and squeezing them with genuine affection.

"I do know it. Here's why." She uncurled her fingers. The marble gave her comfort. Perhaps it would give Nodine some as well. "This tells me that there are people out there fighting for us. Lots of people, our sisters and brothers who aren't part of this nonsense."

Nodine stared at the obsidian orb like it was a life preserver bobbing on a storm-ravaged ocean. "Yes, yes. I bet you're right. Of course people are fighting for us. Why wouldn't they? We're their superiors, and we're rich. They know they'll be rewarded."

She bit back a tart response. "Quite right. Now finish your dinner and set your pallet up closer to the heater. You'll freeze to death all the way over here. There's room next to mine."

She gave the shoulders another squeeze, then moved on. It took her an hour to work through the room, listening to everyone's concerns and suggestions, giving solace when needed and her undivided attention always.

Finally, she sank down onto her own pallet between Agathe and Nodine. She slid a notebook and pen out of a hidden blouse pocket, scribbled a few sentences, tore off the sheet of paper, then tucked it all back in.

Then she closed her eyes, thinking she thought she might toss and turn. Instead, she fell asleep almost immediately.

***

"Jox, wake up." Agathe was jostling her, cutting short a lovely dream about a dark-skinned woman with braided hair and a musical laugh. There had been some hilarious joke about a stick, but she couldn't remember what was so funny.

"They're back."

She struggled to sit, her errant spine stiff from sleeping on the hard surface, then got to her feet. Most of the women were already awake. Everyone shivered. The ethane had run out during the night, and no simulated flames leapt inside the heater.

"How did you manage? Are you freezing?" Jox asked her friend.

"No. Ralork's coat kept me warm enough. I suppose I should thank him for it, but I'd just as soon spit in his face."

The hostility was an encouraging sign. Agathe must not be in too much pain or she would be quiet and withdrawn.

"Greetings, ladies," the first guard said. There were only two of them this time, one pulling the cart and another carrying a blaster. She was relieved to hear the voice of Blue Eyes.

"I hope you are well today," she said to him.

He gave her an indulgent smile. "Please, Jox. I know you're wishing we'd all die of chime-Ra. There's no need for false pleasantries."

She found herself returning the smile with a genuine one of her own. She maneuvered as close to him as possible without looking suspicious.

"We've run out of ethane for the heater."

"Yes, I've brought more. Enough to last *twenty-four hours*." He looked at her intensely now.

"Twenty-four hours?" she parroted, picking up on some subtle message hidden in the last sentence.

"Precisely." He gave her a curt nod and turned away to unload the wagon.

The other women moved about, getting their morning meals ready and taking turns in the privy. Jox waited for Blaster Man to look away. Finally Nodine's imperious voice and beautiful face caught his attention. He pivoted. Jox pressed a note into the hand of Blue Eyes as he turned to face her. His expression gave away nothing.

She released a lungful of air she didn't know she'd been holding in. He might well have made a scene, demanding to know what she was doing and letting his partner in on her transgression.

"Very good, ma'am. You have supplies for *twenty-four hours* this time. Make them count."

The men were gone the next moment.

"What did you give him?" Zania said. She had witnessed the covert transfer.

"A missive to my husband. I feel that he is involved in some way because of the marble. He's the smartest person I know. If he was able to get it to me, he'll somehow send a reply as well."

Zania nodded. "What do you suppose happens in a day – besides the ethane running out?"

"You noticed that, too?"

"Yes."

"I think he wants us to give them twenty-four hours. Not to try any kind of escape or retaliation."

"I think you're right. My instinct is telling me the same thing."

"I don't know how I can sit here doing nothing for that long."

"Patience may not be a choice."

When she shared their theory with the rest of the women, for once everyone was in accord. They would wait, either because they believed there was significance to the subliminal message, or the notion of being chosen for a scouting mission down one of those eerie tunnels was too abhorrent to consider. Jox herself would have volunteered, despite the likelihood of spiders.

"There's plenty of food and water," Tova said.

"Too bad they didn't include some cards or embroidery thread," Agathe muttered, scrawling the new items onto her inventory list.

"We'll just have to create our own diversions. Let's take the opportunity to get to know one another better," said Jox, with a glance toward Zania.

"Horrendous." Nodine sniffed at her bowl and grimaced. "I know all I need to about the rest of you. And what's in this? It smells like it's been eaten and regurgitated."

"Yes, I'm sure they put vomit in the porridge." Tova rolled her eyes.

"She makes a point, though." Zania eyed her own bowl now. "Perhaps they slipped something in our food to sicken us. Or some kind of drug to make us more compliant."

"Did anyone suffer any ill effects from dinner last night?" Jox asked, alarmed now and also disappointed in herself. The notion of drugs or poison hadn't occurred to her.

A round of shaking heads gave her some relief.

"I didn't have a bowel movement this morning, but that's nothing new," Agathe offered with a smirk. "That's your future, ladies. You pee when you don't want to, and you can't poop when you do want to."

"Do we really have any alternative to eating and drinking the food and water they give us?" Tova said after the laughter faded away. "We could go without calories, but not without hydration. If they were going to poison or drug us, I think they would have added it to the water. Eat your porridge, Nodine. It's fine. I've had worse."

"Indeed? That's interesting," Jox said. "Tova, I know you're an excellent cook, so whatever unappetizing food you ate must not have been prepared by your own hand." It was a statement designed to get the conversation going.

Eventually, she would work her way to the mysterious, clever Zania, but she would start somewhere else.

"I wasn't born into affluence, like you all." Tova's thick plait of blond hair evoked images of Easterners, many of whom were fair-skinned and pale-eyed, as was Tova. But that was where the similarities ended. She was heavyset, enjoying her food more than most, whereas the citizens of the Eastern Quadrant tended to be thin. Quite thin.

"Indeed? How did you come to achieve your status, then?"

"It's a tradition in my family for the women to marry only once, which limits income, as you may well imagine. My ancestors emigrated from the East before immigration became banned in the Zone. I worked my butt off through middle and upper school, then went even further to attain my accreditations. Academics, not a pedigree, is the reason I sit at the Table." If it was meant to be a barb, it went unnoticed. Nodine was busy being disgusted with her food.

"How fascinating. I never knew that about you. Agathe, tell us about your childhood. How many siblings did you have?"

"I had two brothers. Didn't we all have brothers?" she laughed. "I loved them so much. Like Tova and myself, they achieved advanced accreditations. One became a successful engineer, and the other a scientist. They both entered into civil partnerships and have never produced offspring of their own. We enjoyed those youthful, carefree years near the border of the Western Quadrant, where my ancestors originated. You could probably discern that from my dark skin. It was always the plan for me to become a member of the Table, coming from one of the Exalted Families, like Nodine's. But I've always felt the position should be earned rather than bestowed. Well done to you, Tova. I admire your determination."

No one made eye contact with Nodine. Most of the women at the Table felt the same way. Yes, their female birthright and familial connections opened the door, but recent generations of Table members were achieving educations conducive to leadership. It was easier to fill the twenty-five Chairs now that females were finally rebounding. The citizenry could be choosier these days, voting for women with skills and knowledge over heritage and fiscal assets.

"Yes, yes. I see where this is going," Nodine said. "And I don't care. I know plenty, even if I don't have the accreditations. Now it's my turn for the privy. Everyone stay out. I need at least thirty minutes."

She turned her back on faces that weren't looking at her anyway, squared her shoulders, and disappeared into the dark tunnel carrying one of the lume-tubes the guards had included with their supplies.

"That wasn't very nice, Agathe," Jox whispered.

"Too bad. She's not very nice and utterly unworthy of her post, as well as our good will."

Jox didn't respond, turning to Zania now.

"Zania, what about you? You're new to the Table, and we know very little of your background. Tell us about yourself."

The woman looked to be the same age as Jox herself, still within childbearing years. Had she borne children? Jox felt her own biological clock ticking, and despite many attempts with all her husbands, she had yet to conceive. Perhaps that was for the best. In a world with so few women, society pressured every female to produce children, even less than perfect ones. Those women's families who succeeded in delivering females became more Exalted with each one. It was the pathway to elevated status, and with it came opportunities and wealth. Just as obsidian was rare and sought after, so were baby girls.

There was nothing more precious in a world glutted with boys.

"I wish I had a fascinating story to tell," Zania said with a level gaze. "My family is not Exalted, but there was money to send me to the best schools, and my brothers and I always had enough food. Our mother and fathers treated us well. It was a happy childhood. Praise Him," she added, almost defiantly.

Those two simple words told a story of their own. The mystery of Zania was being revealed. No wonder she hadn't been forthcoming. The archaic worship of deities was uncommon, and in cases where it still continued, it was generally scorned by the secular population.

"I had no idea you were a Divinist."

"I realize that sort of thing is looked down upon in these days of existential enlightenment. But it gives me comfort to believe in a Divine Creator. Now that's really all

I have to say about it. Let someone else take a turn." Zania stood, thrust her chin out, and walked away.

Jox exchanged raised eyebrows with Agathe.

The older woman whispered, "She seems so intelligent for a Divinist."

"Oh, Agathe." Jox was mortified by the narrow-minded comment. And yet, hadn't her own internal reaction been one of surprise?

"I've never heard your story, Jox," Tova said. It was a daring statement. Most people didn't broach that subject with the one who currently occupied the Tallest Chair.

The women's eyes looked everywhere but upon Jox's physical defects.

She had come to terms with her appearance a long time ago. Others were curious – perhaps morbidly so – about why she looked the way she did, and that was normal. Humans love to witness horror from a safe distance.

"I suppose it's only fair. Most of you have been forthcoming, and it will put some of the more outlandish rumors to rest. Although I have enjoyed some of the especially creative and bizarre explanations for my unfortunate physical state." She took a deep breath. "No, I wasn't burned in a kitchen fire or injured in a transport accident. And no, I wasn't part of some genetic cross-breeding experiment gone awry. That one is my favorite. The truth, as is often the case, is rather boring. This," she gestured with her good hand to the other claw-like one, "and this," she touched the droopy, purplish side of her face, "are merely birth defects. There's a reason you haven't met my mother. She looked just like me. Sadly, she never came to terms with it. But as all patriotic females on our planet, she understood the societal directive to procreate. I never met my grandmother, but she looked like us, too. It's quite callous to expect a woman to risk giving birth to monsters like me. But that's how a family becomes Exalted, after all. The face and limbs don't matter. Only the reproductive organs." She grinned, hoping to dispel any unintended bitterness attached to her speech.

"You're not a monster, dear," Agathe said. Unshed tears made the amber eyes more luminous than ever. Even an elderly Agathe was more beautiful than Jox would ever be.

And it didn't bother her one iota.

"Thank you, my friend. I don't mind, really. I know that's difficult to believe, but it's true. I was given gifts to compensate for my appearance. I wouldn't change a thing."

When she said the words, she acknowledged the utter truth of them. It was a self-revelation, and it felt joyous.

"Perhaps we've had enough conversation for this morning," Tova said, filling the uncomfortable pause. "I don't have cards or embroidery thread, but I can transform the cutlery into pieces for Fox and Hounds. Who's up for a game?"

***

The hours passed slowly. Jox knew the time of day because an antique watch held a place next to the ever-present notepad and pen. She obsessively wrangled with the implications of their abduction.

What was going on in the outside world?

Just when she thought she might lose her mind from impatience, the doors to the terminal banged open. The women, many of whom had been napping out of boredom, jumped to their feet. It was late afternoon, exactly one day since arriving at their repurposed prison.

Something dire was about to happen.

Ralork charged into the chamber wearing an even grimmer expression than usual. "Anyone interested in getting some fresh air? I'll take one volunteer." He was alone this time, but he held a blaster.

Where was Blue Eyes? Had her note been discovered? Was he in trouble?

She stalked toward him, her face equally grim. "By *volunteer* do you mean *sacrifice*?"

"Not you. Anyone else." He dismissed her with a wave of his hand.

"I'm your volunteer. I won't allow anyone else to go."

"Your Tall Chair means nothing to me. I doubt it matters much to the others now, either."

"You're wrong, Ralork." Agathe scurried over to stand beside her. "It means everything to us. The Tall Chair isn't merely symbolic. It has always been filled by the person most suited to its burden...its occupant elected by those most qualified to identify her. We will follow Jox anywhere. Right, ladies?"

Cheers echoed off the crumbling walls.

"You won't get a volunteer besides me. Now let's go," she used an imperious tone not dissimilar to Nodine's. It was a voice she despised.

"Wait a minute." Nodine herself emerged from the crowd of women. "I'll go." She glided over the concrete floor to stand by Jox. Her lustrous auburn tendrils were disheveled, but still lovely. Even Ralork seemed taken aback by beauty that hadn't come from jars or tubes. None of her toiletries had made the journey.

Jox imagined the proximity of angel to demon was quite dramatic. "Nodine, this is no pleasure stroll. Surely you realize that."

"Yes, of course, I realize that. I'm not as obtuse as you seem to think I am."

"Let me go," Agathe said, wedging her fragile body in front of the taller Nodine. "I have a foot in the grave already. You know my pills aren't for arthritis…"

"Listen, old woman," Nodine interrupted. "This is my one chance to prove myself worthy. I won't let you take it from me."

Agathe looked kindly at her once-despised peer. "Child, this is serious. Deadly serious. Do you understand that?"

The violet eyes watered. "I do. I also understand that I'm the most expendable member of the Table. I didn't just discover that during your delightful conversation earlier. I've known it all along."

"Take me," a third voice came from the huddled group. Zania didn't bother addressing Jox. She went straight to Ralork. "You'll want a Divinist for maximum impact. I assume you're trying to prove a point? Let everyone know you're not afraid of using violence? If you want a sacrifice, I'm your choicest lamb, one who has sworn a blood oath never to raise a hand against another human being."

With a sense of dismay, Jox watched Ralork's gaze slide from Agathe to Nodine, and finally fall upon Zania. He began to reach for her arm, then pivoted back to Jox's dearest friend.

"Come with me, ma'am," he said to Agathe. Rather than grabbing her, he offered his arm. A frail hand, laden with jeweled rings, didn't hesitate in resting upon it.

"Stay strong, dear," Agathe said to her. "You will prevail. I know you will." She pressed a still-lovely cheek against Jox's marred one. Then she was gone.

Just before the thudding of the door echoed down the entrance corridor, Agathe's voice floated back to them.

"I suppose you'll be wanting your coat back, you irksome savage."

**

"I wonder if our decision to wait was unwise," Jox muttered hours later. Worry over her friend ate away at her. It may be that Agathe was already dead. Had they lashed her to a wooden post and set her on fire? Cut off her head and displayed it at the City gates? Were blackbirds pecking at the eyeballs even now?

"Are you suggesting we try to escape down one of the tunnels?" Zania replied from a nearby pallet, interrupting Jox's morbid thoughts.

"Perhaps we misunderstood Blue Eyes' message. Maybe he's not an ally."

Zania nodded. All the other women were asleep, it seemed. Or at least they had retired to their pallets. After a sparsely eaten dinner, no one had been interested in conversation or games.

"Blue Eyes looks Eastern," Tova whispered from a few feet away. "I would know. Does that tell us anything useful?"

"He looks so familiar," Jox said, closing her eyes and picturing the handsome, young face. Suddenly it came to her. "I know who he is! He's the partner of Guard Scordin, the friendly one from TR1's security detail."

"How do you know what Guard Scordin's partner looks like?" Zania asked.

"Vyg has a monthly dice game. I haven't given it much notice, and I never intrude. My husbands have their own diversions, of course. I remember seeing Blue Eyes leaving with Guard Scordin one evening a few months ago."

"But what does it mean," asked Tova, crawling over sleeping bodies to get to the other women.

"Maybe their dice game wasn't a dice game. Maybe they were plotting," Zania mused.

"Plotting what? What are you thinking?" asked Jox.

Zania continued, "In the beginning, we assumed this uprising was motivated by the disparity between Palantine and the outer Quadrants. The rumor about potential cuts to the Altruism Budget had no doubt leaked out. One of the first things I learned after coming to the Table was that Falsten couldn't keep a secret if her life depended on it. I'd heard some talk of unrest. One of my own husbands told me as much, but with no details. What if that was a different movement from the one whose machinations we're caught up in now?"

"Two rebellions happening simultaneously?" Jox murmured. "Why didn't you say anything about this unrest?"

Zania shrugged. "I had just arrived at the Table and barely knew you women. I was biding my time, seeing what you were going to propose."

Jox frowned. "I planned to propose sweeping changes to our antiquated systems, but they didn't include elevating men to positions of legislative power. The notion never occurred to me, frankly. And then Ralork and his crew burst through that secret door."

"What is the significance of the marble?" asked Zania.

Jox had been thinking about the marble ever since Blue Eyes slipped it to her. "Perhaps Vyg is the leader of this other rebellion…"

"You said he was the smartest person you knew," Zania said. "Would such a person be content to idly sit by, playing dice and reading books, while people suffered? If Blue Eyes' family immigrated here from the impoverished Eastern Quadrant, would he have Vyg's ear?"

"Yes, of course. Vyg is as kind as he is intelligent," replied Jox. "I'm trying to imagine two sparring factions: contentious men who crave equality to women, and egalitarians who seek to correct societal disparities. Maybe both are reasonable in their desires. Perhaps we've had it wrong all along."

"Chime-Ra happened a very long time ago," said Zania, her voice thoughtful. "How long do we punish the ancestors of those who brought its wrath upon us?"

Jox sighed. "Does five hundred years seem about right?"

"Their aggression in space and their need to dominate nearly killed humankind when they brought chime-Ra back with them." All heads turned to Nodine now, as she sat up on her pallet and joined the whispered conversation. "It decimated our population, thereby disrupting our technologies...our advancements and science...very little of which has been duplicated even half a millennia later. Does that horrible lack of judgment deserve a place at the Table? And what if they want more than equality? What if they want to dominate again, as they did in the old times? You know we can't have that, Jox. They can't be trusted. And don't be so shocked. I know as much of our history as the rest of you. At least the parts that matter."

"How would you feel if the roles were reversed, Nodine?" asked Jox. "I know it's difficult to imagine men lording power over us, but isn't that precisely what we're doing to them because of events that occurred five hundred years ago?"

"Men haven't changed their natures. They still carry the Y chromosome. They're still aggressive. Too impulsive to rule wisely. We all know this."

"Maybe they've evolved beyond that. People can change. People can grow. People can transcend their natures," said Zania.

"Not all can. Ralork and his ilk exemplify that," Nodine replied, then lay back down on her pallet and closed her eyes.

"She's right about that," Tova whispered. "Poor Falsten."

Jox nodded. What should she do?

"Sleep on it," Zania said, reading her thoughts. "You'll come up with a solution in the morning. Vyg may be the most intelligent person you know, but you are the most intelligent person *I* know."

Jox nodded, then lay back down on her pallet, hands behind her head, staring at the ceiling, while gentle and not-so-gentle snores echoed off the walls. Her eyes never closed that night.

***

Early the next morning, Jox visited the privy tunnel before anyone else awakened. She did her business, then continued down the length of the tunnel for a few minutes, using one of the lume-tubes to light the way. It was exactly as she had dreaded, full of spider webs and skittering, long-tailed creatures. She shuddered, then stopped and turned back toward the circular room. Not out of fear, but out of resolve to do this thing correctly.

Several of the women greeted her as she reemerged from the tunnel. It was a bittersweet reminder of the times she appeared in the Table Room, ready for the day's work in the Tallest Chair.

"Ladies, we must take matters into our own hands."

"You're planning an escape, then?" Zania said.

"No. A reckoning, but not the type Ralork has in mind. We'll be having company soon, I expect."

She stood, arms crossed, waiting for the sounds of people coming through the terminal entrance. It didn't take long.

She wasn't surprised when she saw Blue Eyes and several others emerge from the corridor. Nor was she surprised when she saw Vyg among them.

"Greetings, husband," she said with a smile.

"Greetings, wife. You're not angry with me for taking so long?"

"Not in the least. You still had a couple more hours. How bad is it out there?"

"Bad enough," Vyg replied. The grim expression he wore reminded her of Ralork's. "They're contained, though. We're holding the leaders."

"Ralork?"

"Yes. And the others who took you."

"Excellent. Is Agathe alive?"

"Yes. We're caring for her now, but..." He didn't finish the sentence.

She swallowed hard. "How are Durbin and Sawl?"

"Sawl is fine. Durbin is inconsolable," he grinned.

Jox smiled too. "Did you tell him you were coming to rescue me?"

"Of course. He didn't believe we could do it. He thought he had lost you forever."

"Does he know about your rebellion?" She gazed at him steadily when she said the words.

Vyg's eyes opened wide. "You know about that?"

"Yes, but first things first. Let's get out of here. There are spiders, Vyg. Someone will have to pay for that as well as for Falsten."

Six months later...

"Here we go, Brutin," Jox said as she approached the massive doors of the Table Room.

"They're ready for you." The smile on the man's face stretched from ear to ear.

She stopped, lowering her voice. "Is it done, then?"

The smile vanished. "Yes. The sentence was carried out. Falsten has found her justice."

"Very good," she replied, then continued through the doorway and into the Table Room. She wore her confident, crooked smile as she looked at the Members assembled there. Some of the ladies were familiar. Zania and Tova were seated in their normal chairs. Nodine was absent, but that had been her own decision. Vyg sat in the Tallest Chair, the result of the popular vote put forth at her insistence, not only to the citizens of Palantine, but the Eastern and Western Quadrants as well. Women were given extra votes to offset the disparity in their numbers. Still, Vyg had edged her out of the Tallest Chair by fifty-three votes.

It was a running joke between them now. Did it chafe? Yes. But it was the will of the people.

Henceforth, the three nations would make decisions together to the betterment and well-being of all. Blue Eyes, now known to her as Cedric, sat in Agathe's chair. The sight still evoked a lump in her throat.

Jox missed her old friend. Today, especially. Agathe would have been proud to vote for the dozens of progressive reforms, inked on parchment, and stacked upon the stone Table before her.

She smiled.

"There you are, Jox," Vyg said, waving her toward the seat next to his. "Ladies and gentlemen. Let's get started."

The In Between

This time, when her consciousness manifested in the black void, something felt different.

She supposed it should. Her seventh incarnation had ended after an exceptionally long life on Centauri Proxima. People lived longer there than on Earth, and she had needed the extra time to get everything done. There had been a lot of lessons to learn that last time: Kindness, Compassion, Empathy, Patience, Benevolence, and Tolerance. She'd definitely gone out with a bang.

Now that she was back in the In Between, she wondered what to do next. Should she materialize in the body from her most recent life, as she had done six times before? For some reason, that didn't feel right. Instead, she created a kind of amalgamation. She closed eyes that didn't yet exist and thought of them all. Johnny. Jamila. Jun-Tak. Julietta. Jaeda. Jacob. Jox.

J didn't know how she would look when Sarah came for their discussion, but it didn't matter. It felt right. For the setting, she did something different as well. She did nothing. She left the black void exactly as it had first appeared to her when the process began. And waited.

She didn't have to wait long.

"There you are," came Sarah's lilting voice. It always filled her with such happiness, and she allowed herself to bask in it now. She finally realized who that voice belonged to.

"Hello, dear Sarah."

Sarah returned her smile, looking more radiant than ever. In fact, she was glowing, like a celestial body in the cosmic space of the black void.

"How do you feel?" Sarah said.

"Honestly, a bit shaky. That was the seventh, you know."

"I do know. Did you get it all done?"

J thought about the question for a long time. Perhaps a few minutes or several millennia.

"Yes. I got every bit of it done. Do you want to hear how?"

Sarah shook her head. "I think that part is unnecessary this time. Don't you?"

"Yes," J said. "I know who you are, now. Or should I say, I remember who you are. Or were, I guess. Johnny's mom, Jamila's leper, Jun-tak's Onya, Julietta's Francesca, Jaeda's Tana, Jacob's Asha, and Jox's Zania. You were always with me, helping me on my journey."

Sarah simply smiled.

"So what's next? I believe I've completed my goal of becoming sublime, since perfection is unattainable." She remembered those words from her first time in the In Between.

"Do you feel sublime?"

"Utterly."

"Very good. You're really going to like this next part."

Epilogue

Shoemowetochawcawe knew he had died. Had felt the moment his soul left his worn-out body back on the Dakota plains. So when he found himself in a black void, he was confused. He figured he should be soaring through the sky in the body of an eagle or floating down a raging river as a leaf.

He didn't expect to be in this mysterious non-place. It didn't feel uncomfortable, though. He waited for whatever was going to happen next.

"Hello, Shoemowetochawcawe." The voice floated to him through darkness that slowly become lighter. He realized he was sitting on the ground next to his tepee – the first one he had set up near Jacob Payne's sod house, not the larger one that followed when he married Miriam. Soon the prairie surrounded him, but beyond, the black void remained.

"Hello," he said. The woman who appeared before him didn't look like anyone he knew – she had a lithe body, a pleasant face, and long dark hair. But there was something about her that felt reassuring. Familiar even. "Where am I?"

"You're in the In Between. Are you comfortable? Do you need anything?"

He shook his head. "I am fine. Am I dead?"

The woman nodded. "It's true your physical body was left behind in that other place, but it serves a purpose to take on its form again now. It will make all this easier to get through. Do you think you can manage that?"

Shoemowetochawcawe closed eyes he didn't yet have, then opened them. He felt arms covered in fringed sleeves and a soft leather tunic on his torso. He glanced down at bison-hide moccasins.

"Perfect," the woman said.

"What is your name?" Shoemowetochawcawe asked.

"You may call me Jox."

"And you may call me Shoe. It is easier."

She smiled. "Let's talk about your life, Shoe."

"There is not much to tell, really."

When he heard her laughter, it reminded him of his mother's beaded necklace, clinking while she made their morning meal. It was a lovely sound.

"Do you remember a Pivotal Moment when you felt your life had just taken a Very Bad Turn or a Very Good one?"

Shoe smiled. "Oh, yes. There was this white fellow named Jacob Payne…"

THE END

Dear Reader,

I hope you enjoyed this book. I'd love it if you posted a review about it on Amazon and Goodreads. Reading a well-written book in the company of snoozing doggies is my favorite pastime. Receiving feedback and reviews from readers about my own books is my second favorite pastime. Which scenes did you like best? What character could you relate to the most?

On a side note, if you've spotted a typo, please email me a nicki@nickihuntsmansmith.com. I hate those insidious little buggers as much as the next reader.

Follow me on Facebook at https://www.facebook.com/AuthorNickiHuntsmanSmith/ or read my blog (Eating the Elephant) at http://nickihuntsmansmith.com/.

I look forward to hearing from you!

Nicki Huntsman Smith

Made in the USA
Las Vegas, NV
24 February 2021

18403585R00193